ALSO BY DAVIS MACDONALD

The Hill *(set in Palos Verdes), Book 1 in the Judge Series*

The Island *(set in Avalon, Catalina Island), Book 2 in the Judge Series*

Silicon Beach *(set in Santa Monica and L.A.'s West Side), Book 3 in the Judge Series*

The Bay *(set in Newport Beach), Book 4 in the Judge Series*

Cabo *(set in Cabo San Lucas), Book 5 in the Judge Series*

The Strand *(set in the South Bay beach communities of Southern California), Book 6 in the Judge Series*

The Lake *(set in the Lake Arrowhead community of Southern California), Book 7 in the Judge Series*

The Cruise *(set on the open sea), Book 8 in the Judge Series*

Vegas *(set in Las Vegas), Book 9 in the Judge Series – Due out in the Fall, 2021*

I hope you enjoy The Cruise, and if you do, please drop a brief positive review on Amazon for me. Your review will be greatly appreciated.

Watch for announcements for future books on my Website: **http://davismacdonald-author.com/**

THE CRUISE

A Mystery Novel

BY

DAVIS MacDONALD

"We like to think of ourselves as fallen angels...

But we're merely risen apes..."

Paraphrased from a quote by Robert Ardrey

"Dum vivimus, vivamus."

While we live, let us live.

"I'm not bad, I'm just drawn that way."

Jessica Rabbit, from
Who Framed Roger Rabbit?

A Note from the Author

This story, and its characters, organizations, businesses, events, locations and scenes, are completely fictional.

PROLOGUE

Charlie Westerman was just drifting off to sleep beside his wife. It had been a late night with difficult business decisions. He had cut some managers loose, disciplined others, and re-set the priorities among his minions. His instructions, rubber stamped by the Board and officers, would be drifting down, percolating through the organization, reaching the overseas branches in the Far East; being read now. Later, London would open to the news and then New York. Here, in the Valley, part of the great Los Angeles sprawl, his immediate staff would be the last to know.

He had just entered REM sleep when a disturbance in the ether startled him back to consciousness. His dark eyes fluttered open, trying to focus. Someone was sitting beside him on the bed, softly shaking him. Through the blur and illumination trickling from the bedroom window he made out the shape of Jay, the youngest.

"Dad, Dad. Wake up! I've got something to show you. It's important. You must come look."

Jay sounded excited. He tended to be an excitable young man. Just turned twenty and still living at home. Floundering around UCLA, trying to decide what the hell to do with his life. Recently distraught over a breakup with some Cuban princess Jay was too ashamed to bring home to meet the family. An artistic and sensitive soul like his mother. Charlie could see none of himself in the face of this young man staring down at him earnestly. *Well*, he thought, *there wouldn't be*.

Jay would be a taker, never a producer. Shirt sleeves to shirt sleeves in three generations. That's what they said. Someone pulls himself up, makes a lot of money, is hugely successful through pure grit, hard work enormous focus. And then his children come along, the spenders, living lavishly under the father's tent, spending their inheritance willy-nilly, accomplishing little.

As to their children, the grandchildren… well, it was back to the street for them. Back to shirt sleeves. Back to scrabbling around in the herd trying to make ends meet. Trying to satisfy a dominant boss at work; trying to scratch together money here and there for a modest vacation and to put something away for savings and retirement. It was the way of the human tribe.

He didn't understand people like that. People like Jay. Helpless people with no vision, no drive. He'd tried to educate, mostly by example; but he'd failed. If a person had no fire in their belly you couldn't manufacture it there. He was older now and had given up on changing the nature of Jay, or any of them. Spenders all. But of the three young people in his family, Jay had always been the irritation.

"Come on Dad, hurry. This is important. Just throw your robe on; it'll only take a minute."

Charlie rolled out from under the covers with a sigh, nude, how he slept. He cast an envious glance at his wife, still sound asleep, purring slightly. He threw on his robe and slid into his slippers. This had better be good.

"It's down here Dad, downstairs, out on the driveway. Hurry!"

"Jesus Christ… on the driveway?"

Jay led the way down the stairs, across the sprawling living room and toward the front door which was standing open. He reluctantly followed, shaking his head. Muttering to himself under his breath, still half asleep, he stumbled out of the front door, across the grand porch, down the steps on to the driveway.

"You stand here, Dad. Right here. See? X marks the spot."

He walked toward the little pink chalk X faintly visible on the asphalt. He was a large man, six foot two, with broad shoulders and a prodigious stomach which might have benefited from suspenders to keep his pants up. He loved to eat. His bulk cast a shadow in the moonlight, hiding the pink X, forcing him to guess where it was. Where he was supposed to stand? *Shit! This was hair-brained!*

Jay crossed diagonally to the other side of the driveway, twenty feet away. He stopped beside a Folgers Coffee can sitting on the asphalt with the top missing. Jay put his hands out, palms up, flat. "You stay right there, Dad. This will only take a minute."

He'd already heard that before, five minutes before. *Humph!*

Jay reached into his pocket and brought out a silver lighter. Shit, that was his lighter. It had gone missing a week ago. Damn it, this kid was turning into a kleptomaniac.

Jay paused for a minute, starting to hyperventilate. He was more excited now.

"Here's what I want to tell you, Dad." Jay took a big breath. "You're a mean, greedy son of a bitch. An ugly man with an ugly soul."

The father started to sputter. No one talked to him that way. Particularly some useless pup suckling under his roof. He could feel the rage in him, never far from the surface, rising, warming his face.

"You can't talk to me that way, Jay. You useless pieces of shit. A weak good-for-nothing just like your mother, sucking up my money to fund your lazy lifestyle. Your hands out to beg for your big-boy allowance but bad-mouthing me behind my back. You are twenty and you've accomplished nothing. Never will. You'll always be just a useless dependent. Look at you. All I see is failure and deceit for as far into the future as you last."

Jay smiled grimly. "I knew you'd say something like that, Dad. You are so predictable. You have mistreated me, Mom, and the other kids brutally in your pursuit of money and power. In your headlong dash for wealth, you're destroying the oceans, maybe the entire food chain of this planet. I'm so ashamed to have come from you. I would stop you and your company if could, but I can't. All I can do is disassociate from you forever."

"Tut… tut. You can't survive without my money, Jay."

Jay swooped up the Folgers coffee can with his right hand, brought it above his head and turned it upside down, soaking his hair, his face, his t-shirt, his workout pants with some sort of clear liquid. Shit, it was gas; the damn can was filled with gasoline. Jay flicked the lighter in his left hand and brought the flame to his chest.

The flame caught and spread instantly up across Jay's face and into his hair, across his t-shirt and down the length of his pants, turning him into a towering fireball that whirled and danced in a screaming jig for seconds, then collapsed into a flaming lump on the asphalt.

CHAPTER 1
Six Months Later
DAY 1
6:25 PM

The cruise ship was well on its way, having left an overcast Los Angeles mid-morning, steaming out into the vast Pacific, heading for Hawaii. Land was long gone and there was nothing but a circle of blue. The Judge leaned against the deck rail outside the main dining room and watched the small whitecaps tufting the blue-green swells that gently undulated around the boat. He could smell the salt. and the hint of tung from the oiled decks. The waves gave the ship a slight corkscrew motion. Not unpleasant if you were a sailor; and he was.

The Judge looked out to the horizon. The sea was beautiful, alive, rippling and curling, sending its windy breath over the ship in a slight breeze that bespoke freshness and renewal. Its colors were deep blues, snowy whites, and gold sprays of sunlight stretching back from the disappearing sun to the hull below. He watched the orange orb lower itself into the sea.

He looked back over his shoulder at the ship. It was a tawdry mass of hard juts and angles, layers of floors, windows, and rails, populated here and there with bobbing heads traipsing around on one mission or another. The deck oil didn't hide the scent of confined human animals, spread across the tops of the ship's seventeen decks like layered sardines in a can. He could hear raucous sounds drifting around him, loud conversations mixed with the chords of the piano bar, interior elevator music, and the dissonance of the rock band screeching out their last set on the pool deck.

The ship was everything the sea wasn't: cramped, smelly, preoccupied and arrogant. Like some painted whore who'd inadvertently wandered into an ancient cathedral to stay the night without the capacity to see or appreciate its sanctity and beauty.

And the ship's passengers? Well… wherever the tribe of man travels together, even when they've climbed aboard a glitzy tub of a ship for a six-day cruise, they bring along their emotional trappings. Pride, pettiness, fear, frustration, bitterness, jealousy, competitiveness, greed, revenge, and out and out orneriness; all on display if one looked.

He had no clue then his inquisitive nature would shortly put him square in the path of such emotions and nearly do him in.

The Judge was a tall man, broad shouldered and big boned with a slight paunch around the middle, hinting at an appetite for fine wines and good food. He had piercing blue eyes, intelligent and restless, which continuously swept the space around him. He had the ruddy and chiseled features of Welsh ancestors, a rather too big nose, large ears, and bushy eyebrows on the way to grey. He wore tan slacks and a Tommy Bahama shirt with a large floral pattern on a baby blue background that matched his eyes. He carried his blue blazer over his shoulder, but now slipped it on as cool moistness in the soft breeze settled around him.

He had a given name of course, but some years before he'd been on the bench and people began calling him just "Judge". Even old friends he'd known for years affectionately adopted the nickname. He'd later lost his judgeship in an arguably rigged election, but his nickname had stuck just the same.

Five more days and nights on this boat before Hilo. He wondered how he'd keep busy. There wasn't much to do. He could eat himself into oblivion. He could lay beside the pool and sunburn. He could drink himself under the table to assure he'd gotten his money's worth from the expensive drink package he'd been pressured to buy.

Katy, his young wife, had signed herself up for a spa treatment every day. Good for her. That was her thing. But the Judge had no interest in being pummeled and beaten by an overly steroidal Polack who was a woman but looked like a man. Certainly not on a daily basis.

This trip had been Katy's idea. She had lobbied long and hard, determined to get him away and all to herself. He'd dutifully acquiesced, lugging aboard her heavy suitcase stuffed with two bottles of champagne, a bevy of fancy cocktail dresses she rarely wore, a ton of makeup for practically every occasion, wet and dry, and a new negligee he wasn't supposed to have seen. He'd noted the nighty, if you could call it that, more 'froth than cloth', when he stumbled in on Sophia, their Malaysia cabin steward in their stateroom. Sophia'd been unpacking Katy's suitcase and was holding the lacey negligee up to the light, shaking her head in amazement. Sophia's face turned a satisfactory shade of red when she realized the Judge was watching.

But Katy's idea of getting away by themselves had been a dubious undertaking from the start. They were hardly by themselves, packed in this giant tin can with a press of souls determined to have artificial fun, eating, sun burning, drinking, gambling and… and yacking. That was the worst. It was like being penned up for a week in an overcrowded chicken coop.

The Starfish carried 2,600 guests and 1,150 crew. Registered in Bermuda, she was 951 feet long, 118 feet wide, boasted seventeen decks, four pools, a spa, a casino, and a theater. She averaged twenty knots and was over a hundred thousand tons. God help them if the stabilizers went out.

The ship was old, which made the trip cheap; a good thing he supposed. Built in 2002 and refurbished in 2018. But the refurbishment didn't extend to the common guest areas or the staterooms. Everything had stale and dated finishes, colors, and tiles. The pools were old and tired, with large patches of rust and cracks here and there. The pool steps were dirty, the pool furniture torn and worn, and the surrounding walls needed a good cleaning and a coat of paint.

The lounge areas were worn as well. The theatre had wall covering peeling in one spot. And when the Judge had settled into his theatre seat to listen to the introductory welcome talk the cushion had been so beaten down he'd almost slid off to the floor. Some would say this all gave the boat character; the Judge thought it just looked tired. But Katy was happy, delighted to have the Judge with her and not working. He supposed that was the main point; he would do anything to make Katy happy.

At their first formal lunch after they'd gotten underway that morning, Katy and the Judge had sat at their assigned dining table with eight retirees. They'd mostly gotten to hear about their companions' medical problems and surgeries. Through the cocktails and appetizers, and extending into the salad course, Katy and the Judge were pretty much brought up to speed on their entire medical histories in vivid detail. During the second course they heard the medical histories of parents, mostly deceased. '*Genes are important you know, and deceased parents can portend what the future may hold.*'

By the time the dessert menus were passed fellow diners had moved on to the operations and medical issues of brothers, sisters, and cousins, some alive, some not. The Judge was now so enlightened he was certain he could personally pass the Medical Licensing Examination and enter medical practice.

The Judge had excused himself after dessert for a pow wow with the maître d'. After two large bills smoothly changed hands, Katy and the Judge had been reassigned, thank God, to a new dining table for evening dinner and the balance of the cruise.

In telling the story later, the Judge would usually mutter at this point, "Out of the frying pan and into the fire!", accompanied by an eye-roll for effect.

The Judge was now almost through his first day 'at sea', a polite description for a day spent traversing the ocean, no stops, no sightseeing. Nothing but the blue horizon, a rash of fancy alcoholic drinks, and a parade of overfed people prowling around their floating cork, stepping on each other's toes and working on their sun burns. Oh. And accompanied by ear-grating music piped everywhere, making it impossible to hold a conversation with anyone below a shout.

When Katy had left for her spa after lunch, the Judge had wandered aimlessly around the decks in his bright orange trunks that wouldn't stay wet. Trunks he'd cut the inside netting out of because it was fouling his plumbing. Katy was appalled when she spotted him later in his trunks. She'd scolded him; demanded he sit in chairs more carefully in public, and sprawl on lounge chairs with his knees always together. She said his shortcomings were not to be exposed. Frankly, he didn't give a damn. But when Katy was around he tried to obey her rules. Keep her happy.

His ensemble had been completed with a triple-large green t-shirt of doubtful pedigree, which hung over his paunch like a tent, mostly hiding his snazzy trunks. It was one of his favorite shirts, perhaps because it appalled Katy so much. And because it had a breast pocket into which he'd stuffed his reading glasses, pens (black and blue), a pencil, an Indian ink marker, and a small spiral notebook in case he had an idea. The poor pocket bulged with complaint all day, sagging, and looking very pregnant, perhaps even past due.

He had worn his canvas hat, a Tilley, although its label was long gone and sun was starting to show through the threadbare material in splotches here and there. The chin strap was missing too, requiring him to periodically scrunch the hat down hard on his head against the breeze. It made it difficult to see out from under the brim. He'd not walked into anybody this afternoon, but it was so crowded around the pool deck, what with people carrying heaping plates of sloppy food, pizza, drinks and whatnot, there'd been close calls. God could his fellow passengers eat.

He was confident he projected a certain elegant style as he'd wandered the decks. He could tell because he could see heads turn and eyes start here and there as he walked by. But no one approached to talk.

Well, you couldn't talk anyway. Not over the trashy noise they were streaming out pretending it was music from some punk band one deck up. He'd scurried back for his cabin in the late afternoon when a stacked, sweaty blonde named Lola and an anorexic Indian kid named Ajay started setting up microphones at the pool's edge, readying themselves to begin blasting stupid participation water games at the pool crowd. The Judge was already grinding his teeth; if he'd stayed he'd have ended up toothless.

Katy had been less than complimentary about his ensemble on his return to their cabin. He had hoped to go with jeans for dinner, but it wasn't to be. Katy was adamant he put on slacks, his 'old-guy' Tommy Bahama shirt, and his blue blazer. Now he stood out on deck, taking in the breeze while she was down in their cabin frantically applying eyeliner, eyelashes, magic creams, powders and God knew what else, all as a prerequisite to meeting their new dinner companions. And blaming him for her inadequate time to prep… of course.

He beckoned a passing waiter from his perch at the rail and asked for a piña colada. The young man, blue-eyed and all smiles with a fiery crop of red hair and freckles that said Irish, wore a name plate marking him as Sean. He happily took the Judge's order, again assuring the Judge, as he'd done around the pool earlier, that the piña coladas were 'low-cal'. The Judge had had four of them at the pool. It was amazing how good they tasted for being low-calorie. Almost like ice cream.

He hoped the drink would make him a bit numb before having to listen to the new and no doubt equally boring companions they'd meet at the dinner table and endure for the balance of the trip.

He turned back from the now dark horizon, feeling Katy's presence behind him, catching the scent of her perfume, Chanel No. 5. And there she was, her face alight with a smile just for him.

Katy was twenty years his junior, five foot eight, slender, all arms and legs. She had light brown hair which she wore long and had small delicate features and smile lines. Her nose was a bit long and narrow, but in that it matched her head, also more oblong than round, but all very delicate. Her face was pale white, as though never in the sun. And she had the most extraordinary eyes, vivid blue like the Caribbean, large and intelligent, with long lashes.

She had picked out a stunning aqua dress to wear to dinner, long, and cut open and down at the front almost to her navel, showing a large pelt of skin between her small breasts. This seemed to be all the fashion. It was a bit too much skin for his wife to be showing, the Judge thought, though he readily admired the style on other women.

But over eight years of marriage he'd learned to keep his mouth shut about such opinions. Besides, he knew she had taken special care to dress just for him. She loved him with a passion which burned bright, warming what had been a drab and solitary existence before he'd found her.

CHAPTER 2
DAY 1
7:00 PM

Charlie Westerman marched into the dining room at the head of his little group like some large oriental potentate at the head of a parade of minions. And minions they were:

A worn-out wife who barely talked to him except to pick fights, still brooding about the lost son. A business partner angling to unseat him in some manner. A jolly Chief Operating Officer, more marketing playboy than operating whiz, whose stupid ideas for spending money had to be continually checked. His CFO, little more than a glorified accountant really, who didn't know how to count. His CEO, a man from an aristocratic family who opened his mouth each day only to change feet. And his spend-thrift kids, a daughter and a son. The former a tight-ass who at thirty had never had a boyfriend and might be gay. The latter a twenty-four year old who had an enormous ability to talk and talk without saying anything.

He sighed. What a dreary entourage, although he was somewhat fond of his daughter.

The last of his little group was the only bright spot; his Executive Assistant, an ambitious young girl with legs that went on forever under her plaid skirt and a passion for hot sex. He smiled with satisfaction as he contemplated his intimate knowledge of both. She wasn't interested in business and had nothing much intelligent to say. But that was okay. Her other attributes fully made up for that… and more.

The maître d' had said the two empty seats at their assigned table had been filled, a necessity because the stupid dining room did not have enough tables to go around. He was certain the two seats would be taken by a pair of beefy heifers from the Midwest. No doubt a retired and boring couple with little to contribute to conversation beyond anecdotes about their garden and their grandchildren.

He even wondered about the wisdom of setting up this trip and funding it. He had been pressured into it by Kennedy, his COO; a perk for the senior staff after a particularly profitable year. Charlie had picked the cheapest cruise he could find, a tired boat and a pedestrian destination, Hawaii. They all seemed satisfied. Well, who wouldn't? Escape from the office and nothing productive done for six days, and even better, at the boss's expense. *God damn he hated vacations!*

He flounced himself down at one end of the table, watching cynically as Ross Hamilton, his obsolete business partner, angled behind him, maneuvering into the seat at the opposite table end: the second power seat. Ross was a weaselly bastard but had been needed for additional capital when Charlie'd first launched his takeover bid for the soda company years before. Charlie had long outgrown Ross and his capital. Now, as a five percent shareholder, Ross was frequently a nuisance. Ross hungered for power; Charlie knew the look, could see it in Ross's eyes. Ross would try to cross Charlie at some point. When he tried, Charlie would have to put him down.

He was going to be sixty-two this year. He'd accumulated more money than God. He was the majority shareholder in the largest soda bottling company in the world. Even better, he wasn't an officer, and he wasn't a director. He was the controlling shareholder. His name only showed up on one small line in the company's public reports as holding the controlling block of the company's stock.

But nobody made a move, the board didn't meet, officers didn't act, nothing happened in his company until he showed up and told people what they would do. His officers were the public face of the company. But he controlled everything with an iron fist. He'd found it safer to be behind the scenes, particularly after the SEC investigation into alleged irregularities in the early years; and later as his carefully choreographed acquisitions turned into sharp-toothed traps sprung on the owners of a series of target companies he'd acquired.

All fun and games. All very profitable. All leaving a trail of disgruntled victims who'd been outfoxed. And a corresponding warm glow in Charlie's gut. God, how he loved to do business.

Charlie waved his arm petulantly around in the air, and the waiter, Sean something, was instantly at his shoulder to take his drink order.

"A Jack and Coke," he muttered, girding himself for meeting Ma and Pa Midwest.

CHAPTER 3
DAY 1
7:15 PM

The Pacific sky turned to deep purple and Katy linked her arm with the Judge's and they turned and entered the dining room, Katy curious to meet their new dinner companions. As they approached their assigned table, the Judge had immediate misgivings. It was a family table with two open seats into which they'd been shoved. As the Judge circled the table shaking hands and vainly trying to remember names, its members mostly looked at the Judge without interest, their attention mainly focused on the head of the table where the family oligarch sat.

Charles (Charlie) Westerman, or just Dad, sat at the end of the table holding court. He examined the Judge with cold dark eyes as the Judge and Katy approached. He didn't bother to rise but lifted a meaty paw up behind his head to disinterestedly half shake the Judge's proffered hand.

Westerman was a bulk of a man; tall, perhaps six-foot two, broad shouldered, with a big chest and a belly to match.

A little older than the Judge, mid-sixties perhaps, he had iron grey hair, and plenty of it, worn long and streaked back along either side of his square block head. His features were mostly lost in his fleshy face, except for the square jaw that jutted out and looked to brook no interference… and except for the eyes… dark, dark eyes, devoid of pupils. Westerman had the eyes of a predator, moving constantly, seeking advantage.

He wore grey slacks and a black sports jacket with the sheen of silk and a fit perfectly cut to his body; custom made and expensive. Underneath he wore a light grey silk shirt with an over-large collar, open, no tie. A black forest of curly hair lapped out at the open top of the guy's shirt and crept toward his neck.

The Judge moved around two steps behind Westerman to meet Charlie's wife sitting to Charlie's right She stood to greet the Judge, a short brunette with cropped hair, faded blue eyes, and squint lines that burst out as she produced a perfunctory smile. She looked mid-fifties and hard rid; her perfunctory smile little more than a grimace. The layer of pancake cosmetics on her face only emphasized lines of pain and frustration etched there. She wore an expensive silk cocktail dress, metallic cobalt blue, open at the neck and partially down her chest; not as far as Katy's. Small rises tucked under the silk to either side were barely enough to be called breasts. The chiseled bones of her throat and chest protruding here and there across her bare expanse suggested a scrawny creature underneath.

The wife introduced herself in a soft voice as Alice Westerman, barely audible over the racket of the dining room as over one hundred people rattled their china, crashed their silverware together, and yelled at each other across the din in an effort to restart empty conversations begun at lunch. Alice extended a small thin hand emanating a musky scent of citrus and woods, nails perfectly done in clear polish, a large diamond ring sparkling on one bony finger.

To Charlie's left, a man of similar age to the Judge, as tall, but thin, almost bird-like, stooped a little as he rose to meet the Judge. He wore a brown tweed sport jacket over a pale brown shirt that matched his deep tanned complexion and clashed with his grey slacks. Color blind mused the Judge. There was a patrician air about him hinting at Ivy League schools and old money.

"My CEO," muttered Charlie by way of introduction.

The man said softly, "George Walker," smoothly extending a thin spidery hand in a pretend shake. As he felt Walker's dry slippery skin brush across his palm the Judge repressed a desire to immediately wash his hands. Walker had cold green eyes. The Judge had seen friendlier eyes in the snake cages at the zoo.

"And my Executive Assistant," muttered Charlie, pointing with his soup spoon at a young woman in her mid-twenties to the left of Walker, a blonde with soft brown eyes and a bright lip-sticked mouth almost too small below her perky turned up nose. She rose at the sound of her boss's voice and turned to give the

Judge a vigorous pumping handshake, a surprise coming from such a small delicate hand and wrist. "Maddy Stevens," she said. She wore a plaid kilt in bright blues and blacks, a tad too short in the Judge's opinion, exposing long slender legs covered in sheer grey pantyhose.

"My Chief Operating Officer," muttered Charlie, using his soup spoon again to point to the man sitting across the table toward its other end. The COO stood to shake as the Judge dutifully walked around the table. The COO was a plump man in his early fifties, dressed in a white shirt, grey suit, and red bow tie. He had a salesman's smile that easily covered all emotions hidden in the folds of his round chubby face. But the dark eyes that glowed there reminded the Judge of a grizzly, recently disturbed from its winter slumber. He wasn't the sort of man the Judge would turn his back on. "Kennedy," he said. The Judge assumed it was his last name.

Kennedy turned and moved off toward the direction of the men's room, muttering, "excuse me" under his breath.

"And my worthless son," said Charlie, nodding across the table to his right at a young man approaching the table from the direction of the kitchen with a young woman in tow. Charlie's mouth twisted in a smile, suggesting he was almost joking, but not quite. It was a smile that didn't reach his eyes. "Danny and his sister fancy themselves to be cooks, and went off to view the kitchen, or galley, or whatever you call it on a boat."

The son looked to be mid-twenties and favored his mother. Thin, not particularly tall, faded blue eyes, an open face, flushed now at his dad's joke/criticism. He extended a hand to the Judge, introducing himself as Daniel Westerman or "Just Danny", and then sat down. He sported a corduroy jacket in dark blue over a paler blue dress shirt, no tie, and soft charcoal slacks. There was a guarded look in his face that stained his eyes and was repeated in the beginning nasolabial folds around his mouth, despite a brave smile pasted on his lips. His handshake was determined.

The young woman behind Danny extended a small stiff hand hesitatingly to shake. "Laura Westerman," she said softly. She briefly touched the Judge's hand before yanking hers away… as though scalded, then slid into the chair next to her brother on the opposite side of the table.

Laura looked late twenties, a younger, taller version of her mom, streaked blond hair turning to brown. Blue eyes again, watching the Judge suspiciously. She was dressed in a white linen skirt and a bright yellow blouse buttoned up to her neck.

"Laura's my oldest, Judge," said Charlie. "Likes to make unannounced inspections of kitchens. She's an expert cook, takes classes, has certificates, wants to open her own restaurant someday." There was a new tone of warmth in Charlie's voice, missing in his introduction of his son.

"Crab curry soup is on the way, Dad," said Laura. "And it looks yummy."

"That's my CFO, Larry Cain, next to Danny," said Charlie, pointing again with his spoon, looking anxious now to feed his bulk. The Judge continued his saunter around the table as Larry Cain stood to greet him. Cain had strands of black hair, combed with precision over a balding pate, contrasting with his tight mustache fixed like an appliance under this nose, its appearance suggesting it got combed a lot. He was thin, and a little rickety, wobbling as he waited for the Judge to reach his outstretched hand. His handshake was firm, the hand boney and callused, and his brown eyes met the Judge's with squinted precision as they shook. He looked mid-sixties, or perhaps older, dressed in a pale blue shirt with a large open collar and designer jeans.

"And last and perhaps least, at the end of the table, my business partner, Ross Hamilton." There was that smile again, noted the Judge, the one that never reached Charlie's eyes.

Hamilton had a lean face, defined by his hawk-like nose and prominent jaw, softened only by bushy black eyebrows which looked to never to have been clipped. He was a slender man, tall and willowy, dressed in a blue blazer and white cotton shirt open at the collar, and tan slacks. Hamilton did not get up, and declined to shake the Judge's proffered hand, instead turning in his chair to look at the Judge with hooded eyes. "I know you, Judge. All about you. You are an unsavory character. Preying on females and such."

The Judge blinked. As far as he could remember, he'd never met the man in his life. He retracted his hand, shrugged, and turned to watch Katy. She was behind him, dutifully shaking hands in turn. Then she slipped around him to settle herself at the far end of the table next to Ross Hamilton, as far from Charlie as she could get. This left the Judge with an empty seat between Katy and Maddy Stevens, the executive assistant.

Charlie watched him with a touch of disapproval now he was adjacent to the hot young assistant. Tough darts, thought the Judge, giving the assistant a closer look since Katy was distracted initiating conversation with Ross Hamilton to her left. He hoped these people didn't have medical problems to relate, and again wished he'd been successful in talking Katy entirely out of her cruise. Flying to Hawaii in business class would have been so damn more civilized.

Maddy Stevens fluttered her dark eyes framed by large lashes at the Judge, and sat a little straighter in her chair, thrusting her chest forward slightly. The Judge wondered if it was for him. Whatever halter she had on underneath her white blouse must have been sheer and flimsy, as hard nipples showed through the silk provocatively at him; twin points his eyes couldn't miss.

The Judge suddenly felt Katy's stare boring into the back of his head, her conversation with Ross Hamilton apparently paused. He quickly pasted a mild smile on his face as he made a show of swinging his head around the room to gaze at the festive tables and their animated guests dining in the distance. Surveying the room as if that had been his only intent.

Damn! Caught again. Katy watched him like a hawk. And had a memory like an elephant for each infraction, of which unfortunately there were many. Hell, he was still a red-blooded American male. Looking was supposed to be okay as long as he didn't touch, wasn't it? He leaned slightly away from Katy lest one of her pointed elbows came in the direction of his ribs. She wasn't real tolerant about 'just looking'.

Charlie had been watching him carefully too from under bushy eyebrows, his disapproval gone, replaced now with a triumphant smile. Happy his 'executive' assistant had made the intended enviable impression. Alice Westerman's expression had changed too, moving slightly to the sour. As though the Mr. and Mrs. Westerman had completed another act in a morality ritual performed together on a frequent basis.

CHAPTER 4
DAY 1
7:30 PM

"You always take your staff along when you cruise, Charlie?" asked the Judge, making his voice light-hearted and conversational, trying not to get off on the wrong foot. He apparently failed, wincing as Katy's disapproving elbow sliced into his ribs beneath his arm resting on the table. Christ, he would get to the table early tomorrow and choose a seat between the daughter and son, away from Katy's elbows.

Charlie's eyes raised to the Judge's. Examining the Judge as though he were some sort of newfound beetle, some slight interest beginning in the back of his dark, dark eyes.

"Yes… err…Judge… you said your nickname was Judge, right? I like my staff handy. I never stop working. To do so is to risk your entire business. The world moves at an extremely fast pace these days. And competitors are in the wings always, ready to pounce on your smallest mistake. What is it exactly you do, Judge?"

"I mostly lawyer these days, Charlie. It's good fun and it pays the rent."

"A lawyer, huh. Don't have much use for lawyers. My experience is you pay them a lot of money, only so they can make a lot of trouble for you, thereby requiring more of their time to fix the trouble they've made, and so you have to pay them even more money. Kind of a closed feedback circuit, and expensive. Lawyers are useless creatures who produce nothing of value. Like a leech, they attach themselves to your business and just suck."

"So, you don't use lawyers?" asked the Judge, keeping his tone deliberately neutral

"Oh yes. I have to. I use a lot of them, and all the time. Trapped into it because I'm in business. I just don't like them."

"They probably don't like you either, Charlie."

Jesus, Katy's jab was even sharper this time. He bet no one elbowed Charlie in his ribs.

"Is your business profitable?" asked the Judge.

"Oh yes. Very profitable. I've got a lot of money as a result."

"And what do you do with all your money, Charlie?"

"What? What do you mean?"

"How do you spend your downtime, Charlie? What do you do for fun?"

"This isn't a date, Judge. Making my money is my fun time." Charlie snorted at the stupidity of the Judge's question, then turned to whisper something to his wife.

Charlie then turned back to look at the Judge again. "I remember now, Judge. You're the lawyer who got those filthy pedophiles in that pre-school off. The

Sand, or the Strand, or something. What a disgusting piece of work that was. How do you live with yourself?"

"They were innocent, Charlie. They should have never been charged. There was no evidence they'd done anything wrong. Tried in the press by yellow journalists, pursued in a criminal case by a politically motivated D.A., dogged by rigged testimony from young children who were coached to "remember" things that never happened. These were children exploited by psychologists who had their own pre-determined narrative of what ought to have happened, anxious to garner business for their sloppy therapy practice. It was a travesty, misplaced lynch mob mentality.

Yeah, Charlie, I got them off. And proud of it."

"Hah," snorted Charlie. "Two hung juries. Someone must have thought they were guilty."

"It's the essence of our judicial system, Charlie. Innocent until proven guilty. My clients were innocent, are innocent. The State couldn't prove different. Because there was no different."

"Sure, Judge. Sure."

Charlie's sarcastic refrain cut through the air, crackling with animosity, bouncing off the Judge's thick skin and causing him to smile with wonder at the depth of hostility in the man. He felt Katy stiffening by his side. He turned to look at her, saw color raising in her face, her aqua eyes glittering. She wasn't one to sit quiet while someone tried to belittle her man.

"So, what's the name of your company, Mr. Westerman?" Katy asked in a tight voice.

"Charlie, please Ma'am. Just Charlie." Charlie rattled off the household name of a well-known soda brand. "We own, make and bottle several of the most famous sodas in the world. Right now, around the planet, every minute, every day, thousands are lifting our bottles to their lips and enjoying the refreshing taste."

Charlie was starting to purr now. There was nothing better than talking about his business.

"You bottle in those single-use, soft plastic bottles?"

"Yes, of course."

"Why?" asked Katy.

"What?"

"Why? Why are you polluting the world with your plastic bottles?"

"Oh, come now, Katy. People like the plastic bottle. They're convenient. Easier to lift. Simple to dispose of. Nothing to return. They look chic. And if we used glass, as we did in the old days, well… we'd have to raise our price considerably. We're saving the consumer a lot of money." Charlie gave Katy a condescending smile, confident he'd satisfactorily answered her question.

"You ever hear of the Great Pacific Garbage Patch?"

Charlie's smile fled from his face as his eyes narrowed. "That's purely a myth, Katy. Propaganda from tree huggers who are against every advance that makes life better and cuts costs for the consumer."

"From what I hear, there are about one point eight trillion, that's trillion with a T, pieces of trash in the patch, and they weigh in the aggregate about eighty-eight thousand tons. The equivalent of five hundred jumbo jets."

"Well, the U.S. recycles. The U.S. is not contributing anything to this patch… if it exists."

"You said you bottle world-wide?"

"We do."

"So, your bottles are in lots of places."

"Of course."

"Places like China I suppose. And Indonesia, the Philippines, Vietnam, Sri Lanka, maybe Thailand?"

"Yes. There and all over. We do a lot of business in the Far East."

"Most of the trash in the Pacific Garbage Patch comes from those six countries."

"Well, maybe that's so. But it doesn't mean it's our soda bottles that are a part of the trash."

"Oh, but it does, Charlie. Cigarette butt filters and food wrappers make up a portion of the trash, but plastic beverage bottles are the third most likely trash to be found in the patch, and the plastic bottle caps from your bottles are the fourth. In terms of rate of increase, some studies suggest plastic drink bottles are increasing at a much higher rate than any other trash item."

"Well, I don't know about those statistics, young lady. I mean, statistics can be massaged to prove anything. And we have programs focused on ways to reduce our products' impact on the environment."

"Let's face it, Charlie, your company does very little to solve the problem your bottles are making. Particularly in the Far East where you are raking in all those profits from soda sales. You may talk the talk on sustainability, but the enormous rate at which you pump out your single-use plastic bottles shows you really have no interest in the consequences for our oceans.

In fact, I looked into your company last year, read your annual report, did some research on your business. I had to speak at a special conference on sustainability for the high school where I work. Your company turned out one hundred and ten billion plastic bottles last year… that's thirty-four-hundred bottles a second… a second… Charlie. A ton of money for you. But your company refuses to assume any significant responsibility for its role in the pollution crisis you're creating in our oceans."

"You didn't see those numbers in our annual report, Katy. We don't disclose the volume of plastic packaging we put into the market."

"And why don't you disclose your exact numbers?"

"Well, eh… It's not really relevant. It's a small part of the cost of our product. And, well… our lawyers say it's a little too commercially sensitive to disclose."

"I'll bet." But you're right, Charlie. I didn't. It was an estimate by a knowledgeable expert in your market."

"I don't think this discussion is getting us anywhere, Katy. I'm the only real expert in my market.

Your so-called expert is clueless. Anyway, here comes the soup."

CHAPTER 5
DAY 1
7:40 PM

Sean, the young Irish waiter who'd gotten the Judge his drinks earlier at the pool, delivered the soup, delivered his cheerful spiel about the soup, and delivered the table from further descent into open warfare. He put the bowls down in front of each diner with a flourish. It was a delicious smelling crab bisque, Creole style. Kennedy returned from the men's room to his seat just as Sean put the last bowl in front of the Judge. The steaming bowls were immediately dug into by the entire table, the music of soft slurping joining the similar cadence across the dining room.

The Judge was just tipping his bowl away from himself to corner the last dribble when Kennedy, sitting across from Katy, suddenly gave a strange, gurgled cry.

"Ahhh… aaa... ouf... ouf…"

He staggered up from his chair, pressing his hands to his throat, eyes bulging with pain. One shaking hand reached into his inside coat pocket and came out with an EpiPen. He desperately fumbled its cap off with his thumb and leaning down, plunged the pen through his slacks into his upper thigh. He stood there, gasping, waiting, needing the epinephrine to take effect. His face was contorted with pain now, turning from red to purple.

As the Judge watched, the expression in Kennedy's eyes turned from pain to panic. He savagely yanked the EpiPen from his thigh and plunged it in again with vengeance, rocking the pen around in his leg, enlarging its hole.

Horror spread across his face as the pen apparently had no effect.

Alice Westerman jumped up, screaming, "Oh no. Oh my God. Help him! For God's sake somebody help him! Do something, someone do something. He's got a terrible nut allergy. He told them, 'No nuts.'"

Kennedy threw his head back with a strangled cry, then fell forward, sprawling head-first across the table, his face crunching down, scattering china and stemware in all directions. A veritable flood of water, soup and cocktails slid like a tsunami across the table and over its edge, soaking the Judge's lap as he belatedly scooted his chair back from the table.

There was suddenly pandemonium in the room. People standing from their seats to get a better view, waiters dashing from all directions toward the table, Alice Westerman screaming, "No… No…No…"

Shock was etched on Charlie's face. His daughter looked like she was going to throw up. Katy turned wide-eyed to the Judge.

The Judge jumped up and moved to help, as did Danny Westerman.

They eased Kennedy off the table and flopped him back into his dining chair like a lifeless doll where he stayed, not moving. Then Kennedy's head fell back, his face bleached white, his eyes rolling back into his head.

A man from a table across the room appeared at the Judge's arm and said he was a doctor. He went to Kennedy's side and put two fingers to his neck for a pulse. Then he put his ear to Kennedy's chest.

The table waited expectantly along with the rest of the room, everyone holding their breath.

The doctor looked up at them and shook his head.

"He's gone."

CHAPTER 6
DAY 1
7:45 PM

Two men in white uniforms came storming into the room and over to their table as though shot from a cannon. As the Judge discreetly took a couple of pictures with his cell phone, one of the men put quick fingers to Kennedy's neck, then shined a small flashlight into his eyes. Finally, he twisted a stethoscope on his neck and listened for a heartbeat. He frowned and shook his head. The other one unfolded a portable stretcher he was carrying on the floor and they lifted Kennedy over and onto it. As they hoisted the stretcher up between them, Kennedy's arms flopped out to hang down at either side, and a burst of bad air slurried out from under the body, perfuming the air as muscles in Kennedy's colons released their tension.

Kennedy was a big man. The stretcher buckled slightly, as did the crew members shouldering their load. The Judge snapped another picture with his cell phone just before Danny Westerman rushed forward with a tablecloth from an empty table and flung it over Kennedy's head and chest, creating some modicum of privacy.

The men with their burden disappeared as quickly as they had come like some automated vacuum service, leaving the room in shocked silence.

The first waiter to reach the table had been Sean, the young Irishman, towels in hand to clean up the mess. His blue eyes looked stricken now in a face so red it made his freckles vanish. Sean started clearing the broken and turned-over dishes where Kennedy had sprawled. He picked up the EpiPen, only to drop it again as though a hot potato when the Judge's voice rasped, "Don't touch that EpiPen. Get me a plastic bag to put the pen in, and a container for some of the gentlemen's soup as well."

The implication of the Judge's words hit Alice Westerman like a physical blow. She started to wail. Charlie leaned over close and in an audible whisper muttered, "Shut the fuck up, Alice. You're supposed to hardly know Kennedy."

Alice's teeth closed with a crunch and she sat back in her chair, stifling further noise with a handkerchief she produced from her small purse.

Sean scurried off like a crab, scuttling among the tables toward the safety of the kitchen while the Judge brought his cell phone out again and snapped several pictures of the EpiPen from different angles.

The Judge turned to Sean as he returned with a small plastic bottle and a small plastic bag. The Judge put the EpiPen in the plastic bag and poured some of the soup into the bottle.

"Did you take the gentleman's dinner order?" the Judge asked, nodding at Kennedy's empty chair.

"Yes sir." Sean looked calmer now, if you ignored the slight shake in his hands.

"Did he tell you he had a nut allergy?"

"Yes sir."

"What did you do about it?"

"I noted it on his meal card and turned it in at the kitchen."

"Turned it in to who?"

"There's a big metal wheel. We clip the meal card to the wheel, one card for each seat at each table. The kitchen staff pull the wheel around and work through the cards, trying to make sure each table's orders are ready about the same time."

"Let's go see your big metal wheel," said the Judge.

The Judge followed Sean as he weaved his way back through the collection of tables in the dining room, all abuzz about Kennedy, to the room's rear where twin doors led into the kitchen.

The kitchen was stainless steel and bright; busy hands everywhere rattling pots and china, stroking flat irons over flaming burners filled with burbling sauces and meats, busy fingers plucking green lettuce leaves from rapidly diminishing balls of iceberg to deposit on chilled plates. Organized chaos. The Judge supposed it had to be like that.

A large metal counter ran down the side separating the work area and creating a narrow corridor against the wall. A portion of the counter had cabinets above with heat lamps imbedded to keep plated food warm. And plates there were, a great many strung along the counter, each with its own meal card under the plate; perhaps twenty plates ready but not yet picked up and served. Waiters flowed around the Judge, dashing in to pick up plates and out again, making him feel like a sedentary rock in a stream. The Judge took a picture of the counter and wheel with his cell.

"So, anyone could have dumped peanut oil into Kennedy's soup while the soup sat here?" asked the Judge, turning back to Sean.

"I suppose so, sir. But who would do such a thing?"

"I don't know, but we need to find out if that's what happened. Did you see anyone lingering around this counter? Perhaps waiting for Kennedy's soup to come out?"

"No." Sean's demeanor turned from calm to worried.

"No one?"

"No."

"You know, if you're lying Sean, it could make you an accomplice to murder. You could go to jail."

Sean's face went red again. "No. I saw no one, sir."

"Did you see Miss Westerman, Laura Westerman in the kitchen taking a tour?"

"Oh, well, yes. She came in with a man just as I left to take an order to another table."

"Danny Westerman?"

"I guess so."

"Did you see them leave?"

"No."

The Judge snapped another picture with his cell phone, trying to get most of the cooking staff. Then he inspected a large trash can at the end of the counter. He lifted the top layer of paper wrappings in the container with his finger. After a bit of looking he found a small bottle three layers down. The brand on the side of the bottle read, *Pure Peanut Oil Concentrate, Gujarat Farms.* Using a pen from his pocket, the Judge lifted the empty bottle out, placed it on the counter for a picture on his cell phone, then placed it into a plastic baggie quickly supplied by Sean; Sean's eyes were wide saucers now.

They walked back into the dining room where some sense of decorum had returned, though the Judge caught idle chatter here and there about the dramatic collapse and death across the room. Snippets that they "didn't want to eat in this dining room again" and "a bad omen for the rest of the cruise" trickled up to the Judge's ears. One old lady was jabbering it was "like the death of the albatross in The Rhyme of the Ancient Mariner." Probably a retired English Lit. teacher, mused the Judge.

When they reached the table, Alice was still hyperventilating into her handkerchief. Charlie sat immobile at his end of the table as if frozen in time, his face a mask of blankness concealing whatever emotions were bouncing around inside. Katy was pale and had lost her appetite, backing her chair several inches away from the table, looking for a polite way to flee.

Daughter Laura Westerman was digging with gusto into her charred swordfish, flinging chunks into her mouth as if there were no tomorrow. Kind of like a push lawnmower chopping. It was hard to tell if this was a stress reaction, or the normal way she ate. The CEO, George Walker, and the CFO, Larry Cain, both looked pale, crunching the remains of their salads like spooked rabbits, trying to avoid looking at Charlie or anyone else. Guilt or terror? The Judge couldn't tell.

Ross Hamilton, the business partner, sat at the end of the table, one knee folded over the other, and watched the crowded dining room behind the Judge with studied disinterest. His face was calm and relaxed as if nothing had happened. Apparently the loss of Kennedy meant nothing to him.

Charlie's face suddenly softened. He stood up and reached over to help his wife up from her chair, her frame still bent with racking muffled sobs, and escorted her out of the dining room, nodding at the Judge as he passed.

Katy reached over to the Judge's hand, saying, "I've lost my appetite too, Judge. Can we go." He slipped the small 'to go' bottle of soup, and plastic bags containing the EpiPen and empty peanut concentrate bottle into his sport coat pocket and they glided out of the dining room, ignoring the nosey stares from diners they passed.

The Judge helped Katy through the door of their narrow cabin and into the relative peacefulness beyond. But peace and quiet were likely to change soon. The young kids in the neighboring cabin on the left were not married but rather on a 'get to know each other' extended date. They'd been partying much of the afternoon, drinking and blasting music out their open veranda door before settling into noisy lovemaking on what must have been the floor of their veranda. That fortunately didn't last long. Stamina lost by all the booze, the Judge supposed. But they'd be back after their dinner and God knew what the night was going to be like.

It was a refurbished ship, and their narrow cabin was supposed to be fitted with a queen bed. But the cruise company website had lied. The cruise ship had taken a page out of the airlines' handbook, making everything smaller, tighter and more restricted. His oversized butt didn't fit well on the narrow toilet seat, leaving a painful pink ring if he spent any time on it. And the shower was the size of a coffin stood on end. The narrow 'veranda', as they called it, had two undersized chairs and a small coffee table squeezed onto it. Blinder partitions on either side extended from the exterior wall to the rail, cutting the view to a forty-degree arc unless you stood right at the rail.

Earlier that day out of curiosity he'd leaned out over the rail to look around the partition on the right. His eyes made surprise contact with a woman quietly sitting in her chair, perhaps late seventies, wearing oversized bikini bottoms the size of a tank, but topless, taking the sun on her weathered boobs. She gave the Judge a look that could have peeled paint.

He'd whipped back around, flushed, thinking about the changes going on in his own body, his large paunch, jowls beginning to sag, the artificial parts he now had to use: orthotics that allowed him to walk with his fallen arches, hair dye to keep his hair medium brown, the teeth replaced with crowns, the reading glasses he detested but was forced to use. He hated getting old. But there seemed no good alternative.

At least the lady next door wouldn't be noisy.

Katy sat the Judge down on the bed. "Now, Judge," she started, using her schoolmarm voice, "This trip is my treat, and it's to get you away from the stress and angst of practicing law for a week. This isn't about chasing mysteries; it's about chilling out and relaxation. I don't want you running about, wading into this accident the way you like to do, hunting for a murderous explanation. Just stay out of it and let the captain and his ship's officers handle things. Can you do that?"

The Judge opened his baby blue eyes wide and gave Katy his big boyish smile, a non-committal smile all the same. She knew what that meant. Like some enormous salmon coming out of the water to snap up that perfect fly, he was already hooked. It was his nature. And she hadn't been able to change him. She'd pretty much given up trying. She sighed and headed for their miniscule shower.

The Judge watched his bride depart, reading her resignation to his desire to pursue what had happened to Kennedy. She knew him well. It was bound to be a hell of a lot more interesting than just lying around the boat.

He decided to take a quick walk around the deck, soak up the ocean breeze, and reflect on what he's observed. He headed upstairs to the promenade deck. When he returned a half hour later, both sides of their bed had been turned down by the maid. And Katy was fast asleep on her side.

Not yet sleepy, on a whim, the Judge decided to try the jacuzzi, officially open till midnight, and perhaps reasonably quiet now it was eleven p.m. He needed to work down the stress of the evening. He donned his fancy trunks, his green t-shirt, a ship's robe from the closet, and crept out of the stateroom.

CHAPTER 7
DAY 1
8:30 PM

Charlie deposited his wife in their suite, suggesting she take a sedative and go to bed. Her eyes were puffy from crying and she didn't seem able to speak. She simply nodded absently and began rummaging through her purse for her little purple bottle.

Kennedy's death had been a shock, but Alice would get over it. All the same he'd keep a close eye on her. As he kept a close eye on everybody in his family, particularly now he'd lost his youngest dependent, Jay, some months earlier. He looked down at the faint scars still on the top of his hands and forearms. Second degree burns.

Alice hardly spoke to him since that night. Just looked at him with her narrow flinty eyes, cold, hard. She blamed him for the loss of Jay, he knew. Charlie'd taken all his feelings and placed them in a mental box in his head, which he sealed and stored in some deep corner for later retrieval. There was too much business to be done; he wasn't going to be distracted by things he could do nothing about.

"I'm going for a cigar, Alice," Charlie called over his shoulder, as he fled the cabin and Alice's grief. He took the stairs four flights down and walked out on the promenade deck and along toward the bow. He took his cigar out, clipped the end over the rail into the sea, and brought his lighter to his face, drawing his breath and the flame in as the cigar's tip began to glow. It was the same silver lighter from that night. The wind whipped most of the white cloud away, dissipating some of his satisfaction from belching out the cigar's smoke.

Kennedy'd been something of an asshole, he thought. A debutante really, fussing about this and that, having to have press releases and product brochures all just right, afraid to take any risk. And God could he spend out an advertising budget.

He suspected Kennedy'd been sleeping with Alice. In fact, he was certain of it. Course he really didn't care much, so long as it was discreet, and he wasn't publicly embarrassed. Alice and he hadn't had sex in years. She'd turned into a dried-up prune, all wrinkles and saggy breasts, a stretched-out pouch of a belly, her once pretty face lined and wrinkled, her butt wizened and boney. If Alice's little affair with Kennedy made her happy and kept her out of his hair, well and good.

But he still found it comfortable to sleep together with Alice in their common bed. He found other outlets for his other drives these days. He smiled at that thought, thinking of Maddy Stevens, with her long legs. Legs that seemed to go on forever under her skirt, or stretched up around his neck when he stood over her on her back.

He thought now and then about that night, six months back, when Jay had killed himself. He'd been hard on Jay, he supposed. Hell, he was hard on everyone. It was the way he'd been raised. His drunken father, Joe, beating the shit out of him periodically, just for fun. His large diabetic mother just watching, afraid, wringing her hands, wondering when it'd be her turn.

It hadn't been easy. And he'd leaned hard on the children in his household, trying to toughen them for the real world so they'd understand. Go out and never be poor. And they'd all hardened a little, except for Jay. The weak one. Like his mother. Soft, emotional, artistic, sensitive. No discipline. No ability to accomplish anything, really. So many times, he'd berated the young man for his laziness, his lack of drive, lack of follow-through, lack of discipline to accomplish something. Jay had shaken off his criticism like water off a duck. Well, perhaps some of it must have stuck. Jay'd managed to accomplish his own suicide in one try, kind of surprising really since it was Jay. He smiled bitterly.

He looked down at his hands and wrists again. He'd rushed across the driveway that night, whipping his robe off, throwing it around Jay, trying to snuff out the flames. 9-1-1 had gotten Jay to the UCLA burn center over the hill in Westwood where he'd lingered for a week. Then infection set in and that was that. Alice had lived at the burn center that week; refusing to sit with Charlie when he was there, just glaring at him across the waiting room. After the first night, Charlie'd gone back to his office to work. The business couldn't wait. And sitting around moaning at the hospital was a waste of time. Jay'd screwed up, as Charlie knew he would. Best to get over it and move on.

CHAPTER 8
DAY 1
9:00 PM

The Judge shed the green t-shirt and projected his rotund body toward the jacuzzi sunk into the deck of the boat at its bow. It was a beautiful night, a calm sea, stars twinkling overhead, and the twenty-person capacity spa was jammed to the gills with twenty-eight capering revelers in assorted suits, hair colors, bare and covered chests depending on declared sex. They were nestled in tightly, like graham crackers stacked in a box, the murky green water lapping over the side periodically as they leaned about.

The Judge wasn't sure he would fit, and even more doubtful anyone would ever get out again if he tried. But an older man with a paunch that put the Judge's to shame managed to extract himself from the fray and scramble out over the side of the jacuzzi, standing and leaning down to extend a hand to help his friend, a horse-faced blonde with a scrawny ass, younger, perhaps late forties. Well, well, guess there was room after all.

As the Judge approached, winding his way amongst the last teak loungers scattered across the deck at all angles like a cosmic jigsaw puzzle, he was joined by a wing-man also intent on the hot water, its vapors now assaulting the Judge's nose with the scent of chlorine that demanded a drink, just to cut the smell. The man was shorter than the Judge, maybe six feet, a little chubby, and a lot younger, late twenties probably. It was dark and they were both in shadows so he was difficult to see. His swimsuit was a replica of boxing shorts, large and bulky, bright panels of satin red in front and back, matching panels of white on either side. They didn't look quick-dry like the Judge's suit, and probably still had the netting inside. He looked to have light eyes, likely blue, and very white skin that lapped over the top of his boxers.

"Do you suppose there's room for two?" asked the Judge.

"I'm sure," Boxer Shorts muttered. "Those two just left," jerking his thumb at the departing occupants leaving a trail of drippings across the deck.

Boxer Shorts started to clamber over the spa side first, intending to squeeze in next to a cute brunette. She looked mid-twenties, the top of her two-piece suit little more than two patches and a string semi-covering modest breasts, her silky hair curled up in a bun at the back of her head. Startling blue eyes evaluated Boxer Shorts for three seconds; then she slid way over, forcing the black gal next to her to scrunch up against her neighbor, creating a space and a half for Boxer Shorts and then the Judge to squeeze in.

They settled in, the Judge feeling unreasonably close to a middle-aged lady to his left who didn't seem to mind. She gave him a bright Midwest smile and seemed to enjoy the invasion of her personal space, the cloudy water filling around him lukewarm, disappointing, belying the promise of heat in the vapors raising from the pool. He looked across the spa at a man hunched down, his knees pulled up so the water was up to his neck. The man scowled back at the Judge. His face was vaguely familiar. Of course, one of Charlie's people at the dinner table, Les or Ross or something. He'd been a bit rude to the Judge for no reason. Oh well, to hell with him.

The Judge settled down, ensconced in the lukewarm water up to his nipples. He downed an extra dry Bombay Sapphire gin and tonic and managed to avoid meaningless chit chat with the Midwest lady by responding in mono-syllables to each of her questions. She finally gave up in favor of the older man to her right, chatting his ear off in a desperate effort to use all her words for the day. The sultry breeze sweeping rearward from the bow blended with the lingering taste of Sapphire and the sparkling stars above to drain all anxiety from the Judge's psyche; he started to nod off.

Suddenly there was an enormous disturbance in the water beside the Judge, as though some wiggly creature had jumped in. The Judge's eyes fluttered open to catch the sight of a small hand, loaded with angry venom, delivered as a slap across Boxer Trunk's cheek. His head flew back with the force of the blow, slamming him into the Judge as the young brunette screeched through the cluttering noise of the jacuzzi, "You fuckin asshole. Keep your hands off my butt."

Boxer Trunk quickly slunk down deeper in the water, tight against the Judge, seeking shelter. The voice of a young redhead across the tub rose with indignation. "He did the same thing to me this afternoon. He's a groper. Get the perp the fuck out of here."

There was a general muttering among the other females jammed in the jacuzzi, and the redhead continued. "They're together." Pointing at the Judge. "Get both the assholes the fuck out of our spa".

Ross, Charlie's partner or whatever, pointed an angry finger at the Judge from across the tub, and hissed, "I know him. He's a registered sex offender!"

Ms. Midwest to the Judge's right, her smile replaced by a snarl reminiscent of a maddened wolf, began shoving at the Judge, almost pounding, yelling at him to get out of the spa. Boxer Shorts was similarly attacked by the brunette. The two men rose up out of the spa together in self-defense, hoisting themselves into sitting positions on its shadowy rim and then twisting their legs up and over on to the deck, sloshing water onto a pair of smart white leather shoes which had suddenly appeared there. The Judge looked up to see the tall figure of a ship's officer standing in the shoes, his face in shadow under his captain's hat, a lot of heavy braid on his cardboard squared shoulders. *Oh, Shit!*

"I'm the third officer," said White Shoes in a clipped English accent that had a touch of India, matching the brown skin of exposed forearms and the jaw jutting out from under his cap and picking up light. "What's going on?"

There was an immediate babble of female voices, octaves rising into a crescendo, small hands with painted nails jabbed threateningly at Boxer Shorts and the Judge.

"Are you two friends?" asked White Shoes.

There was an immediate chorus, "No" from the Judge, and "Yes" from Boxer Shorts, who leaned in closer to the Judge in the shadows, seeking to validate his credentials.

"I've never seen this man before in my life," shouted the Judge, his voice rising an octave, pushing the man away.

"We're friends," yelped Boxer Shorts. "We had a conversation about the condition of the spa before we got in together. All the tits and ass packed in there… You know, guy talk."

"We had no such thing," snarled the Judge. Semi-ballistic now.

White Shoes gruffly handed Boxer Shorts off to a junior crew member, no braid, who appeared out of nowhere at his side with brawny tattooed arms. Boxer Shorts was hustled around the corner, apparently to be separately interrogated.

White Shoes then turned his attention to the Judge, demanding identification. The Judge suddenly felt panicky, realizing he'd left his room card/ID card in his room. He had no way to identify himself. This seemed to make White Shoes even unhappier.

"All right, all right. Crewman Stevens is going to see your special friend to his cabin," said White Shoes, nodding toward the corner around which Boxer Shorts had disappeared. "He'll be confined in his room until the Captain can deal with this. We've had complaints about him already and we're not even a full day out."

"As for you… err… Mr. X, put your t-shirt on and let's go wake your wife up and see if she can identify you."

The Judge pulled his green t-shirt over his head and down over his paunch, watching it soak up the water from his chest, giving the shirt a more pleasing, darker green color. White Shoes had no time to be bothered, thrusting the Judge's robe at him, which he put on.

The Judge was marched across the deck, past the jacuzzi, where several mean little fists came out of the water to be shaken at the Judge, as though he were a common felon. Ross, or whatever his name was, seemed all smiles now, taking his hand out of the water to point his forefinger at the Judge, then wiggling it in a classic 'Shame on You' gesture.

The Judge was marched inside and across the lobby bar, heads turning, eyes staring, leaving a trail of droplets across the carpet to the elevators, his sandals squelching as he walked. By the time they reached the relative protection of the elevator bays, the Judge wasn't sure he had any teeth left from all his jaw clenching.

The Judge and White Shoes rode down two floors and walked along the corridor to the Judge's stateroom, where White Shoes rapped on the cabin door with authority. After a second rap, and then a third, Katy's muffled voice came through the door, "Just a minute." The minute seemed like an eternity.

Finally, the door open and Katy peered out from inside her cabin robe, her blond hair tousled, her aqua eyes filled with sleep. They narrowed quickly though, focusing first on the Judge in his soaked green shirt under his open robe, and then at tall Captain White Shoes with his grim face.

"You know his man, ma'am?" asked White Shoes.

Katy paused for what seemed forever, and then said in a mock doubtful voice, "Do I get a prize?"

"Oh, for Christ sakes, Katy. Don't dick around. Just tell him it's me and let me in. I'm going to catch pneumonia."

"Yeah, he's mine. What's he done now, Captain?"

White Shoes shook his finger at the Judge, like Ross had. "You should be more careful of the company you keep, sir. Good night."

He spun on his heel and marched back down the corridor, leaving the Judge standing in his puddle in front of Katy, who had her hands on her hips with that 'this is going to be good' look on her face.

Damn, damn… damn.

CHAPTER 9
DAY 2
7:30 AM

The Judge awoke to sun light blasting into the room. He'd forgotten to close the curtains. He sat on the edge of bed and squinted through the glare to the small chair where he'd slung his sport coat the night before. He'd set the plastic bags containing the empty peanut concentrate bottle and the used EpiPen under the chair where his coat had been dumped. But there was no sport coat there now, and no plastic bag under the chair.

He quickly moved to the closet and found his coat hanging there primly on a hanger. He reached into side pocket, feeling for the plastic bags with the EpiPen and the peanut concentrate bottle. They weren't there. He quickly went to the other outside pocket, then to the inside pockets. No pen, no bottle. No bags. He moved to the tiny refrigerator where he'd put the small sample of crab bisque soup. It was gone too.

The Judge looked at all the surfaces, then moved to the drawer beside his bed and pulled it out. Nothing. Katy's side drawer was equally empty. The evidence was gone.

He grabbed the phone and rang for housekeeping, then threw on his clothes. Ten minutes later the pretty dark-skinned maid with the flashing white teeth knocked on the suite's door and the Judge ushered her in.

"What's your name again?"

"Sophia."

"Sophia, I'm missing something."

Sophia clutched her pass key to her chest, her eyes getting big and round. She looked like she might faint.

"No, Sophia. Nothing like that. Nothing valuable. But something important just the same."

"Yes, sir."

"I had a zip lock plastic bag, see-through, which had a small empty bottle, and a used EpiPen. I put it under that chair last night, and my coat on top of the chair. And in the refrigerator, I had a small bit of soup from last night's dinner in a container. Have you seen any of them?"

Sophia looked confused. "What's an EpiPen, sir?"

"It looks a little like a fountain pen."

"Oh. Yes. I saw your plastic bag with the pen and the empty bottle. The pen looked broken. I put them in my trash container."

"And the soup?"

"Yes, the old soup. It smelt really bad. I threw it out too, sir. I didn't want you or the missus to get sick."

"Damn," muttered the Judge. "Where did you throw it out, Sophia? Is there a big trash can down the hall where we can go find it, retrieve it?"

"I don't know."

"You don't know? Jesus, Sophia, you don't know where you threw it away?"

"I don't know where it goes, sir. There's a big hole in the wall, a… a… a chute. We all throw trash from the rooms down the hole, and it goes down somewhere below. And I guess it gets taken care of somewhere down there."

Damn… Damn… Damn. Now he was going to have to go dumpster diving.

"Can you take me to your supervisor, Sophia? I need to talk to him about where the trash goes."

Sophia nodded uncertainly, her face flushed, and slowly turned to lead the Judge out into the corridor, her body hunched over like she was going to her own hanging. She led him down the long hall to a small cubby at the end of their section where a large black man was squeezed in, filling out paperwork.

"This is Mr. Jeff. He's the boss."

The black man looked up at the Judge with soft eyes, then carefully unwound himself from the tiny desk and wiggled out of the cubby and into the hall. His skin was a true black, offsetting perfect ivory teeth in a loose smile. He was dressed in the same steward colors as Sophia and the other staff on the floor.

"Did you get yourself in trouble again, Sophia? What'd you do now?"

"Nothing like that," said the Judge, feeling Sophia back away behind him in fear. "Something important from my room got discarded as trash by mistake and went down the trash chute. I was hoping to retrieve it."

"Not likely, sir. But come with me. We'll go talk to the engineer fella."

Jeff led the Judge back along the corridor to the elevator bank and hit a down button, flashing his ID to the scanner beside the control buttons. The elevator whisked down in a steep drop, two floors below the last passenger deck. Jeff led the Judge down another long corridor, and opened a door marked *Sanitation Engineering.* Inside, a technician sat at a desk with various displays blinking above him amongst a sweeping bank of instruments, controls and live video cameras.

The man turned to nod. "Hi Jeff. What can I do for you?"

"You supervise the waste collection and disposal for the ship?" asked the Judge.

"I do. About ten tons of it every twenty-four hours, mostly leftover food and poop."

"There were two plastic bags thrown down the trash chute about eight hours ago. One had an empty glass bottle, the other a plastic EpiPen. And there was a plastic container with liquid in it. They were put down the trash chute in error. Is there any way I can retrieve them?"

The engineer smiled, then slowly shook his head.

"We immediately sort stuff that comes down the chute. Glass goes into our glass grinder. The plastic is immediately bundled with other plastic and stored for later off-loading. We have thirty-six hundred people on this ship so that's a lot of bundled plastic. There's no way to find your plastic now."

Damn! Damn, damn, and double damn!

CHAPTER 10
DAY 2
8:30 AM

The Judge was escorted to the elevator and whisked back to the guest decks. He had intended to return to his cabin but decided to let Katy sleep and headed instead for the assembly line breakfast laid out toward the back of the boat on the Pool Deck.

He got off the elevator into a flood of people flowing in both directions at once, some trying to escape on to the elevators, others trying to get to the dining room. He elbowed his way into the dining room and found himself in the middle of a horde of tubby people scurrying and scuffling to get in the buffet line. Others were on collision-risk cross-courses balancing flat plastic trays loaded with food that tilted dangerously in one direction or another as they scrambled for tables.

Some were abandoning trays filled with empty plates at tables and endeavoring to swim upstream, back to the tail of the food line for seconds. After all it was free food, wasn't it? At least sort of. No wonder over thirty-six percent of Americans were obese. You could certainly prove it by the chubby people on this boat. God could they eat.

The food was pretty bad too. Powdered scrambled eggs, likely left over from yesterday's breakfast, bacon burnt to a crisp, processed ham and sausage filled with nitrites and nitrates, mushy looking fruit even though the boat was only one day out, baked cinnamon rolls that would break a toe if dropped.

The Judge settled for coffee and some dry toast. He managed to snag a table by the window just ahead of a 200-pound lady, about four foot tall, who had made a desperate dive for it, nearly toppling her mile-high piled plate into the Judge's lap.

He settled in and tried the coffee. It had the right color but was diluted and tasteless, barely warm. *Yuck!*

He was just thinking about heading for one of the fancier restaurants aboard when a shadow cast over his table, and then the looming bulk of Charlie Westerman maneuvered around him and settled into the other chair facing him.

Charlie gave the Judge an ingratiating smile, the sort you expect from a leering shark. He wanted something. There was no rollicking chit-chat conversation in the man.

"So, you're something of a private detective as I understand, Judge."

"Yes, at times I've played that role," admitted the Judge, "with some modest success."

"And you suspected something last night, the way Kennedy died. You thought it suspicious."

"Well, it was odd. Particularly how the EpiPen didn't work."

"You collected samples of the soup and took the defective EpiPen with you, wrapped in plastic."

"Yes. I was going to give them to the police, or the coroner, or whoever will determine the cause of death, but…"

"But what?"

"They've gone missing from my cabin."

"Everything?"

"Everything."

"I see. Isn't that even more suspicious?"

"Not necessarily. The maid threw them out."

Charlie just looked at the Judge then, not saying how stupid that sounded. He didn't have to. His look said it all.

"Well, Judge, I'd like you to look into Kennedy's death further. I want to know what really happened. Was it just a freak accident? Or was it something else. I'll pay you whatever your hourly is."

"I'm not cheap, Charlie. And what I find goes to the authorities, regardless of who may be involved. Even if it happens to be you."

"You think I had something to do with it?" Charlies' eyes widened.

"From the reaction of your wife, Alice, and your whispered comment to her to be quiet, it sounded like a little hanky-panky was going on between Alice and Kennedy. If that were so, that would give you a motive."

Charlie laughed then. A mean cynical laugh that said more about him than he intended.

"Alice and I haven't had physical relations for years. And yes, I know about them. I don't give a damn. As long as it was discreet, and it was. Investigate that angle all you want, it'll lead nowhere. But if you drag our names through the mud, you'll regret it."

"Perhaps Alice threatened a divorce because of her tryst with Kennedy, or perhaps because of your relationship with your Executive Assistant. That would be a different motive."

"You don't miss much, do you Judge? Alice and I have a prenuptial agreement, iron clad, and besides, where would Alice go? She'd have some of my money, but who'd want her now?"

"Kennedy, apparently, if he hadn't died."

Charlie laughed his mean little laugh again. "Kennedy was a convenient windbag for Alice's R&R. A showboat without much substance. Alice wouldn't have contemplated a future with him. But you're partly right. I like having Alice around. We share our kids and being married precludes pressure from other females who might want to formalize a casual relationship. Alice is kind of like an old pair of socks you get used to and don't want to give up."

"So, if I investigate, there's nothing off limits?"

"No, nothing off limits, insofar as foul play goes, but if you go blabbing extraneous sexual details about me or my family just to spice up the story, I'll sue you so hard your great grandchildren will spend their lives bottling my soda in Thailand."

The Judge digested that threat but didn't respond. "I'll take the job, Charlie. There's nothing much else to do on this damn boat; and I do like a good mystery."

Charlie extended a huge paw across the table to shake the Judge's hand, carefully so as not to crush the Judge's fingers. Then he put both hands on the table, hoisted his bulk out of his chair, and lumbered off.

The Judge marveled at how quickly Charlie could switch positions without a care. First, he hated attorneys, now he needed one. First, he didn't care for the Judge, now they were pals. The Judge suspected their pal status wouldn't last.

CHAPTER 11
DAY 2
9:30AM

The Judge returned to his stateroom to find Katy up and out on the balcony in one of its small chairs. She'd ordered room service for two. The little balcony table was straining under the load of pastries, an omelet, hash browns, English muffins, bacon and sausage, fruit, orange juice and coffee. He squeezed in across from her, delighted to share a second breakfast. The sea was calm and the sky blue, giving truth to the name The Blue Pacific. He could smell the salt, and from somewhere overhead the hint of smoke from the ship's stacks far above.

It looked to be the beginnings of another nothing day aboard; a horde of feeding, drinking, dancing bodies scrambled together on the floating speck in the middle of the vast ocean. Katy had her spa to look forward to. The Judge…? Raucous noise and sunburn around the pool, or old movies in their suite. Katy of course was lobbying for him to go to the gym, but it was the last thing he felt like doing. And now… now he had a real mystery to work on, or perhaps just a freak accident. It was hard to tell. But he mentally rubbed his hands together anyway in anticipation. And perhaps he'd have some more of those no-calorie piña coladas, just to keep his mind clear.

He squeezed out of the small chair and stood up, throwing his hands above his head in a stretch, touching the ceiling above the veranda. Their stateroom telephone buzzed. The Judge took two steps into the unit and picked up the phone.

"Hello, sir. This is the First Officer. The Captain would like to see you in his office."

Jesus. He thought he'd adequately explained about the jacuzzi last night. Christ sake, was this going to be another inquisition?

"What's this about?" he asked

"Not at liberty to say sir, but the Captain would like to see you sooner rather than later."

"I'm not dressed yet. Give me fifteen minutes."

"That will be fine, sir. I'll have a steward call at your suite and escort you up to the Captain's office in fifteen."

'Escorted' mused the Judge. Practically a prisoner.

Exactly fifteen minutes later there was a sharp rap on the door. When the Judge opened it he saw a young Indian standing stiffly in front of him, dressed in the white uniform of the stewards. At least he didn't have a side-arm. Looking more closely, he recognized the scrawny kid from the pool who led the silly pool games. He was certainly all gussied up.

"I'm Ajay, steward for the Captain this morning. They've asked me to accompany you to the Captain's office," he said in a soft Commonwealth accent.

"Okay. Let's go."

Ajay marched him along the corridor toward the bow, then into an elevator bank. They rode up six floors, to the top. Off the elevator, Ajay led the way through a door that said *Crew Only*, and onto a walkway surrounding the ship's bridge. The Judge was getting more and more anxious, particularly as Ajay insisted the Judge go first at each step and watched his every move like a hawk.

They moved forward from the elevators, stopping at the back of the bridge where a teak door was set into the corridor with a polished brass plate which read, *Captain's Quarters.* Ajay rang the buzzer, then stood aside, nudging the Judge to stand in front of the door. They waited. In due course the door opened and there stood the Captain, offering his hand to shake the Judge's and inviting him in.

The cabin was traditional and lush, thick green carpet set off by hand-rubbed teak walls that defined three sides of the quarters, the fourth given over to a bank of large windows looking out over the sea

Captain John Quincy Smith was about the Judge's age, but an inch taller and considerably thinner, and buff the Judge had to admit. He seemed cordial enough, intelligent dark eyes examining the Judge carefully, listening to the Judge's each word, focused. He had a receding hairline, salt and pepper hair, cropped short, and bushy salt and pepper eyebrows. He was in his uniform whites, the placards on his shoulders emblazoned with the emblem of his captain's rank.

He waved the Judge to a large leather sofa in soft caramel, and plunked himself down in a matching chair, a small round coffee table between them.

"Would you like a drink… 'Judge', isn't it? May I call you Judge?"

"Of course, Captain. And yes, a gin and tonic if you have it."

The Captain touched a buzzer at the side of the small coffee table and a panel slid open in the teak behind them, exposing a small galley and another steward, a black man of indefinite age, shuffled out and took the Judge's order in English clipped by a slight East Indian accent. This didn't look to be a bad life… serving as the captain of a cruise ship.

"Just a Diet Coke for me, Tony," said the Captain, turning back to the Judge. "On duty you see."

"Yes, well…"

"You're wondering why I've asked to meet with you."

"Yes. If it's about last night and that mess in the front jacuzzi, I..."

The Captain held up his hand, silencing the Judge with a smile, twinkles in his eyes. "No. No. We and the crew had a good laugh about that one. But I know you weren't involved in any hanky-panky. Wish I could say the same for your newfound friend. Don't know what we're going to do with him. Something of a menace around our spas. The way he's going, he may be permanently confined to his quarters through the end of the voyage."

"Oh."

"Yes. I asked you here because I have a favor to ask."

"I'm all ears."

"We don't have a budget for this and can't pay you. But I know of your reputation of late in solving tricky cases. I was hoping you would participate in our investigation of what happened to Mr. Kennedy. We'd like to know if it was a freak accident, or something more sinister."

The Judge sat straighter in his seat. Not only did he have a real live case to work, here, on the ship, but the actual captain of the boat wanted his help.

"That's a capital idea, Captain. I'd love to," the Judge blurted out.

"Yes. I thought you might, Judge. I've heard rumblings perhaps sea-going life isn't your favorite thing."

"I love the sea. I just prefer a boat with more sails and fewer people."

The Captain smiled. "My First Officer, Rex Edwards is available to answer any questions you may have about our ship"

"That will be helpful."

"Good. And I understand you've already collected some evidence, a sample of Mr. Kennedy's soup, and his EpiPen which seemed not to work."

The Judge shifted uncomfortably in his chair. The Captain was silent now, letting the silence linger, waiting for the Judge's reply.

"I did take both the soup sample and the EpiPen from the table back to my cabin, as well as an empty peanut extract bottle from the galley. But they've now disappeared."

"Oh?"

"Yes. I left them out in our stateroom and your ship's maid, who is very efficient on our floor, threw them out."

"I see. That's most unfortunate."

"But I can still look into it, Captain. I have pictures of what happened, and I can investigate to see if it was a stupid accident or premeditated."

"Excellent, Judge. I would greatly appreciate it if you would do exactly that."

"Where did you take Kennedy's body?" asked the Judge.

"To our morgue. We have a six-body morgue aboard. We have to. We have a lot of older passengers, and invariably someone will die aboard. Worldwide, three people a week die on cruise ships. Our morgue is on deck four. We have body bags there and can store a corpse for over a week at four degrees centigrade in the narrow metal cupboards."

"How do the bodies get off?"

"At the first major port, in our case Hilo, the body will be taken off and delivered to the onshore medical examiner, who will issue a death certificate.

From there it's up to the family to pay the freight and ship the body home."

"Your ship company doesn't pay to air freight the body home?"

"No, I'm afraid not. We move the body off the ship, and from there it's the family's nickel."

"I see."

"We also have a brig with several holding cells, should it turn out we need one."

"You think it was murder, Captain? And not just some crazy accident?"

"I don't have an opinion. I'm hoping you'll tell us what happened, and why."

"I'll do my best."

"Thank you Judge. I'm counting on you. Ajay is waiting outside and will introduce you to Mr. Rex Edwards, my Executive Officer."

The Captain stood, indicating the Judge's interview was over.

Ajay led the Judge further along the corridor outside the Captain's quarters and through another door, taking them onto the actual bridge where the ship was manned. Ajay introduced the Judge to an officer, mid-forties, standing behind various crew operating the controls at the helm and keeping track of their progress on radar.

Edwards stood stiffly, in a braced position, monitoring each of his minions with a sharp eye, his hands clasped behind his back. The Judge supposed if he had responsibility for the safety of 3,600 plus souls on this piece of flotsam in the middle of the Pacific, he'd be the same.

Edwards unbent to give the Judge a solid handshake, a smile lighting up his grim face and his brown eyes twinkling. He was a 'what you see is what you get' sort of guy underneath his command posture, open and friendly. The Judge liked him immediately.

"I have to attend to my duties here, Judge, but perhaps we can meet for a drink later, after I'm off at two bells. Sorry, five p.m."

CHAPTER 12
DAY 2
10:40 AM

The Judge returned to his room and went straight to his telephone, obtaining Larry Cain's room number and putting in a call. Larry was quite cordial, as though expecting the call. He agreed to meet the Judge in the ship's piano bar in twenty minutes. Charlie must have told his officers to cooperate.

Twenty-five minutes later the Judge sat down at a small table in one corner of the empty piano bar, opposite the grand piano. It was 11:05 in the morning and the room was dark, very dark. Black walls, black teak wood floor, black piano, black chairs, and tables. Hardly any light, most of the ceiling's down-turned spots turned off. Walls were curved so no light came from the outside port windows and doors. It wasn't a morning room by any means. The smell of stale beer and pretzels faintly flavored the air and the floor under the Judge's feet was a tad sticky.

Larry Cain arrived five minutes late and lingered at the room's entrance, looking for the Judge, his eyes adjusting from the glare outside. The Judge noted Cain's shuffling gait as he moved across the room. As he got closer the Judge could see Cain was considerably older than he'd first thought. Cain's hair was dyed black, what was left of it, and so were his eyebrows and short mustache. It was a do it yourself job for sure. There was a hint of cosmetics under his eyes, possibly Retinol cream designed to hide the pouches, the cream not rubbed in quite enough.

Cain produced a half smile, displaying a perfect set of white teeth, too perfect and too white to be his own. He was dressed in a slimming, blue-checked shirt with a large collar, open, hinting at a forest of white chest hair underneath. He wore grey designer jeans. His face was framed by steel-rim glasses that magnified watery blue eyes but didn't change their shape, slits narrowed with age, peeking out at the Judge with suspicion.

"Charlie said I had to come talk to you. About Kennedy, and our company, and whatever you wanted to talk about. But I don't see why. I don't know you. I don't know much about Kennedy, and I don't know anything about what happened to him. I actually never liked the man." Cain folded his arms across his chest, signaling that was about all the Judge was likely to get.

"You did know Kennedy some. You worked with him."

"I didn't know him well. I don't know anybody well anymore. My friends have all died off."

"How long have you been with the company?"

"Almost five years."

"You look like you've had lots of experience in the corporate world."

"You mean I look old, Judge." Cain smiled. "You're right, I am. I've had several careers. I retired about seven years ago. But then my wife suddenly died. It was no good being home alone. Charlie was an acquaintance. We used to play as partners in a bridge club. All guys, the group went on for over ten years.

Anyway, Charlie took pity on me. Knew I was entirely lost without Ann. Leaned on me to become his Chief Financial Officer. I said no way at first, but he persisted; finally prevailed on me. Best thing that could have happened. Gave me a whole new life, new energy, got me out of the house, out of myself, out of feeling sorry for myself. I owe Charlie big time."

"I understand Kennedy worked for the company before, maybe twenty years ago or so. And left. Then recently came back."

"So I was told, Judge. I joined the company five years ago. I didn't know Kennedy from before, only now, since he came back."

"About a year ago?"

"Yes. He came back about a year ago."

"Kennedy's title was Chief Operating Officer, but what did he actually do?"

"Kennedy was more like a marketing guy. He didn't know money very well, but he knew how to spend it. He'd chew up my budgets just fine. Totally undisciplined. I had to ride him a lot."

"He'd go over budget?"

"Like a sky diver. He was always over the top. I'd have to pull him back, explain that if further money was needed to complete whatever the hell the project of the month was, he'd have to use his own money. He didn't like to hear that. He used to get quite angry with me. Try to go over my head to Charlie. But Charlie always shut him down. Every time."

"Marketing, you said?"

"Yes. I guess in some ways he was the face of the company, at least to the public."

"Tell me about the single use plastic bottle your company uses."

"Charlie originally came up with that idea. Changed the dynamics of our industry."

"How so?"

"Well, of course originally the plastic bottle was heavier. Thicker plastic. But now it's been refined down so it's very lightweight. You've probably noticed. The plastic's so thin and light it practically falls over when you stand it up. It just barely keeps its shape when it has our soda in it. You can crumple an empty bottle really easily."

"So lighter is cheaper."

"Oh, yes. Much cheaper. The old glass bottle used to cost a dollar-fifty each. The new lightweight plastic bottles cost sixty cents. Then there's shipping. We save in shipping because of less weight. You add it up, we've moving a lot of additional money to the bottom line.

"And since there's only a five-cent payment for returns at most, Larry, and only at recycling centers, most customers don't bother with making returns, and in any event your company doesn't have to get involved in returns."

"Yes. That's good too, although in many ways the sale of our soda is inelastic; our customers will buy our product regardless as long as the cost isn't too high."

"So, your company is very profitable."

"Very."

"I understand the son, Danny Westerman, works in the company. Does he work for you?"

"Yes." Cain's face turned suddenly guarded.

"Is he a good employee?"

"He shows up."

"Oh, come on now Larry. Charlie asked you to be candid with me. Leave nothing out."

"There might be things going on that even Charlie doesn't know."

"Like what? Tell me."

"I've got nothing concrete yet. I'm still investigating."

"Okay. I want to hear what you're investigating."

"Well... is this off the record?"

"Yes. Off the record."

"Off the record from Charlie too?"

"If it turns out to have nothing to do with Kennedy's death, I'll have no reason to talk about it with anyone."

Larry nodded, accepting the Judge's reasoning. "Danny is in charge of running our cash, our float, keeping it working on a twenty-four-hour basis, as it washes in and washes out as cash flow. He interacts with the banks and other sources that pay short term rates."

"Okay."

"Well, someone outside the company hinted to Kennedy last week at a conference that in running this cash around our banks and collecting interest, there might be a small kickback paid to someone in our company."

"Danny?"

"Yes."

"Have you confirmed that?"

"No. I was about to look into it, but then we all left on this stupid cruise."

"Did you ask Danny about it?"

"No. You don't accuse the son of the principal shareholder without solid proof to back it up."

"Does Danny know you're investigating?"

"Not from me. I don't know if Kennedy said anything to him."

"So, Larry, is it fair to say Danny might have a motive to see Kennedy disappear?"

"I don't know that. It's all idle speculation right now. I need to dig into our cash investment numbers, make some outside inquires, and see what's what. I'll do that when we get back."

"Was there anyone who might have been out to get Kennedy? Anybody who strongly disliked him?"

Cain looked uncomfortable again.

"Come on, Larry. Someone is dead. I'm trying to find out if it was a stupid accident, or something more."

"Well. For whatever reason, I don't think Laura liked Kennedy."

"Charlie's daughter?"

"Yes."

"Why do you think that?"

"She always tensed up when Kennedy was around. Refused to shake hands, avoided sitting near him, pretended not to hear if he said anything to her. I don't know what was going on there. But she clearly didn't like him. There must have been something."

"Was her attitude recent?"

"No. It was immediate, as soon as he came back into the company. So, whatever it was, I suppose it must be from before."

"From before Kennedy's hiatus from the company?"

"Yes. I guess so."

"That was how long ago?"

"I guess over twenty years."

"So, Laura would have been around nine back then?"

"Yes."

"But you don't know why the bad blood?"

"No."

CHAPTER 13
DAY 2
11:30 AM

As the Judge left the piano bar behind Cain he caught sight of Laura Westerman as she slid into the nearby Calypso Bar that had just opened. He followed her in. It was mostly empty, a quiet refuge away from the crowded pool. The Judge hopped himself onto a small bar stool welded to the deck under the porpoise sign, wishing the seat was wider so his fanny didn't overlap. But it wasn't and he did. He looked up at the huge white canopy above the bar, like some giant plastic crown, embedded with gaudy blue tile here and there in the shape of teardrops, and wondered if he weren't really at Disneyland, or maybe in Wonderland.

The Judge ordered a piña colada and glanced at Laura Westerman. Her bottom was settled on one of the leather stools three stools away, lapping over as much as his. She was shorter than the Judge, but broader, dressed in loose white shorts and a pale rose blouse buttoned again to the top of her neck. When the bartender delivered his drink, the Judge took it, slid off his stool, and moved around to climbed onto the stool next to Laura's.

"Are you enjoying the cruise so far, Laura?"

Laura turned to look at him suspiciously, slowly recognizing him from the dinner the night before.

"Mr. Judge."

"Just Judge."

"Sorry. Well, Judge, frankly it's a little slow for my taste." She gave the Judge a shy smile. "I think cruises like this are for more mature people. Like you, I guess."

"Ouch," said the Judge.

"Oh, I don't mean you're old or anything, Judge, but it's just… you know."

"What would a more exciting trip be like, Laura?"

"Well, my last trip was solo, on a train, across India, all the way from Calcutta to Ahmedabad and Gujarat. Now that's an exciting trip."

"I'll bet. I can see how this trip would be a little more inhibiting since you're traveling with your mother and dad."

Laura gave a little snort, muffled by a slug from her gin on the rocks. "You get used to tuning them out; although it'd certainly be more fun if they weren't along."

"Your dad seems quite a character."

Laura Westerman's face broke into a quick smile. "Dad's a little overbearing at times, but he's more bark than bite."

"So, you get along with him well?"

Laura snorted again. "I don't know anybody gets along with him well. He's very hard to get close to. But he's stuck with mom through thick and thin, funded us three kids through college, no student debt or nothing.

And despite all his bluster, he takes care of his people, his employees… that is as long as you're performing. My dad is fond of saying 'a busy ship is a happy ship.' All his employees have Cadillac Medical, generous vacation time, time off for new births, and retirement plans the company funds to the max. His employees love him… from afar of course since they don't really know him. But from what I've seen, the morale in the company is great; they all feel well treated."

"That must cost a pretty penny."

"It is calculated, Judge. Dad says a happy employee will make you three times what a grumpy one will. In the end, for dad, it's always about the money."

Laura twirled two fingers in the air, signaling the bartender she'd have another gin rocks.

"Why is that? Did Charlie grow up poor?"

"Very poor. It was an abusive home, I think. He doesn't talk about it much. My grandparents are all long dead. Never met them. But I think money's like a security blanket for Dad. He wraps it around himself. He only feels safe when he's got it in his hands."

"There was a famous comedian like that, Laura. It was the new age of the TV, and he successfully transitioned from vaudeville and theater into it, along with Milton Berle, Bob Hope, Jack Benny, and the other legendary greats. But when he was live on stage and later on TV sets, he could only go out and perform, make people laugh, steal the audience for his own, when he had his assistant just off stage in the wings holding a black satchel filled with a hundred thousand in cash. That was his security blanket. Without that he wouldn't go on."

"That sounds like Dad. The numbers are bigger, but the principle's the same. It's funny. The amount in dispute can be a million dollars on the table in a contract, or an overcharge of ten dollars for parking. Charlie responds with the same fervor regardless of the sum. Like some large marlin coming out of the water. He's fierce."

"You said there were three children. I met your brother. You have another brother or sister?"

"Jay. My brother. Jay died last year. Killed himself."

"Oh. I'm sorry, Laura."

"It's old news. Though I think Mom hasn't recovered. It was tough on all of us."

"Including your Dad?"

"Good question. I don't know. He never talks about Jay. Jay had it tough growing up, always in trouble with Dad, didn't seem to do anything right. I guess I've always been the favorite. That's how it worked out. Jay was different, not interested in money, not interested in the company, not interested in Dad. I guess the feeling was mutual."

"And Danny?"

"Danny gets along with Dad pretty well. Danny talks a lot but doesn't say much. And Dad likes that, never feels threatened by Danny. I guess it's because Danny's so transparent, like an open book."

"Did you know Kennedy at all?" asked the Judge.

Laura's face puckered up, as though she'd tasted something sour. Her cheeks were turning a bit flushed, from the gin guessed the Judge.

"Yeah. I knew Kennedy from the beginning. Never liked him. A creep."

"Really?"

"Kennedy was around when my dad first started building his control position in the company. Seemed like Kennedy was always around. I was just a kid then. But he made me nervous the way he looked at me and stuff. Dad would be off on his business trips all over the world. I'd come home from grade school and there'd be Kennedy, just hanging around the house, drinking with Mom. There's something about him, he was always a little off."

"So, Kennedy was with the company. Left. And then was hired back?"

"Yeah. Something like that. I don't really know. I just know Dad didn't want to hire him back, but Mom worked on Dad. It was one of her campaigns. She can be like that. Just kept bringing it up, pushing and pushing, wearing Dad down. Like a dental drill. Finally, Dad just gave up, gave in. I guess Kennedy was pretty down on his luck when Dad hired him back."

"How long ago was it that Kennedy was with your dad's company before?'

"Let's see. Danny's twenty-four. Jay wasn't around yet; he'd be twenty now, still. I guess Kennedy left about twenty odd years ago. I was about nine."

"Did anything... physical, happen back then, between you and Kennedy?"

Laura's eyes closed briefly as she straightened on her stool. "I don't want to talk about it, Judge."

"Kennedy was back for how long?"

"About a year."

The ship's bell sounded from through the atrium and down the hall to the bar, counting off twelve bells.

"Whoops, that's me. Got to go. Meet Mom for lunch. Nice talking to you, Judge."

Laura threw a quick squiggle on her bar tab, jumped off her bar stool and disappeared down the corridor toward the elevators at a panicky trot, not looking back, shaking slightly.

CHAPTER 14
DAY 2
12:30 PM

"Hi sailor."

The words startled the Judge awake from his slumber in an out-of-the-way corner of the pool deck on a well-toweled chaise. He knew the female voice… intimately… but couldn't quite place it.

He sat up and turned to look behind him. Oh shit. It was Barbara. His pre-Katy ex-girlfriend. She tended to turn up in his life like a bad penny. Katy was not going to be pleased.

Barbara and the Judge had been locked in a passionate affair behind Barbara's husband's back, a year two before he'd met Katy. An affair so hot it'd burned itself out of its own heat. Wild images floated into his mind, too wild to put into words. The affair had ended when the Judge insisted Barbara either choose him or her husband. Barbara, always practical, had opted to hang with her husband, planning for divorce and a hefty property settlement to be initiated only after hubby made partner in his national accounting firm.

The last time the Judge had run into Barbara had been the year before in Cabo. And Katy had been in

Cabo with him. The resulting cat fight had shaved several years of his life.

Katy took a dim view of Barbara. Was it because Barbara was beautiful? Or perhaps oversexed? Barbara exuded a feminine sensuality that hung like musk in the air when she entered a room. Perhaps it was because Barbara was still infatuated with the Judge. Or because Barbara was now single and on the prowl again for her next husband. 'Marrying up', as they called it in Beverly Hills, was a blood sport for Barbara. But the Judge suspected it was mostly a territorial thing between females. Unfortunately, he was the territory.

Barbara had on a bikini, the top half of which looked three sizes too small. The bottom half was cut low and very tight. The Judge wondered if she had to get it wet to wiggle into it. Her body was still perfect, and so were the rollicking brown eyes, appraising the Judge with a mixture of humor and lust.

"How you doing, Judge?

Barbara's eyes searched his, finding what she wanted there, memories of a past that tied them together forever. Barbara had been a wild ride… all the way. They'd shared the most intimate parts of their bodies, joined, panting, gasping, heaving together like some single organism, cresting together and sliding down the back side of ecstasy. *La petite mort.*

Like many old lovers, they looked at each other differently; saw each other filtered through memories of past revelries. Once you were lovers, it was forever different between a man and a woman. Some part of her was in him still, and some part of him was certainly in her.

"Still married to the anorexic chippie?" Asked Barbara.

"Still married to Katy and still quite happy."

"Won't last, Judge. Sooner or later you'll be back. Back for a real woman… perhaps me. We had lots of fun together. Remember that night we got drunk and waded into that fountain on City National Plaza in downtown L.A., the one with the bright red stairs sculpture, going uppity up up and then backety back down. We were going to climb the damn stairs to the top. We didn't know the surrounding pool was so deep. The water came damn near up to my neck when I slid over its wall into the pond. You had to get under me and shove my ass back up over the parapet to get me out. It was a race between you getting me out of the pond and the old security guard catching up with us. Remember him trying to run across the plaza, huffing and puffing, shouting at us. I thought he was going to have a heart attack."

The Judge felt himself smiling. That's the way it was with Barbara.

"You're looking pretty good for yourself, Judge. What's it been, twelve months since we ran into each other?"

She was spot on. Practically to the day.

"How are you doing, Barbara? Did you find the new husband you've been searching for?"

"Oh, well. You know how it goes, Judge. Lots of competition in West L.A. So many men seem only to care how few years a girl has on her. They don't give credit for experience, maturity, and a natural talent in the bedroom honed to a fine point."

Barbara rolled her eyes for emphasis.

"But I've got a hot one, Judge. Finally, a serious one who has semi-proposed. He brought me on this cruise. He's going through a nasty property settlement with his ex, so we have to be a little low key right now about our relationship. So, if you run into us together, pretend you don't know we're in love."

"I'll be discreet, Barbara."

"And keep that hellcat wife of yours away. She'd love to torpedo my chances with this guy.... Unless of course, you'd like to cancel Katy's ticket and pick up with me where we left off. We'd could have some real fun."

As he smiled at Barbara, he suddenly felt eyes boring into the back of his head. He turned to see Katy on tiptoes at the other end of the deck, peeking over the heads of the pool revelers, staring at him. She been watching his repartee with Barbara. He blanked his face quickly, too quickly. Caught!

"We've both moved on, Barbara. Fond memories are great to reminisce about occasionally, but I'm firmly committed to my new life."

Barbara pouted, but quickly slid into her public happy face as the Judge felt a shift in the atmosphere around them.

Suddenly, Katy was beside him, placing her hand territorially on his shoulder so there was no mistake to whom he belonged. Showing all her teeth to Barbara in a smile that was more threatening than friendly. In another context he was certain Katy would have gone for Barbara's throat.

There was tension in Katy's hand, and she was pinching his shoulder a tad too tight. He would no doubt pay later for engaging in this little tête-à-tête with his old flame.

Barbara made an excuse about needing her sunglasses and quickly melted into the relative safety of the pool crowd, placing several bodies between herself and Katy's smile.

CHAPTER 15
DAY 2
1:00 PM

The Judge read his mystery novel by the pool for a while, Katy beside him on the adjacent lounge. Then they meandered back to their stateroom to share a nap.

As the Judge swung the door of their stateroom in and stepped into the mini space, his shoe settled deep into the carpet and its pad with an audible squish. His momentum propelled him forward and under a stream of water coming from the ceiling, washing over his head and down the front of his shirt. Son of a bitch, the ceiling was leaking.

"Katy, Katy, I'm getting soaked," he yelled.

"Oh… what? What, Judge?" Katy lifted her head from fumbling with something in her purse, still out in the corridor.

"I'm getting wet."

Katy took one look and then backed herself out into the corridor, screeching, "Oh my God, Judge, we're sinking. We're sinking! Where are the damn preservers?"

"No, no, Katy, it's nothing like that." The Judge stuck his finger into the stream and sniffed suspiciously. "I think its chlorinated. Like pool water."

After an hour, beginning with a flurry of excited calls back and forth to the desk and to various technicians, followed promptly by a string of experts and management poking their head into the stateroom for a better look, it was finally determined there was a leak in the ship's pool amidships one deck above. The leaking pool water had traveled laterally to a point above the Judge's ceiling where it had decided to accumulate and leak through on top of the Judge's head, as well as across his carpet.

Further time went by before the ship's welder appeared, fully equipped in his flame-proof jumpsuit and fold-down glass-pane mask. He traced the leak along the ceiling out into the corridor and along to the connecting passage between corridors. He disappeared into the ceiling after removing several tiles while a small crowd gathered, consisting of ship's staff, and nearby guests attracted by the commotion. Twenty minutes later he emerged from the ceiling, looking victorious and quite ready to take a bow, announcing the leak was fixed.

There was a tangible sigh of relief from the ad hoc little group and then it dispersed, the Judge muttering to Katy under his breath all the way back to their cabin about the stupidity of booking a cheap cruise on the oldest tub one could find.

The door to their cabin was standing wide open, the wet-vac and its attendant gone, a light smell of chlorine permeating the room. The Judge glanced over at the small bureau, and stopped in his tracks, Katy bumping into him from behind. His cell phone, which had been resting on the bureau, his cell phone with pictures of the dinner table where Kennedy died, and pictures of the bottle and of the soup sample, was gone. Everything he'd collected about the death of Kennedy was now gone. Everything.

CHAPTER 16
DAY 2
2:30 PM

The Judge looked into the bottom of his piña colada glass and thought how Charlie and his family seemed so screwed up. A suicide son. An older son stealing from the company. A daughter whose hatred of Charlie's COO dated from childhood; the same CCO who was sleeping with Charlie's wife behind his back… or perhaps in front of his back. Charlie, so rich and yet so poor in so many ways. The Judge almost felt sorry for him.

The Judge decided to try some of the sloppy pizza people were carrying with them all over the ship. But when he arrived at the pizza bar the waiting line for a stool was two layers deep behind the seats. He hated waiting in lines more than anything. Particularly for something as stupid as pizza. He grabbed a table just vacated off in a hidden corner of the pool deck and flagged down Sean the waiter, now serving the pool area. He ordered a Quattro Formaggi.

As the pizza arrived, the Judge felt a nudge next to him. He turned to find Barbara sliding into the chair next to him at the table.

"Hi, Judgie. How's the pizza?"

"Well, since it's the only pizza around here in the middle of the Pacific, I guess I'd have to say it's the best that can be found. Doesn't hold a candle of course to Pizzeria Mozza in Los Angeles, or Razza in Jersey City."

"I'd love to have a piece, but I can't afford the calories. A girl's got to keep trim. But use your fork, cut me a small bite."

The Judge did so and Barbara wolfed it down. She was obviously hungry, perhaps starving.

"I haven't seen you in the dining room, or promenading around the ship with your new friend, Barbara. You been keeping yourself under wraps?"

"Why is it always so damn complicated, Judge? It was complicated with you, and it's complicated now. In fact, it's complicated with every damn man I meet. Ross is in the middle of his divorce. He and his ex are pretending to be dear friends, while fighting tooth and nail through their attorneys over terms of the property settlement. Meanwhile, he's in the middle of this financing to whisk control of an extremely profitable company into his hands. It's what makes him such an attractive mate for me, Judge. If he succeeds, we'll be one of the wealthiest couples around.

"That sounds exciting, Barbara."

"Maybe too exciting, Judge. Meanwhile, he's having dinners aboard with the company officers and this controlling shareholder he's targeted for extinction. I'm relegated to the damn conga line at the aft-deck buffet. I have to sit out under the stars and have my dinner alone. It sucks. Course you could sneak out and come join me."

"It sounds all very iffy, Barbara."

"Oh no. Ross is solid. He loves me I know. It's just this dragon of an ex-wife he has to maneuver around and this business deal that he needs to complete. Then it'll be smooth sailing. Not sure I would have come on this cruise though if I'd known I'd be mostly by myself. All I get is the nights, and then he's usually too tired to talk much. All he wants to do is fuck my lights out."

"Did you tell him I was aboard, Barbara?"

"Oh yes. I saw you and your used-up wife boarding and immediately told him everything, Judge. He was a little jealous. Doesn't like you very much. He's a very territorial male. I like that."

"I guess we all have pasts."

"Our past was a lot of fun, Judge. I'd pick it up in a heartbeat if you want to start again, Ross or no, Katy or no." Barbara flashed her warming sun smile at the Judge, all teeth and gums.

"I saw your anorexic wife at the gym. She's aging, Judge. Lots of lines around the eyes, a bit of a bulge at the stomach from the kid. Mot the spright young thing you married."

"Oh, come on Barbara. She's still a spright young thing. Twenty years younger than me. Ten years younger than you."

"Just saying, Judge. The wear and tear shows. Don't think she knows how to keep herself up. You should be sending her to health spas more, better salons, kit her out in more expensive clothes. Maybe get her a pool boy for the afternoons when you're working late." Barbara collapsed into rollicking giggles.

"When she gets to be your age Barbara, maybe I'll start thinking about those things."

Barbara's pout was immediate.

"You really know how to hurt a girl, Judge. Anyway, I wanted to ask you a legal question."

"Okay."

"How is it that a man can own only thirty-two percent of the stock in a public company and yet he still controls it?"

"Well, Barbara, that depends on the company. Usually in more mature public companies, the original founders and key early executives have sold off their shares. And the current management owns an infinitesimally small portion of the company's outstanding stock. The bulk of the shares tend to be held by a zillion individual investors and a handful of institutional investors with no one having a large block. Only about 27 percent of the so-called retail investors, the small ma and pa investors, actually vote their shares at shareholder meetings. Institutional shareholders do better, perhaps because they have to report to their clients. About 85 percent of institutional shareholders vote their shares."

"Okay, so?"

"So, posit a public company with 50 percent of its shares held by a ton of ma and pa shareholders, 18 percent held by institutional investors, and 32 percent held in a single block by Mr. X. And remember if things are going along okay, most voting shareholders just vote to keep the recommended management in place."

"Go on."

"So if you do the math, the ma and pa shareholder will typically cast 13.5 percent of the outstanding shares at the meeting, the institutions will cast about 15.3 percent of the outstanding shares, and Mr. X will cast 100 percent of his shares, or 32 percent of the outstanding shares at the meeting. In effect, Mr. X will cast a majority of all the shares cast at the meeting and control its outcome. That's even before you consider the preponderance of votes by ma and pa shareholders will go to continue current management recommended by the board. A board that would typically be handpicked by Mr. X and in his pocket."

"So, someone who owns 32 percent of the stock of the company could actually control it?"

"Yes."

"How would you gain control for yourself in such a company?"

"Well you might already have accumulated a large block, quietly through purchases in the market, and perhaps own, say, just under 5 percent, the threshold for reporting. Then you could initiate a public tender offer. You'd offer to purchase a large number of shares from existing shareholders, from the institutions and from ma and pa shareholders, offering them a favorable price. In a large public company, you'd need serious financing to back your play, but it's done a lot. You might also start a proxy fight in an effort to dislodge the existing management, seeking to get a higher turnout of voters who actually vote their shares, and vote against re-election of the existing board."

"Wow. It sounds complicated."

"It can be."

"It better work. I'm staking my future on it. Well, got to go Judge. Remember, if you see me with Ross, pretend you don't… don't see me, don't recognize me, don't approach, don't wave, don't say hello."

"Got if Barbs. Your fiancé's name is Ross?"

"Shhh. Yes. You didn't hear that."

"I'll be Mr. Invisible, Barbara."

Barbara surprised him by leaning over to throw her arm around his neck and give him a sloppy kiss on the cheek. Then she got up and left, doing her stage model walk across the deck… her swinging bottom turning heads as it always did.

CHAPTER 17
DAY 2
3:40 PM

The Judge returned to his stateroom to find Katy there, stepping into the tiny shower. "How are you doing, Hon?" He shouted through the steam clouding the small bathroom proper. "Getting ready for your afternoon spa treatment?"

There was a muffled response through the water and steam the Judge couldn't quite make out, but for some reason it didn't sound friendly. It was the tone in the voice, the sharp way the response was delivered.

He headed for the mini-bar and poured himself a Scotch on the rocks, Johnny Walker Black Label, just in case.

Katy came out of the bathroom fully dressed, white shorts and a yellow sports bra, disappointing the Judge. He enjoyed watching her put on her underwear and dress as she well knew. Her chin was cantilevered in the air and she was wearing a frown. The Judge took a big slug of his Scotch.

"Was your morning masseuse too rough?"

"Don't give me your bull shit, Judge. You know full well why I'm mad."

This was female logic the Judge had encountered before. It was a sort of female interrogation game, much like interrogation by the Nazis in occupied France. The Judge had no idea why Katy was upset. But if he proceeded with the guessing game, he was sure Katy would find multiple reasons, likely not even related to his original trespass.

"I give up, Katy. What'd I do?" It was his only move. To play the game was suicide.

"You… You… You were necking with that woman!" Katy hissed out. Using a towel to dry her hair with such force the Judge was afraid he'd soon have a bald wife.

"What woman? What are you talking about, Katy?"

"That… that… that tarty female… Barbara…!"

The Judge opened his mouth, but no words came. He just couldn't imagine… wait… wait… the peck on the check Barbara gave him on the pool deck, at the table. Well, it was a sloppy kiss really, but safer to call it a 'peck'. And it wasn't really public, they were hidden way back under the upper deck. Not private enough apparently. He'd best not bring up the secluded surroundings for the peck; that didn't work to his advantage.

"Ah, honey, you mean that sudden peck Barbara gave me as she left the table. That was a complete surprise. I didn't know she was going to do that. It was absolutely meaningless."

"And in public, where everybody could see," muttered Katy.

"Well, yes Katy. In public. You wouldn't have wanted it to be a secret meeting would you?"

"*Harrumph!*"

"Look, Katy, I can't help she still has feelings for me. That she's so terribly jealous of you. I don't encourage it. We just seem to run into each other occasionally is all. I didn't kiss her. It was just a surprise peck she gave me. I wasn't expecting it at all. We're just old friends now. There's nothing there to worry about."

"I'm going out to flirt after my spa with the first likely candidate I see. Then we'll see how you feel."

"Oh, Katy…"

"And mark my words, Judge… Mark my words. That tramp is no good. She's not your friend. She's never been your friend. She'll sell you down the river first chance she gets."

With that, Katy turned and marched out the door of their stateroom, muttering she was going to the gym to do her steps on the treadmill.

CHAPTER 18
DAY 2
4:00 PM

The Judge slipped into his no-wet swim trunks and his puke green t-shirt, plopped his Tilly hat on his head, took the elevator up, and wandered out to the pool. He couldn't think of anything else to do.

He spotted Laura Westerman on a lounge, shaded by the upper deck, and walked over, easing himself into the lounge chair beside her just vacated by a black woman, beating out another potential occupant, a guy who came tearing around the pool in a mad dash to snare it. There weren't enough lounge chairs for everybody on the Tub.

"Hi, Laura. What's your best thing so far on this cruise?"

"Hi, Judge. The ice cream of course. The all-you-can-eat ice cream. The way I'm going on this cruise I may as well scoop it out of the dish and apply it directly to my thighs. But it's sure good. How about you? What's your favorite thing."

"I'm addicted to the piña coladas, Laura. Do you really think they're as low calorie as that waiter, what's his name, Sean, says?"

Laura looked at him skeptically. Then smiled and said, "It's your cruise, Judge. I think the coladas have whatever calorie count you want them to have."

The Judge gave her a rueful smile.

"Is that a Bombay Sapphire, Laura? Is that your favorite drink?"

"Yes, I picked the liking up in India."

"Can I ask you a little more about Kennedy, Laura?"

Laura's smile slipped from her face, as though a magician waved his hand across her countenance. She visibly stiffened and her eyes grew cautious, careful.

"I don't know. Depends on what you ask."

"You said back when you were nine and Kennedy worked for your dad's company before, you didn't like him. That Kennedy was around a lot and made you nervous."

"Yeah."

"Can you elaborate on what made you nervous?"

Laura grew silent, considering how much to say. Finally, she spoke.

"When you're nine you don't like some old asshole coming into the bathroom while you are taking your shower, peaking at you around the shower curtain while he pretends to be making conversation."

"Did Kennedy ever touch you?"

"No. Not physically. He alternated between making it clear he wished I wasn't around when he came visiting and ogling my body when he thought I wasn't looking. He creeped me out. Course Mom always found reasons for me to leave. An overnight stay at a friend's house, shopping with my aunt, whatever.

But when I was there, Kennedy wasn't very nice to me. Teased me about being fat. Said I was going to have whoppers for boobs. I don't know what happened there." She looked down at her modest chest, then smiled at the Judge. "But I was very sensitive about my breasts. Nine-year-old girls are."

"What was going on between Kennedy and your mother? Were they just friends? Or something more?"

"You mean was Mom sleeping with him?"

"Yes."

"I don't know. Why don't you ask her?"

"How was it for you when Kennedy came back to the company?"

"I hated him every time I saw him. He looked at me with hungry eyes, like he was mentally undressing me; like he wanted to take me, force me. The way he looked made my skin crawl. Made me want to run away and wash, wash the scent of him away. Ugh...!"

Laura bit her lower lip, then took a large slug of her gin and tonic.

"Did you dislike Kennedy enough to kill him, Laura?"

Laura gasped, her face shading to pink, her eyes wide, unfocused now. She sat silent for the count of ten; he could see she was mentally counting the seconds. When she spoke again, her voice was calm, level, her breathing relaxed, only her blue eyes flashed fire.

"Kennedy was destroying Mom, destroying my dad, destroying our family. He was a fuckin' troll who crawled out from under a bridge somewhere after twenty years, bent on pure mischief. He deserved to die. I'm glad he's dead. I'm glad he suffered a little before he kicked off. I'm sure the bastard went straight to hell."

Laura's chin came up as she glared at the Judge.

"But you can't prove I had anything to do with his death. So, Judge, go pick on somebody else. Go pick on Maddy Stevens, the no-panties girl. Leave me out of it."

"You were in the kitchen while the soup was being prepared last night, Laura. And you were in Gujarat, India, last summer. It looks like the bottle of peanut oil concentrate put in Kennedy's food came from Gujarat. And you sound like you had a motive."

"So, what are you saying? I purchased a bottle of peanut oil last summer and laid in wait, even though I had no idea I'd be on a cruise with Kennedy ten months later? That doesn't make sense Judge and we both know it."

Laura got up off her lounge, turned, and swanned off.

CHAPTER 19
DAY 2
4:15 PM

As Laura got up, the guy looking for a lounger was out of position again on the other side of the pool. He scrambled hard to get around, barely missed out again, this time to a well-endowed gal in a large floppy hat that hid her face and a skimpy bikini that hid absolutely nothing as she sat down on the lounge chair with her back to the Judge. Somehow her body looked familiar.

She suddenly turned around to look at the Judge full on from under the dramatic hat and the Judge was startled to see himself looking into the sparkling brown eyes of Barbara again. Three times in one day.

"I do like the way you look at me, Judge. It makes me feel all warm and moist."

"Sorry, Barbara. I wasn't expecting to see you again. I thought you'd got all your questions answered, and besides, I'm supposed to play 'hear no evil, see no evil, say no evil.'" The Judge glanced at his watch, assuring himself Katy was still at her spa treatment, then surveyed the pool surroundings, just to be sure.

"I need some more insight on what's going down, Judge."

"On what Ross is planning to do?"

"Yes."

"Ross is Ross Hamilton, right?" the Judge asked. "Charlie Westerman's partner in the soda company."

Barbara's jaw dropped open, but no words came for several seconds. "You're not supposed to know that."

"I don't, Barbara. I don't. I just forgot it. Nothing's in my mind now."

"Yes, well, there'd better be nothing, Judge."

"So, what's your question?"

"My honey…"

"Ross?"

"Yes, damn it. I never should have told you his name, Judge. Anyway, his plan is to remove the entire board, put himself on as chairman, his own people as directors, and his own people as the executive officers."

"And the problem is Charlie owns the controlling block of stock?"

"Yes, Judge. Almost like you said. Charlie holds a little over 30 percent of the shares."

"So, your boy, Ross, has some uphill work to do?"

"That's what I think too. But he says no. Says he's got it handled. Says he's been quietly buying company shares in the market; holds almost 10 percent. Says he's got a deal with the big investment bank, Anderson & Sparks, to make a tender offer, all cash, for 25 percent of the outstanding shares. That plus his ten gives him more shares than Charlie has; and he says that's control. At the same time, Anderson & Sparks is going to help him start a proxy fight to replace the entire board and all the officers. He says the officers are terrible, loyal only to Charlie, no interest in protecting the shareholders."

"Wow. He's really serious about this."

"Yes."

"So, what's your question?"

"Can Ross really pull it off, Judge? Displace this Westerman guy as the control guy? Or is Ross just pissing in the wind? Will he stay broke like he is now with his Ex hammering him in the divorce and the divorce attorneys on both sides sucking him dry? I'm too old to align myself with a broke loser, Judge. You know that. I've served my time. Now I need a rich husband to care for me."

"I don't know the answer, Barbara. If the investment bank is willing to put up enough money, Ross may well succeed. But there are so many variables. Not the least of which is Charlie Westerman himself. From what I've seen of Charlie, he's a shrewd, mean, down-and-dirty gutter fighter. I wouldn't be quick to pick a battle with someone like that."

"They've been business partners for years, Judge. Ross say he knows Charlie well. Says Charlie will cave once the right leverage is applied."

"Then why are you worried, Barbara?"

"I guess I don't know Ross well enough to trust him."

"Maybe you never will, Barbara."

"Yeah, maybe I never will." Barbara got up, wrapped her towel around her body, and slowly walked away, forgetting to do her model saunter, lost in thought.

The Judge watched her until his view was blocked by the lounge seeker from the other side of the pool; he came tearing around its end at forty miles an hour and slid onto the vacated lounger as though taking second base.

CHAPTER 20
DAY 2
6:45 PM

The Judge and Katy walked along the promenade deck, heading for the entrance to the dining room, Katy in another dress she'd resurrected from her closet, this one a bright pear color with sequins either side of the low décolletage. She looked stunning.

The Judge of course was dressed in his standard uniform, blue striped shirt with open collar, tan slacks, and blue blazer. They walked outside, along the promenade deck to the door opening to the hall leading to the dining room. They were almost to the door when there was a sudden plop beside the Judge's ear. He turned, startled, saw nothing, turned back to see Katy's face going apoplectic with mirth.

She pointed with an unsteady finger through peals of laughter at his shoulder. He scrunched his head down toward his shoulder to discover a seagull had dropped a little gift. A white and grey sticky little gift starting to run down the breast of his sports coat. Son of a bitch! As if he needed another reason to hate this cruise.

She accompanied him into the men's room over his half-hearted objection and wiped him down, first with Kleenex she always kept in her purse, then with a soggy paper towel loaded with warm water and soap. He wished her eyes weren't twinkling so much, almost as if she were enjoying his situation. The biohazard seemed to go away, leaving only a swath of darker color on the sport coat from the water. But he suspected he didn't smell quite the daisy anymore. Damn, damn, damn.

As they moved out of the restroom and across the set of wide stairs that deposited guests at the entrance to the dining room from the upper decks, there was a cry of frustration on the stairs above them. A cry turning to fear, tones shifting to higher notes, panicky.

"Oh, what the, fuck, Ahhhh!" rattled down the stairwell from two flights above, followed by several large thumps.

They turned together and rushed up the stairs, practically tripping over Larry Cain, Charlie's CFO, lying in a lump at the foot of the second flight of stairs up. The Judge looked at the stairs above in time to see the flash of a foot in a white deck shoe disappearing behind the rail above. The ankle was festooned with a gold chain tagged with sparkling letters, "MY".

Cain wasn't moving. His eyes were glassy, his arm was cocked at an unnatural angel, and his neck oddly twisted to one side. The Judge knelt beside him, taking his shoulder, and gently whispering, "Larry, Larry". There was no response.

The Judge put two fingers to Cain's neck, searching for a pulse. The Judge shook his head. "Christ, Katy, he's gone. What is going on? This is the second officer of the soda company to die on this cruise in as many days."

The Judge turned and sprinted up the stairs two at a time, reaching the upper floor out of breath, looking around for the fleeting white shoe he'd seen. No one was there. He looked thoughtfully at the first step of the stairs starting down, and then the second step. He knelt down there to pick up a small bit of clear fish line, Berkley Trilene monofilament he guessed, probably 30 lb. He put it in his coat pocket and sat down on the second stair to look around. He saw a small hole in the wall of the opposite side of the stair from its rail. Had an eyelet been screwed in there? Perhaps a bit of fish line stretched across the stair and around the rail post at the other end of the stair?

He inspected the post. There were small scuffs five inches up from the bottom. Perhaps the line wrapped around there and then fed off to a nearby location, the line lying flat on the stair until the right victim approached. There was a chair pulled over near the top of the railing on the upper floor. A perfect place to sit and watch, ready to pull up the line and send someone sprawling.

As he stood up, his eyes met those of Danny Westerman, coming down the hall on the upper floor. Danny looked flustered. "Forgot my camera," he muttered, stepping around the Judge and heading for the elevator. He wore white deck shoes. His jean cuffs turned down, didn't show his ankles.

The Judge moved back down the stairs to where Cain lay. White-coated waiters and grey-blazered security people were crowding in on the landing now behind Katy. Ross Hamilton, coming off the adjacent elevator, rushed over to see what was going on. Their murmurings ceased as a small rotund figure in a blue sport coat with fancy gold buttons cut through the crowd and pressed the Judge aside so he could get to Cain, his own two fingers going to the side of Cain's throat. He whipped out a stethoscope from somewhere, almost like a magician, and pressed it to Cain's chest to listen. Then looked up and slowly shook his head. "He's expired. Judging from the angle of his head and neck, my guess is his neck's broken."

CHAPTER 21
DAY 2
11:35 PM

It was pushing toward midnight and Katy was asleep in the cabin, making soft noises which she claimed were purrs; the Judge called them snores, mostly to irritate her he supposed, sort of a mean tease. But the Judge couldn't sleep in the small cabin with its claustrophobic walls and uncomfortable bed, particularly after Katy made him close the sliding balcony doors so there was no longer the sound and feel of the wind sweeping into the cabin from the undulating sea.

He'd wandered around the pool deck twice now, sniffing the wind, wondering if it portended a coming storm. On his second trip he stopped to glance down a deck to the promenade deck below. Two figures had converged there in the shadow of a lifeboat. He recognized Charlie at once. Shielding his eyes from the overhead deck lights, he saw the girl beside Charlie was Maddy Stevens, the young executive assistant. They were engaged in earnest conversation, quite far from the ears of anyone in their party or aboard. Maddy was talking animatedly.

Maddy looked up and down the promenade deck, carefully scanning for any people. Then she reached up and threw her arms around Charlie's neck and with a little leap, hoisted herself up onto his standing frame, throwing her legs around his hips and hooking there, her pelvis pressed hard against his pants. He tottered back against the rail with the weight, but held, his hands coming under her short skirt to the soft pads of her buttocks to help support her.

She peppered his face with kisses, ending in a mouth to mouth kiss that made CPR seem puny. They seemed to be exploring each other's dental work. Maddy's undulating torso slid up and down the plumbing bulge in Charlie's slacks. He bent back further against the rail to increase the friction.

Maddy reached down with a hand to jerk at Charlie's zipper. After a bit of mutual fumbling they joined, Maddy's strong legs propelling her body up and down Charlie's hips in an ever-increasing rhythm until Charlie let out a gasp and sagged farther into the rail. They held like that for a time. Then Maddy slid down and off, smoothing the front of her wrinkled skirt with both hands and anxiously looking around the deck again to assure it was vacant.

Charlie tucked things back together, gave her a peck on the cheek, then turned and disappeared under the Judge's overhanging deck toward doors leading to the ship's interior. Maddy watched as Charlie staggered off, happy but spent. Then she reached down into her small purse discarded on the deck and brought out a clutched of Kleenex nestled there. After looking around furtively she hiked her skirt and shoved the tissue into the crotch of her silk panties.

The Judge stepped back from his position at the rail, feeling like a voyeur. He continued his walk along the pool deck, wondering what Maddy saw in an old fart like Charlie… beyond… beyond… beyond what? Beyond all the money in the world. All the power in the world. All the prestige in the world as the controlling force behind one of the world's largest companies. The Judge also wondered whether Alice Westerman was aware of the dual role played by the pretty executive assistant. Maddy was hot.

CHAPTER 22
DAY 2
11:59 PM

The Judge rode the elevator to 17, the top floor, and wandered into the Sky Bar there, settling into a back-corner table for a night cap, still not ready to face his cabin and its mean, pretend queen bed. There were only two people in the bar drinking, not enough to people-watch. As his drink arrived, Maddy Stevens wobbled in. She looked worn from her adventure on the promenade deck, and more than a little smashed. She spotted the Judge at once, despite the shadows in his corner, and floated over to settle into the other chair at his table uninvited. She ordered a single malt, straight up, two fingers; a Macallan 12 Year Double Cask, heavily advertised. The Judge didn't think much of Macallan, preferring the strong peat and smoke taste of a Laphroaig, or the silkiness of a Bowmore from Islay.

"How are you, Judge?" Her words were slightly slurred, confirming his assessment.

"Relaxed, a bit bored, not a great fan of sea voyages on large cruise ships."

"Did you enjoy the show on the foredeck?"

The Judge felt color rising across his face. He thought he'd been discreet. He decided no answer was the best answer. He just smiled at Maddy, lifted his drink, and sipped.

Maddy smiled too, as though her self-worth was somehow confirmed. The big sloppy smile across her face registered 'intoxicated'. She took a large swig of her Scotch and swallowed it down to keep her buzz going, her face slightly twisting in a grimace as the alcohol bit.

"Men are such… such… such sloppy animals, Judge. But if you're young and pretty and broke, you have to put up with them. What choice is there?"

"I guess there are other choices, Maddy."

"Yeah, like working the cosmetic counter at Macy's? Hah! Some choice." She raised her glass to the Judge and eyed him over its top.

"Where you from originally, Maddy?"

"Tennessee, Judge. Grew up dirt poor in Tennessee."

"College?"

"Yeah. I pretty much slept my way through the University of Tennessee, allowing my various beaus to fund my education. My family had no money; it was a better than encumbering myself with those ridiculous student loans you can never get out of. Besides, it was damn fun."

"It sounds like you were a little wild, Maddy."

"I'm a modern woman, Judge. Independent and unbound by the old mores that held women back. My body is my own. I can use it anyway I want; just like a football player or an Olympic swimmer."

"That's true of course, but you don't have to grow up all at once, and so young." The Judge gave her a soft smile to lighten his words.

"It's true, Judge. I grew up very early." She stared into the bottom of her glass for a moment, old memories flooding in, then looked up at the Judge.

"See, I had this favorite uncle, Judge. A handsome man with dancing blue eyes. He'd always show up with a small gift for little Maddy. He made a fuss over me every time. Made me feel special. Took my side in any argument, lavished praise on how beautiful and smart I was. I was so very fond of Uncle Tim."

"What happened?"

"It all came to a screeching stop one afternoon while my parents were away working. Uncle Tim came by to claim what he wanted. I was only fifteen. It hurt like hell. But I kind of liked it too."

"I'm sorry."

"Don't be. Of course, it was different after that. Uncle Tim stopped coming around much. At family gatherings he'd ignore me, wouldn't look at me. No more, 'how are you', or 'my you look pretty', or 'boy are you smart'. I was disappointed, hurt, about that. It was my first understanding of how shallow and short-term men can be.

But as I turned sixteen there were lots of schoolboys interested. And damn, there was nothing to lose after that, right? So why not? It was a natural thing after all. What God intended for the human race. And it felt soooo good. It was meant to be."

"And then on to college?"

"Yes. But I started seeing older men while in college. I learned techniques I'd never have learned dating those callow college boys. Techniques I use to entrap and entwine you silly males. I know how to keep a man interested. To draw him in, tighter and tighter, till he's like an addict craving a bigger and bigger fix. I can bind myself to a guy so I become indispensable and he becomes totally dependent." She stifled a hiccup and took another slug of Scotch.

"So, have you bound yourself to Charlie?"

"Some. He's pretty slippery. But I'm working on him. What do you make of Charlie, Judge? You've obviously seen lots of characters in your career."

"Is Charlie a character?" asked the Judge.

"I think so. What else would you call him?"

"Mean." The word just slipped out before the Judge could stop it.

Maddy's head snapped up, lightening in her eyes. "He's no such thing. He has no tolerance for fools… But he's the most generous man I've ever met."

"We all have many facets to our personalities, Maddy. You see generous in Charlie; I see something else. Not necessarily inconsistent. We humans react differently to different people. Do you love him?"

Maddy gave the Judge a rueful smile. "I don't really believe in love anymore, Judge. But I respect Charlie, all he's accomplished, how he's ordered his life, how he treats me with dignity. And he's very consistent; perhaps that's what I like best."

"And you obviously find him attractive. But I have to confess, Maddy, to me he looks a little gross."

"What would you know, someone like you, a broken down old ex-judge? I think you're a little jealous."

Maddy paused to take another slug of her Scotch. Then she continued.

"Women don't see guys the way guys do, Judge. When I look at Charlie, I see four vacation homes, business class travel everywhere, collector cars that turn heads, a large yacht with a crew at beck and call, a butler and a maid, no more cooking, laundry, or cleaning. I see Cadillac health care, a large monthly allowance for incidentals running to the mid five figures, and all the status and access that goes with it. I see Academy Award seats, Olympics boxes, hockey and football suites, and recognition as you walk into the best restaurants across the country. I see new wardrobes three closets deep, Aoud Absolue Précieux perfume like Alice wears, and shoes, glorious shoes, racks and racks of shoes. No more scraping by. That's power. That's security for life. That turns my head.

Did you know Charlie got me out of my windowless crap stateroom and relocated into Kennedy's suite? He's like that, always worrying about my comfort."

"I suppose the soda company booked all the rooms and has to pay the freight, whether someone uses the room or not."

"Well of course, but Charlie didn't have to move me. He went out of his way to take care of me."

"So, where is this affair going, Maddy?"

Maddy paused, took another swig of Scotch, and then blurted, "I'm going to marry Charlie."

"Marry? Wow. But Charlie's already married, Maddy."

Maddy snorted. "That's become a short-term impediment, Judge. Charlie loves me. He wants me. What we have will last. Some people will have to get out of the way, that's all."

"You sure you're not just being played?"

"I'm sure. I'm perfect for him. I like to screw, and I need to be very, very wealthy. I don't need kids. I'm happy as long as we're compatible and my man is reliable. And Charlie is."

"What about love?"

"Charlie loves me."

"And do you love Charlie?"

"Love's an over-rated concept, Judge. A couple of months of starry-eyed fantasy and it's gone, replaced with real things like how to pay the rent, how to get the next raise, how to avoid being laid-off, how to catch your lover cheating, whose turn it is to do dishes. Been there, done that, way more than once."

"So, you believe Charlie will leave his wife for you?"

"Yes. It's going happen." She peered at the Judge, her eyes blurry now. "Sides, I have a secret weapon."

"What's that?"

Maddy put a finger in front of her lips. Went "Shsss… can't tell you."

"Doesn't it feel a little funny, Maddy, Charlie going off to bed with his wife after your tête-à-tête; you left to wander the deck and into the only open bar?"

"Nope."

But the Judge could sense a small kernel of doubt forming in Maddy, deep down. A suspicion that Charlie would never marry her. Maddy would be pressing Charlie now wherever she could, suggesting milestones for moving things forward. The Judge wondered if she would succeed in her quest. Charlie looked to be a slippery bastard if ever there were; he'd be hard to pin down.

"Night, Judge."

Maddy took the last slug of her Scotch, got to her feet by leaning heavily on the little table, threatening its stability, then wobbled off for the door, walking like a teenager trying on her first heels.

CHAPTER 23
DAY 3
7:30 AM

Katy sat by herself at a table next to the window, watching the wake at the stern of the ship roll out behind them, more breakfast than she could possibly eat spread in front of her. Pancakes, waffles, fruit, eggs over easy, ham and bacon, an English muffin, even hot chocolate. She hated hot chocolate. But she'd been caught up in the frenzied line of bustling passengers, piling their plates with everything they could reach under the glass along the extended breakfast buffet. She supposed she was beginning to think like the Judge… God forbid.

There was the clamor behind her of trays set down territorially at open seats, small disputes about who got there first, the rattle of dishes, silverware and glasses piled high and carted away, and the clink of coffee cups set down to claim territory on newly vacated tables. It was mixed with the thunder of a thousand steps, the herd grabbing food and chowing down together. It was all quite organized, and quite sterile, complementing the food, which looked great but invariably had a taste that hinted of cardboard.

A thin gentleman inquired about the open seat at her small table and she felt socially forced to nod her assent though the last thing wanted was company. He looked vaguely familiar, his lean face defined by a hawk-like nose and bushy dark eyebrows. His hair was black, wavy, and thick; she guessed Croatian roots. He was dressed in a dark purple workout suit.

"You're the Judge's wife," he said. "We met briefly at dinner before old Kennedy collapsed."

"You're Charlie's business adviser, or partner, or something…."

"Very good. I'm Ross Hamilton, Charlie's business partner. I was at the end of the table near you but we hardly had a chance to talk."

"Yes. My husband and Charlie are both strong personalities. I think the table was caught up in the drama between the two."

"You had quite a bit to say yourself about single use plastic bottles, as I recall."

"Yes. Well, I guess I did."

"The Judge is quite an opinionated man. Do you find that difficult to put up with?"

"No more opinionated than most men, I'd say. If only women ruled the world, it would be different. We'd get things done."

Hamilton smiled, but without conviction.

"You know, Katy, in some parts people consider your husband a cad and a thief."

"That's ridicules and slanderous." Katy's chin came up from coffee cup with a scowl.

"Just saying. I heard how he destroyed the marriage of a friend of mine. Promised her the moon, wooed her away from her husband and a very secure nest with promises of eternal love, then dumped her once he'd used her. Turned his back and kicked her out into the cold, penniless, alone, distraught.

Now, whenever he runs into her, he makes obscene advances toward her again. Toying with her emotions, trying to give her false hope. It's sad to watch."

"None of that's true, Mr. Hamilton," Katy said crisply.

"Oh, but it is. You see the poor girl he dumped is now my fiancée, or about to be. She's on this trip with me, unofficially of course. So, I can't bring her to dinner. But your husband is already trying to arrange an intimate rendezvous so he can again get into her pants."

Katy opened her mouth with a retort but was stopped by Ross's flat palm extended in front of her face, as Ross continued.

"I hold you partially accountable, Katy. You should do a better job of policing your Judge. Make him keep his dick in his pants around reputable women."

With that, Hamilton abruptly rose and strode off, giving Katy no chance to reply.

Katy sat stunned for several seconds, staring down at her cold eggs. Then a single name floated into her mind… growing larger there like the opening credits of *Star Wars*…. ***Barbara!***

CHAPTER 24
DAY 3
8:00 AM

Maddy sat up in bed suddenly, full awake from the morning light streaming into her new suite. Then she wished she hadn't. Her head felt like a swollen melon, pulsating from the sun's rays bouncing off her forehead. She considered being sick, perhaps a dash to the toilet, then rejected it, sinking carefully back down on her pillow, shifting an arm across her eyes, almost wishing for death.

Later, she didn't know how later, she hobbled up and over to her luggage, grasping desperately for her bottle of aspirin with one hand, holding her forehead with the other. She dragged herself to the bathroom and popped three pills, forcing herself to drink a full glass of water. Then she staggered back to the bed and collapsed there.

An hour later she sat up, feeling better, and surveyed her new suite. Kennedy's suite, now hers thanks to Charlie. The other miserable little room she'd been billeted in was an interior hole in the wall amidships up in the bow, no window, not even a port hole; cramped and uncomfortable.

Back in her former room she'd tuned the TV screen that practically covered one small wall to the live feed from a video camera mounted on the ship's helm and pretended the increasingly frothy view as the sea turned around the ship was really a window. But it was hard to pretend. She had felt closed in. And the increasingly violent scene as the ship's bow rose and then lowered with the cresting waves in some ways matched her own shifts in internal mood, carefully concealed from the world. Her driver's license said she was turning twenty-six soon, but she knew she was inexorably edging on to thirty. *Shit!*

Kennedy's suite was first cabin, with its neat balcony and sliding glass window, a separate seating area, and a queen size bed. It had a fully stocked bar… Ugh. She didn't want to think about that.

She remembered vaguely the night before a bit of hanky-panky with Charlie out on the promenade deck. How delicious; how wet he'd gotten her.

Charlie had gone off to climb into his king bed with the dried-up creature who held the title of wife. Meanwhile, she had made her way automatically to her cheap interior room without the window, forgetting that Charlie had her moved here.

She had a vague recollection of conversation with the judge guy before she'd finally found Kennedy's cabin. The conversation had been in a bar somewhere. But she couldn't remember where or what the conversation was about. She hoped she hadn't said too much.

Maddy got up and began to pace the floor, considering her options and her strategy. She wanted… no, needed Charlie to marry her, and soon. She was tired of hiding their mutual attraction and their affair. Charlie needed to come through with the goods… divorce the wife, marry her. Time was going by and she was aging in place… single. The program needed to move quickly along, and none of that pre-nuptial lawyering crap either.

She thought about her new strategy, considering again the risks and rewards. She'd stopped taking her birth control pills. It was not an ideal path. She didn't really like kids. But Charlie of course only wanted to do bareback, leaving it to her to sort out the birth control technicalities. Typical male. Well, they were sorted out now for sure. One random joust and it could be eighteen years of flush living for her. She smiled with grim satisfaction at her secret.

Her bare foot crunched down on something hard by the nightstand. She kneeled and felt with her fingers in the tall carpet, coming up with an earring, just one, a small white gold pendant with a diamond embedded in it.

She recognized it. One half of Alice Westerman's favorite set of earrings. Worn at lunch on the first day but not at dinner. Now she knew why. Well well…. What had been going on in Kennedy's stateroom behind Charlie's back? She imagined with satisfaction her production of this Exhibit A next time she pressed her case. The fur ought to fly with this.

CHAPTER 25
DAY 3
11:35 AM

The Judge settled into an overstuffed leather chair in the private dining room for first class passengers. He'd been invited by George Walker, Charlie's Chief Executive Officer. Walker has said 11:30, and the Judge had been fashionably late at 11:35. But no George. There was a reservation though and the Judge settled into the assigned table with his back to the window, facing the entrance to the small clubby room.

Cherry paneling on the four walls was offset by a vivid green carpet that your shoes sunk into when you stepped in. There were oils on the walls, scenes of ancient ships and distant shores, all with large splashes of color, each set off by shiny brass lighting above the frame.

The people were different here too. There were only three couples dining here so far, seated at tables well-spaced out, talking in intimate tones that couldn't be overhead. The women were dressed to the nines, bright expensive summer wear, and the men sported the casual look of Ralph Lauren and Tommy Bahama. Short sleeve shirts and tailored slacks. Only one wore a sport coat, an expensively tailored blue blazer with brass buttons.

It was a small crowd comfortable with themselves, perhaps even smug, with a smell of money that assured orderly lives and deferential service. Two waiters, a young man and a young woman, buzzed among the three tables topping off Arnold Palmers or replacing mixed drinks.

George Walker glided through the entrance door at 11:45, looked around, and steered toward the Judge's table. He wore blue Bermuda shorts, cotton, cut just above the knees, and a blue checked sport shirt that reminded the Judge of a pioneer's tablecloth. The Judge thought Walker looked mismatched and stupid, but if you had enough money, he supposed you could do whatever you wanted, and it would still look okay.

Walker was just under six feet, carrying his fifty-plus years gracefully, not quite slender anymore, but active; the movements of a golfer perhaps who still carried his own bag. He wore his patrician veneer like a flag over his perfectly tanned face, giving off the scent of wealth, privilege, and power.

He stood over the Judge to reach down and offer his spidery hand, ivory white with veins showing, hairless. The Judge again felt a dry slippery sensation, as though of a lizard losing its skin, when Walker's hand slid across his. The same green eyes examined the Judge without warmth, as though the Judge were a new specimen of minor interest.

"So, Charlie's hired you. A waste of money if you ask me. Everyone knew Kennedy had that peanut allergy; that it'd be the death of him some day. I guess the EpiPen didn't work. Often things don't work the way they're supposed to in this supposedly modern world."

"And what about Larry Cain, George?"

"Cain was old and clumsy. I'm surprised he hadn't fallen down some set of stairs much sooner. Just bad luck for him he landed wrong on his neck. There's no indication of foul play in either circumstance. I told Charlie as much."

"You don't think it beyond coincidence that two executive officers in the same company die on the same cruise within twenty-four hours of one another? Both in unusual 'so-called' accidents?"

"I don't. I think Charlie likes to romance the things that happen around him, find shadows here and sinister consequences there. I won't say Charlie's paranoid exactly, but he has leanings."

George sat back in his chair primly, folding his hands together on the table in front of him, confident he'd closed the subject, moving to shut off further debate. But the Judge wasn't so easily deterred, plunging ahead with his questions, his chin coming up and his steady blue eyes snapping back at Walker.

"Two people are dead, George. Dead. Each under suspicious circumstances. Charlie's hired me to look into it; and the ship's captain has made a similar request. So, it's what I'm going to do. Do you know anyone who might want to kill either or both of them? Anyone with motive or who might hold an old grudge?"

Walker sat forward again, his hands making a steeple in front of him now. "Alright," he said. "Let's play your silly game, Judge. Let me think for a moment."

The Judge sat in silence, watching the now narrowing green eyes across the small table, waiting Walker out.

"Well, Judge, there's Charlie himself, of course. We all knew Alice was sleeping with Kennedy. It was so casual you couldn't call it a secret. Charlie didn't seem to mind as long as they weren't in his face about it. I suspect whatever passion Charlie and Alice originally shared burned out long ago.

There's Laura, Charlie's daughter. She never liked Kennedy. I don't know why, exactly. But there was always tension in the room when both she and Kennedy were present. I suspect she harbored some sort of dark grudge. And she was in the kitchen before the crab bisque was served. She had opportunity, as well as some motive of sorts.

There's Danny, Charlie's son. He was working for Larry Cain. Larry told me there were questions about possible improprieties in the way our company's cash was being moved around by Danny. Small little nickel and dime shit, charges, fees, payments under the table, improprieties here and there, but they mounted up, perhaps to the tune of a half a million dollars last year alone. If Danny was skimming money through kickbacks and the like and was about to be unmasked by Larry Cain, that'd certainly be a motive."

"Do you think any of those three are capable of murder, George?"

"I think everybody's capable of murder under the right circumstances, Judge. We homo sapiens seem to have a propensity for violence. But this is just a company business cruise, not a game of Clue."

"Anyone else?"

"Ross Hamilton. Hamilton's been doing some secret maneuvering of late. I don't know what it's about, but Cain had gotten wind of it through his men's club in downtown L.A. Said he wasn't sure how it was all put together, but it was pretty big and Charlie was not going to be happy. Said he was still collecting the facts on it."

"What about you, George. Did you have any reason to see Kennedy or Cain leave the scene?"

"No. Of course not. Just more work for me now. I'll have to vet replacement candidates for the two vacant corporate offices."

"Anything else come to mind, George? Think for a minute."

"Well… I guess there's the notes."

"What notes?"

"Charlie didn't tell you about the notes?"

"No."

"I'm not surprised. Charlie treats them as bad omens, doesn't like to think about them, much less talk about them."

"Tell me about the notes."

"We officers get them. Kennedy as COO, Cain as CFO, and of course me, as CEO. Charlie doesn't get them nor Ross Hamilton, the other principle shareholder. The public doesn't generally know about how they quietly control our company."

Anyway, we get notes all the time. Threats about this, threats about that. The typical rubbish. Discrimination against women, discrimination against minorities, alleged sexual harassment, stop ruining the climate, stop polluting the oceans, stop polluting the world, stop poisoning pregnant women with plastics, stop making people obese with our sicky sticky soda formulas, you name it. It's like our officers' fan mail club."

"They come to your office?"

"Yes. Or to our email accounts. We've all gotten a good laugh over them. Kennedy liked to frame the nastier ones and pin them in his little executive washroom at corporate."

"But you sounded like you were talking about a specific set of notes."

"Oh. Well, about a week before we left on our trip, we each got a note in the mail. A little unusual as we all got the notes at the same time and they all said the same thing. Apparently from the same person."

"What did the notes say?"

"The usual tripe. Stop polluting the oceans with your plastic bottles and tops. Stuff your bride would lobby for."

"Was there a threat included?"

"Oh sure. The usual. Death and destruction of you and your company, that sort of thing. Like the Black

Spot out of Treasure Island. All very romantic I must say."

"What did they look like?"

"What do you mean?"

"What sort of paper and envelope? Computer print-out, handwritten?"

"Brown paper, like a shopping bag from the market, stuffed into a plain white envelope, letters cut from a magazine or something."

"And you don't consider them serious?"

"No. None of us takes them seriously, Judge. We get them all the time. Not relevant to our discussion here."

"Do you have a picture of one of these notes?"

"Better than that. I think I have the actual note, this last one, stuffed into the mail file I brought along."

"Where's your file?"

"In my room."

"Let's go get it. I'd like to see it."

"Right now?"

"Right now."

They rose together, Walker scribbling a hasty signature on the check shoved under his nose before making large strides toward the door of the dining room.

"Are you married, George?" asked the Judge as they entered the lift to shoot down four decks.

Walker turned to give the Judge a lopsided smile with a touch of avarice somewhere in its recesses. "In name yes; in deed no. We've been married a long time and now we go our separate ways, meeting up occasionally for family affairs. We have a son on Wall Street. But I decided life is more fun if you aren't chained down. You have a pretty wife, Judge, but I've always found it difficult to restrain my tastes to just one flavor."

They reached Walker's stateroom in first class and George bolted in, going straight to the closet where a briefcase lay stacked against the wall. He opened the case and rummaged through a sheaf of emails and letters, then looked up at the Judge in embarrassment.

"I thought it was in here with my correspondence, but I'm mistaken. I must have left it at the office."

"Tell me George. Your two fellow officers are dead. Are you worried you might be next?"

"Absolutely not. These were both unfortunate accidents. A coincidence they both occurred on the same cruise."

"And only a day apart, George."

"Yes, and only a day apart. But both accidents, Judge, clear and simple. Someone fell down some stairs. Someone had an allergy flare up and his EpiPen didn't work. That's all there is to it. There's no sinister plot here for God's sakes. Charlie loves drama. But I'll be damned if I'll let him spoil my vacation with his unfounded accusations of some conspiracy, some plot to kill people. It's all poppycock."

George leaned his back against the wall of his stateroom, folded his arms across his chest and glared at the Judge. His expression said case closed, interview over.

CHAPTER 26
DAY 3
1:00 PM

The Judge took one turn around the promenade deck to walk off his lunch, then decided to explore some more of the ship. He took the elevator down to Deck two. He realized at once he was no longer in the guests' quarters. The hallways were smaller and there was less access to elevator banks. Peeking into a couple of rooms whose doors were open for maid service, he could see the rooms were tiny, with a single small porthole on the outside rooms, narrow bunks on each side wall, and a miniscule toilet and shower enclosure, even smaller than his room. He was sure there was no way he'd fit into one of the bathroom units. If he tried he'd get stuck; they'd have to use a can opener or something to extract him. Being crew on a cruise ship was definitely a young person's calling.

After walking the twists and turns of the hallways for a while and making random choices at forks, the Judge decided he was completely turned around,… lost. It was like a maze. He needed help. He saw a door with a sign which read *Crew Only-Dining Room*, and in desperation barged in. It was a smallish room with cafeteria style food service running along one side, about the size of a small hospital cafeteria. The food laid out in self-serve trays didn't look appetizing. The Judge recalled the crew ate leftovers from the guest food service above, not yet bad, but perhaps a tad stale.

The floor was a dull grey linoleum tile, clashing with soft aqua walls that looked like they could use a paint freshening. Hospital colors. Beyond the food service was a cluster of inexpensive tables and chairs, reminding the Judge of McDonald's.

Three of the tables were occupied. One at the front had two young women with dark skin leaning over the table talking earnestly to one another. The Judge had the impression a lover's quarrel was in progress, given the intensity of the conversation, the rolling of eyes, and the outstretched hands of one trying to hold the darting hands of the other.

A table in the middle had three people. A young woman and two men shared beers and talked softly. The Judge recognized the woman facing him: Sophia, their floor maid. The man to her left was the scrawny pool guy, Ajay or something. The third man turned his head and the Judge recognized Sean, the dining room waiter. He sat very close to Sophia and had his hand territorially on the back of her chair. The Judge wondered if they were an item. Shipmate parings among the crew were frequent but short term, the Judge had once been told. There wasn't much else to do with your down time if you were crew on a cruise ship.

Sophia was doodling on a napkin which she suddenly crumpled and made into a ball, lobbing it at a nearby waste basket. Missing. The three got up, Sean nodding at the Judge as their eyes met, a perfunctory smile pasted on his face. They sauntered with overt casualness to the back of the dining room and out, disappearing down a corridor. There was a tension in the little group the Judge couldn't explain. Was it forbidden for a guest to wander into the crew's dining area? Was this their private sanctuary away from the guests? Had he blundered across unspoken lines?

At a rear table, three men were seated at a board game. It looked like Monopoly, one of them blowing on dice and then rolling them with vigor up against the torn-out bottom of a cardboard box. There was an intensity to them beyond the mere playing of a board game. There were real dollars tucked under one side of the board where the game's banker sat.

Out of curiosity the Judge walked over and plucked Sophia's crumpled napkin from the floor beside the trash basket. He smoothed it out to reveal a series of three-dimensional boxes drawn across the napkin with the letters, 'ELF' sketched in the face of each box. He shrugged but stuck the napkin in his back pocket.

Beyond the dining area was a lounge, boasting a bar, a pool table, a 65-inch wall screen, and several vinyl couches with offsetting low cocktail tables. A cluster of three people was leaning at the bar, conversing animatedly. It sounded like they were sharing humorous stories about the current guests and enjoying themselves.

The Judge interrupted and asked for guidance back to the elevator bank and salvation from the crew level. The three men smiled and one of them detached himself from the group, a large strapping black man who looked late twenties and spoke with a clipped English accent. "I'm Adam. I'll be glad to help you, sir."

"Tell me Adam, is the crew permitted to cook their own meals down here?" asked the Judge.

"Generally, no. But there is a small galley we can use on occasion. We like to cook home dishes now and then for ourselves and our friends. Yesterday I made some Nyama Choma with Kachumbari and Ugaliand."

"Delicious, Adam. With short ribs?"

"Of course, sir."

"You're from Kenya?"

"Yes sir. Down here the crew tends to fragment into small cliques. Most of the people from each county tend to gravitate toward their own countrymen, building relationships with people who share customs and language. It's only natural. We Kenyans like to get together and share our home food now and then."

"Can I see your galley?"

"Sure. It's this way."

Adam led the way around the bar and through a door into a small room. It boasted a mini-electric range and oven, a microwave, a large refrigerator, counter space and cupboards, and a large sink and dishwasher.

"Very compact," said the Judge. "Who cleans this area?"

"That would be one of the crew stewards, sir. Let's look. There's an assignment chart over here on the wall."

Adam led the Judge to a clipboard hung on the wall in one corner. He leafed through it, then said. "Martha Sandor has the duty for this leg of the cruise. She's from Argentina."

"Can I speak to her?"

"Sure. She's on duty now, probably cleaning at the other end of our quarters."

They retraced their steps back into the lounge and then into another long corridor, partly blocked by a cleaning cart. "Martha, are you around?" called Adam.

A smallish woman, perhaps early forties, poked her head out of one of the cabins further down, cleaning cloth in hand. Her face was tan and wrinkled, framing soft brown eyes that looked at Adam expectantly, and then at the Judge, sizing him up as a guest.

"My companion here was just inspecting the crew's small galley and had a question or two for you."

The Judge stepped forward and proffered his hand, which was quickly taken and given a soft perfunctory shake.

"Other than Adam, has the crew's galley been used by anyone else this week, Martha?"

"Let me think, Sir. Yes. Yes. The Mexicans made enchiladas for lunch. Juan Martinez and his friends. Left a hell of a mess. And someone made an apple pie, I don't know who, but they left me a slice. Real yummy. And, let's see, Ajay made Indian Spiced Carrot Soup for some of his pals. Oh, but that was last week."

"Would you have recipes for the dishes made in the crew's galley?"

"No, sir. But you could ask whoever was cooking. Adam here, for instance makes a mean beef stew. But I don't know who made the apple pie."

"Thanks, Martha," said the Judge.

Adam guided the Judge back into the corridor and then walked him what seemed like three blocks through turning corridors and alcoves, until they finally came to an elevator bank with buttons for upper floors. The Judge sighed with relief, more than ready to leave the bowels of the ship. He punched the button for the main pool deck.

CHAPTER 27
DAY 3
1:45 PM

As the Judge entered the pool area, he spotted Alice Westerman, Charlie's wife, on a lounge chair at the other end of the pool. He moseyed over and sat down on the adjacent lounge. Alice eyed him over the top of her book, a mystery novel.

"Looks like you're joining me, Judge."

"You're the only familiar face I see out here," smiled the Judge.

"Charlie doesn't like the sun, or the people, or to get wet. Fact is, he doesn't like much of anything about cruising. I don't know why he makes the effort. I think it was the officers who took a vote on what to do for a bonus trip after a good year. He could have crushed the idea if he'd wanted. Surprised he didn't."

"How long you two been together?"

"Three decades. I count it in tens, like penitentiary time."

"You sound disillusioned."

"The romance wore off years ago."

"You don't love Charlie anymore?"

"Love? I don't even like Charlie anymore. In fact, the word 'like' isn't a word one would use in talking about Charlie. Rich, self-sufficient, brilliant, ruthless, tricky, mean, these are the words that come to mind."

"Why do you stay?"

"I kid myself it's the prenuptial I signed. But it's not really about that. I stay… I stay… I stay because I've got nowhere to go, Judge. Parents long gone. Charlie engineered things so I never made close friends. There's just Charlie, and the three… I mean the two kids. We lost one last year."

"I'm sorry."

"I am too, Judge. It was Charlie's doing. He so terrorized my youngest son, Jay, that Jay killed himself to get away. Suicide, right in front of Charlie. Guess that tells you something about their relationship. I'll never forgive Charlie for that."

"How well did you know Kennedy?"

"You don't miss much, do you Judge?"

"So?"

"So, I could say it's none of your business. But I don't give a shit. If it makes Charlie look a little bad, well then good. Kennedy was a sweet man. Divorced. She took their two kids when she left, never allowed him to see his kids again. He didn't have anyone; kind of like me. We just slid into this arrangement. Started years ago when Charlie took over control of the Company. At first just a couple of lunches when Charlie was out of town, good conversation, we got to know each other. It felt comfortable. It felt real. It was all very innocent at the start. But it changed, deepened, became a physical thing, like a craving. I couldn't get enough of Kennedy. I'm going to miss him a lot."

"But Kennedy left the Company."

"Yes. I missed him for many years. But then I got him back. Had to lobby real hard to do that. We started right up again, like we'd never stopped."

"And Charlie knew?"

"Of course Charlie knew. He knows everything. Nosey spying bastard. That made it even more exquisite; that I could enjoy myself and piss on him at the same time. Maybe that's the real reason it even happened. I don't know.

Anyway, Kennedy's gone now. Charlie doesn't really give a shit I slept with him. As long as there was nothing public, he could care less. Charlie and I haven't had sex in two decades. It wasn't like Kennedy was ploughing ground someone else'd been tending." She gave the Judge a sad smile."

"Charlie's certainly a one off. How'd you two meet?"

"In college. Charlie was broke back then, going to Stanford for his masters on a scholarship. Living in a shabby little single on the wrong side of town. He was already full of himself though, even then. Bragged to me of the money he was going to make, the power he was going to wield. He swept me off my feet."

"What was Charlie studying?"

"Charlie worked his way through UCLA and got a degree in chemical engineering, then Stanford. Then he just went out and fought his way, rung by rung, up the corporate ladder at various companies, gaining experience. He accumulated enough money to start his own company and to invent and patent the cheap single use soda bottle. His company was acquired by the soda company for a ton of its stock, cash, and a continuing royalty. He used the money to quietly buy blocks of the soda company stock offshore until he effectively had a controlling interest, all told about 30 percent. The next largest shareholder owns only 5 percent.

Charlie replaced the board with his own people and controls the company with his personality, backed by his controlling block of stock. He's not even a director or an officer or anything, and his name never shows up in annual reports, although there are of course rumors now and then.

Company Board Meetings are held, but nothing gets done until Charlie arrives and tells the board what he wants done. He also took over the executive hiring and firing function, working through his milquetoast HR guy. He cut a lot of people last year, pruning the tree and disposing of the weak sisters and the higher paid senior executives, old and tired chickens that had been molting for years."

"That must have generated some enemies."

"I suppose so. One of the people Charlie cut out of the gentlemen's lucrative consulting contract was Ross Hamilton. Ross is a 5 percent shareholder and originally partnered with Charlie to take control of the company. I heard Ross was livid.

You have to be really smart and really tough to succeed in business the way Charlie has, and driven. Charlie's all that… and something more. He takes pleasure in being ruthless! It why he's succeeded where others have faltered, finding themselves trampled as Charlie outfoxed and then steam-rolled over them."

"How did Charlie make the company so successful?"

"Charlie set the company on a new course, manufacturing his single use plastic bottle for soft drinks that replaced glass bottles. He sold the bottle to the other soda companies and to a myriad of other companies for use in food and material packaging. The market was quick to buy. And why wouldn't it be? His products are cheaper, less weight to ship, don't break, and the plastic bottling can last forever. It has made the soda company, and Charlie, very rich."

"Do you think he might have had a hand in Kennedy's death?" asked the Judge.

"You mean it wasn't an accident?" Panic spread across Alice's face.

"I don't know yet. That's why I'm looking into it. If it were premeditated, in other words murder, is it something Charlie might do, given your affair with Kennedy?"

"I wouldn't put anything past Charlie, but I don't think he had any motive. He didn't give a shit about my affair. I think the affair even salved his conscience, allowing him to feel more comfortable with the tom-catting around he likes to do."

"And what about Cain? Would Charlie have any motive there?"

"You think that wasn't an accident either? God. That'd be a mess. But no. I can't think of why Charlie would have any quarrel with Cain."

"Okay, Alice. Thanks for the time, and your frankness."

CHAPTER 28
DAY 3
2:15 pm

The Judge decided to settle in for a snack in the buffet restaurant aft of the pool. He walked into a swirl of people and food trays. Suddenly in the middle of a thundering herd of heifers stumbling around with their loaded treys in blind panic lest they miss some of the tasteless food piled high behind the austere glass panels. He settled for watered down orange juice, an English muffin with margarine, a slice of seedless watermelon, and some more of the discouragingly thin coffee. He found an empty seat near a window, barely beating out of hefty black lady who'd tried unsuccessfully to cut him in the race for the table.

As he polished off the watermelon, he heard a voice from the table behind him.

"You're a complete asshole, Judge."

"What?" The Judge turned in his seat to see who was sitting at the table behind him.

"You heard me. I know all about you." It was Ross Hamilton, Charlie's business partner.

"What exactly do you know?" asked the Judge.

"I know you enticed a wonderful lady out of a steady marriage by false promises of 'forever' when your only goal was to get into her pants. I know you made her commit sex acts against her better instincts, in public, in your car, in an orange grove, even while you were driving down the freeway. I know your sex play with her was mean, kinky, unnatural, and rough. I know you've got a teeny pecker; you have lots of trouble keeping it up, and you over-compensate by talking dirty to embarrass nice females. Every woman you approach finds your crude and offensive."

"And just how would you know all that?"

"The very same wonderful lady happens to be my fiancée."

"Barbara!"

"Yes. Barbara. She's told me all about you, Judge. What you did. What you promised her. What you did to her. You lied to her, painting a rosy picture of how you were going to take care of her forever. But you always intended to dump her after you got tired of using her. And that's exactly what you did. You have no shame, Judge."

"Hamilton, I'm not sure how to respond to all that. My general rule is a gentleman never talks about a past affair. But it seems Barbara has been telling stories about me that are not true."

"*Haaaahhh.*"

"Believe what you like, Hamilton. I will say this, though. I gave Barbara a choice back then. Leave her husband and come with me. Or stay with her husband

and end our affair. She chose to stay with her husband and end our affair. He was about to make partner at his prestigious CPA firm. She decided to stay in her marriage because she wanted to maximize her property settlement and alimony payouts. So, I left."

"Yeah, well that's not the way I heard it."

"I can't be responsible for what you heard, how you heard it, or what you believe. I only suggest you not take Barbara's fantasy stories about the past as gospel. But I'm glad you spoke up. I've been wanting to talk to you about Kennedy's death."

"And why would I want to talk to you?"

"Charlie asked me to look into Kennedy's death."

"Charlie…Charlie…. Whatever authority Charlie has as a non-officer, non-director, is about to be long gone."

"Oh, yes. I think I heard something about that."

Ross's head shot up, his eyes blazing. "What? What did you hear? Where?"

"Just a rumor, nothing concrete. I don't remember where."

Ross stared at the Judge long and hard for thirty seconds, then his face shifted into a poker player's countenance, betraying little, except for his lips, which went tight in a straight line across his mouth.

"How well did you know Kennedy, Ross?"

"Not well."

"But you worked with him at the company."

"No. I've never worked at the company… period. I'm just a shareholder."

"A five percent shareholder."

"Yes."

"You weren't a consultant for the company?"

"For a time, but I got terminated."

"Did you see Kennedy socially?"

"No. Not before this cruise."

"Know any reason why someone would want to kill Kennedy?"

"You think Kennedy was murdered, Judge?"

"Perhaps. Know anyone who disliked Kennedy that much?"

"No. I didn't kill him. Had no reason to. He was just a fat nothing as far as I could see."

"He might have spoken to Charlie about your plans for the company."

"What plans?"

"Did you share any confidential plans with Kennedy."

"Like what, Judge? You're just fishing now, grasping at straws."

"Maybe. Maybe not."

"I'm not saying anything else, Judge. I don't have to talk to you, asshole. You've got no authority over me. Go tell Charlie he can shove it up his ass…. And stay away from Barbara."

Ross sprung out of his chair and stomped off.

CHAPTER 29
DAY 3
2:45 PM

The Judge returned to his stateroom, changed into his never-wet trunks, and took the elevator up to the pool deck. As he arrived at the pool area, the Captain's voice came over the loudspeaker with… well... authority. He was the Captain after all. But his words put a slight shiver through the cavorting bi-peds around the pool.

"This is your Captain. Unfortunately, ladies and gentlemen, an unexpected Pacific storm has erupted across our route ahead. A storm of such proportions they are calling it a Pacific typhoon. Huge winds and waves. Not a fit sea even for our sturdy ship.

So, we're going to outrun it, a detour to the north where seas will be calmer. We'll increase our speed and it's going to get a bit rough for a few hours this evening… well, quite rough really. We expect to encounter large waves and there'll be a heavy blow from the wind. It will be no problem for our trusty ship, but it will get a bit bouncy.

We'll also be a day late arriving in Hilo, our first port of call. And we'll skip our visit to Kauai. The winds won't permit it. The good news is that deleting Kauai will put us back on schedule.

We'll be beyond the influence of this storm in about ten hours. We are now closing our pools. The gym and the spa will remain open, as well as food service. And of course, our casino and our bars will be open, and our music will play on. Thank You."

Skinny young females at the pool in two pieces, never intended to be wet huddled together with big eyes and began to gather together towels, fashion magazines, romantic paperbacks with lurid covers, sunscreen, and nail polish, all in preparation for withdrawal. Young guys with rippling chests and flat stomachs who'd been parading around the pool leaving a trail of pheromones, now began to melt away into the interior of the ship.

It sounded like it was going to be an interesting evening.

CHAPTER 30
DAY 3
3:00 PM

The Judge pulled his trousers over his never-wets, and left the pool area, following the crowd. He cut around the giant hole in the middle of the ship people liked to call the atrium. As far as he was concerned a hole was a hole. In this case this was a hole in a hole in the water. He passed the minuscule library (reading aboard ship was a low priority, well below eating, sunburning, soaking, strutting, shopping, and gambling), and into the casino, a shortcut to his block of elevators.

The Judge looked around as he walked in. Perhaps the rest of the ship hadn't been maintained to the best of 'bright-work' standards, but that wasn't true of the casino. White columns with fluted tops were anchored in a floor of green carpet sporting bright orange seahorses and seaweed shapes. The columns disappeared into a ceiling mirrored like a French whorehouse, displaying a reflection of the carpet and the tops of everybody's head. The Judge looked with distaste at the top of his head with its pink and spreading bald spot, the gloomy harbinger of his future Friar Tuck look, and bit his lip.

He noted in passing that the gaudy one-armed bandits, with their glitzy lights and flashing buzzers, weren't one-armed anymore. In going to electric buttons, the machine purveyors had destroyed half the fun of playing the slots and precluded the English the Judge used to give the lever to fudge the inextricable odds. But they were still noisy and flashy. Spots in the ceiling focused on two glistening green crap tables and a multi-colored spinning roulette wheel.

The Judge felt like he was in King Tut's tomb. Except of course, the room was bustling; hefty guests lapped over small stools at the slots, and numerous players leaned desperately over dice tables to watch the white bones roll down green felt to bounce randomly off padded table-ends. The noise level was high. Slots whistling and beeping, roulette wheels were ratchetting, and customers randomly expelling their breath, some happy, some not, as the machinery turned in methodical order like some giant clock, churning out the house's vigorish. The friendly staff displayed welcoming smiles filled with bright white teeth worthy of a dental commercial.

Winding his way around the slots, arranged so you couldn't walk through the casino on a straight line, he nearly tripped over Danny Westerman in the narrow space, hunched over a twenty-dollar slot machine. Danny had his credit card in its slot and was mechanically pushing the buttons, his eyes dully watching the spinning numbers whirl in the machine's face. Periodically the machine would clink, and lights would flash, indicating he'd won back a small portion of his credit card investment. There was a line of highball glasses down the side of the machine. All were empty except for the closest, half full of a golden-brown liquid. The Judge guessed cheap Bourbon from the aroma seeping up from the heat.

"Winning?" asked the Judge.

"Do you ever?" responded Danny, his speech slightly slurred. "It's just something to do on this stupid boat."

"Why'd you come?"

"Had to. Dad combined family and business on this trip to prove he cares about us."

"Can we talk for a couple of minutes? I'll buy you a free drink, Danny."

"Sure, lets. I'm doing no good with this blinking bandit."

They settled into overstuffed chairs at an empty green felt card table in the back corner of the room. The Judge ordered a Laphroaig straight up; Danny ordered a Mule.

"You work for your dad's company, don't you?" asked the Judge.

"Yeah. Unfortunately."

"What do you do?"

"I'm in accounting. I run the cash for the company, invest it over night at bank rates and stuff. All very technical."

"I understand the company does quite well."

"Yeah. But they don't believe in compensating their employees well. Old Tight-Fisted is, well, tight-fisted. They don't pay me anything like I'm worth."

"I heard Larry Cain, the CFO, was in a shouting match with you before you all left on this trip. Heard there might have been some irregularities in your department in the way certain fees were paid."

Danny scowled. "Larry was old, and a little senile, didn't understand modern ways."

"Why was Cain so upset?"

"Just a misunderstanding. Larry's an old school CPA, doesn't really understand about running cash flow, investing your cash while you're holding it temporarily. He thought something fishy was going on. Thought some money may have gone missing around the edges or something. Totally wrong. I had to show him how everything is accounted for, down to the penny."

"Was he an overly suspicious type?"

"Larry Cain? He was paranoid. About everything, and specially about Dad's money, dude. He knew Dad cares more about his money than anything. If any money were ever missing, Larry knew he'd be axed immediately."

"Charlie is really into his money, isn't he."

"Oh yeah. It's more important to Dad than any of us. Kind of sad isn't it? Dad's a guy with the Midas touch to make money, but all he values in the world, in his life, is the money he accumulates."

"Sometime people identify money as their security blanket, Danny. They get wrapped up in it, frightened it might go away. It becomes the center of their stability. But that doesn't mean they don't love their family too."

Danny snorted. "My dad doesn't care about anything but his money. It's a fact our family has learned to live with. He's dysfunctional, Judge. All he can see, all he can smell, all he can think about, all he values, is his money. There's no room in his soul for people. It's what killed my younger brother."

"How so?"

"Jay committed suicide on our driveway in front of Dad 'cause Jay couldn't stand to be a part of our family, Dad's family, anymore. Dad sucked all the life out of Jay. Belittled him for years. Criticized Jay all the time. Abused him verbally. Destroyed his self-esteem. Made him feel about as important and worthwhile as a gnat."

"Did Charlie do that to you, too?"

"He tried. But I've got a thicker skin. I don't give a shit what Dad thinks. I take his money. I have a good life. But I don't respect the man. I don't feel anything for him. He's just the walking, talking ATM I use. He'll die and go to Hell someday. And we'll all be dancing on his coffin, spending his money with abandon, just 'cause we know it'd piss him off." Danny smiled with grim satisfaction.

The Judge nodded his understanding, stood up, and moved on through the casino with its flashing lights and buzzers, its gadfly gamblers trapped in cycles of loss, its accommodating dealers, its sharp-eyed croupier, and its two scantily clad cocktail waitresses of uncertain vintage trying to prance around as the ship began to pick up more rock in its motion.

Danny watched the Judge's back, wondering faintly through his alcoholic haze if he'd said too much. What a nosey old fart. And that asshole, Cain, spreading malicious rumors about him. But then he thought comfortably of his secret offshore account, swelled to almost a million now from a tiny slice of vigorish here and there every time he ran money overnight. He smiled, the lyrics of Master of the House from Les Misérables floating into his mind.

Charge 'em for the lice
Extra for the mice
Two percent for looking in the mirror twice
Here a little slice
There a little cut
Three percent for sleeping with the window shut.

Perhaps in a former life he'd been an inn keeper. But he had to be careful. His dad had asked some pointed questions during their last argument, as though Charlie intuitively knew what he'd been doing. And after that, Charlie had dispatched Cain to nose around his office, peek into his personal statements, audit some of his accounts. Had Cain discovered his game? Perhaps blabbed about it before his timely accident? No one had said anything, so he assumed not. But he couldn't be sure. It would soon be time to pull up anchor and leave this miserable company. Get out from under Charlie's fucking heel.

CHAPTER 31
DAY 3
3:30 PM

The Judge took a deep breath, one of resignation really, then pushed at a glass door marked: *Ship's Gym.* After Katy's subtle and then not so subtle pressure, she'd finally made an upfront demand. Said he had to stop complaining about his weight and go get some damn exercise on the boat. And not just walking around the promenade deck but at the ship's gym. It was always a little uncomfortable when she was right. He'd reluctantly agreed, negotiating his sentence down to trying a single workout to start. That's how lawyers were. Everything was a negotiation.

He'd passed Alice, Laura and Danny Westerman in the dedicated hallway that led to the gym, all in robes, apparently bound for the spa. Charlie's wife looked as scrawny as ever, bundled up in a ship's robe half open, exposing a one-piece suit that did nothing to enhance her form. Laura had her robe closed tight, secured with a large tight knot at the waist, the collar pulled up hard across her neck. She studied the floor as they passed and muttered only a low grunt to his 'hello'. She didn't look to be having a good time. She had all the earmarks of one forced to go to the spa, just as he was forced to go to the gym. Danny looked hung over. If anyone needed a spa treatment, it was Danny.

The gym was bright, making the Judge blink after the dark corridor. Raucous sound poured out of speakers scattered around the rooming, attacking his ears. Wasn't anything on this boat ever quiet? The room had the same odor all gyms have, stronger here because they were surrounded by water and moist air. A combination of old socks, sweat, damp shorts and mold. It left a foul taste on the Judge's tongue, reminding him how he hated exercise.

A line of cycle bikes stretched across the opposite window wall overlooking the stern of the ship like a line of pterodactyls hunkered down but ready for flight. Three of them were occupied, two by buff guys in their early thirties, and one by a large lady whose flesh lapped over her seat like jello spilling from a bowl.

An attendant behind the desk inside the door stepped around to meet the Judge. He was Chinese, late twenties, dressed in white jeans and shirt, and of course buff. Everybody young seemed to look buff these days. The attendant flicked a broad smile across his round face. Dark inquisitive eyes examined the Judge as though measuring for a suit, sizing up the Judge's bulk, paunch, and the tell-tale signs that he didn't really want to be there. The attendant bowed slightly, asked for the Judge's identity card, took it, and swiped it across the mini terminal on top of the desk, officially registering the Judge's presence and clocking in a charge.

"I'm Jack," the young man said smoothly, "and I'm required to show you around a little and explain our wonderful facility here."

The Judge grunted.

"This is our co-ed gym and workout area, and we have some of the newest and most interesting machines available here."

The Judge looked around. In addition to the five spin bikes, three people, two men in shorts and one woman in workout pants, were sweating away on various complicated contraptions designed to administer pain. The Judge felt his stomach knot just watching. This equipment looked right out of the Spanish Inquisition.

To the left, in the corner, another two victims, guys, were standing around two sets of free weights. They were being instructed on use by a hot Danish blonde the Judge would have liked to take home if he wasn't married. She was dressed in tight, tight athleisure ware, canary yellow, which left little need for imagination. The men, mid-forties, were pretending to have an intense interest in lifting weights, asking for multiple demonstrations which she gave with good humor. Funny, there were no women guests in that corner.

Jack led the Judge through double doors off to the right into the changing room, checkered black and white tile floor, with beautiful hand-rubbed teak cabinets for clothes storage. To its left was the bathroom, fitted with extra wide private stalls and four brass hand basins set into the quartz counter. At its end, there was a steam room on the left and a brass door with a steamed-up window on his right. Jack led him through the brass door into a room fitted with two good size pools, one a bubbling jacuzzi with steam sizzling off its surface, the other marked as a cold plunge whose water surface looked ready to freeze. The Judge shuddered looking at the frosty pool. Jack led the way between the pools to another door on the opposite wall, a door with a brass handle but no window, chattering away like a monkey about the benefits of hot and cold spa therapy.

The new door was marked in heavy letters: *CO-ED POOL - CLOTHES REQUIRED.*

"We privately call this our playroom. That's because guests can rent it out for private time and space during their cruise," explained Jack. Then he gave the Judge the barest of winks.

The Judge stepped into a smallish room, paneled in polished mahogany, with wide moldings. The soothing strains of *Somewhere in Time* flowed over a pair of GoldenEar Technology Triton Five speakers. Two small pools, one with warm air coming off in fumes, the other again looking very cold, occupied two thirds of the room. The balance contained a double chaise lounge in a flat position with a plush looking mattress and fresh pillows on it, and an ice cream table with two high back chairs. The floor was a soft pink Mexican tile, and plastic pillows were attached to the edges of each pool. Behind, against the wall, was a built-in counter with bar, sink, and glass cabinets containing china. The bar looked well stocked.

There were three doors in the room, the brass one the Judge had come through, a brass door on the opposite wall marked *Women's Dressing Room*, and on the right wall a third door, marked *Outside Corridor.* The Judge turned back to read the sign on the inside of the door he'd just come through, *Gentlemen's Dressing Room*, and noted the brass bolt on the room side of the door, permitting it to be locked from inside. The other doors had similar brass.

The Judge bent down and stuck a finger in the water of the warm pool. It was lukewarm bathtub water one could stay in for hours, much more his speed. And there was nobody around the pool to jabber at you. Perfect.

"You can rent this room for a half hour, or an hour, or of course for as long as you want, for use as your private spa," explained Jack. "The bar is fully stocked, room service is just a button away for food, and we send in a private masseuse with her portable table or a training coach immediately at your request." The Judge noted a smaller fourth door to his left, thick glass, clouded with vapor, and to its right, on the wall, temperature controls for the sauna contained behind the door.

"So, my family can come down here and spa privately together?"

"Exactly, Judge. Our Muslim guests find it particularly suitable."

"Why the bolted doors?"

"Oh, well, sometime guests like to meet up quietly with other guests, privately you know, without a record. You rent the room, you let your private guest in through the door opening onto the corridor. Total confidentiality. Your private guest enters and exits by the corridor without signing in."

"You mean like a No Tell-Hotel?" asked the Judge.

"Who knows, Judge. We keep no record of whom you invite." Jack winked again. "But the room gets a lot of use. You'd have to book in advance."

"I'll bet," muttered the Judge.

Just then the door behind them to the men's gym opened, and George Walker came in. Charlie's CEO was dressed in a ship's white terrycloth robe. He wore a large smile and nothing else besides the robe, gauging from the pink and furry legs exposed as the robe flapped open here and there as he walked. Walker was wobbling a little, perhaps from one too many margaritas, an almost empty one in his hand. He looked very intoxicated, judging by his gait and the splashes of pink color across his cheeks and nose.

Behind him a steward (it was the scrawny kid from the pool games, Ajay) carried a tray loaded with a bottle of Ketel One, four small bottles of ginger ale, a bucket of ice, and two glasses. The kid deposited the tray on the little table and backed his way out.

"Ah yes, Mr. Walker," Jack said. "We were just checking out the private spa room to be sure all was in order for you, sir. Enjoy."

Walker nodded at the Judge. It was then the door to the corridor opened and Ross Hamilton,

Charlie's partner, stuck his head in. His eyes met Walker's, then the Judge's, then he silently withdrew his head, and the door seamlessly closed without a sound.

Jack shooed the Judge ahead of him through the door back into the gym, hung a "Private, Do Not Disturb" sign on the gym side of the door, and firmly closed it, securing for Walker his well paid-for privacy. The Judge heard the bolt thud in place on Walker's side of the door.

"He's going to use the room by himself?" asked the Judge.

"What do you think?" Jack smirked.

They retraced their steps back to the gym with its cluttered, giant insect-like equipment, and across to the other side, where a small waiting room had been laid out with comfortable overstuffed leather chairs around a sculpture of large teetering pebbles with water running down them to a pool on the floor. They filled the area with a drip… drip… drip….

A pretty attendant in a white uniform was behind a desk at one end, Spanish guessed the Judge, mid-twenties, with sparking dark eyes and hair the color of night.

"This is where you sign up for your massage, Judge. You'll certainly want to do that. We have wonderful talented people, men and women, who know how to take all the kinks out."

The Judge saw behind her a narrow hall with doors to each side, no doubt soundproof torture chambers where this gal's minions could do their worst.

The Judge tried to hide his physical recoil, coughing lightly into his hand as a cover, stepping back, anxious.

The Judge thanked his guide and said he was just going to hop on a stationary bike and peddle a bit. Didn't need a locker, or anything. Jack looked disappointed, almost hurt, then turned back toward his desk with a sigh.

The Judge marched over to a stationary bike with resignation and hauled himself aboard. A panel of winking and blinking lights embellished the panel between the handlebars, and after some experimentation, he got the thing set to some sort of pattern that read *Irregular.* It was easy pedaling, seemingly like he was going downhill, but then suddenly it wasn't. He grunted under the load on the pedals, finding it difficult to make them move, wondering what he had done wrong. It was his heart that was now irregular. No doubt that's how the machine got its name. This was no fun at all.

Where was the damn setting for continuous downhill? He fiddled more with the controls, coming up with a combination that read on the screen, downhill run. This was much better. He could do this. Katy would be proud of him. He whizzed away on this his downhill ride for fifteen minutes, then his butt began to get sore. He stopped his pedals and swung one leg over the machine, easing off, then stood up, surprised at how stiff he was feeling.

The Judge decide he needed something less complicated, and moved over to a walking machine, stepping on and randomly pushing several of its flashing buttons. Nothing happened. He pushed the buttons some more. Still nothing happened. There was a small magnetic disk hanging in the middle of the operating panel, attached by a string so it could not be lost. Above was a similar circular magnet built into the panel. He reached over and stuck the disk on to the circular plate to see what would happen. Suddenly he was going backwards crazy fast, it seemed like sixty miles an hour. He leaped off the rubber tread to the side just as his feet were about to be swept off the back of the treadmill. He came crashing off, stumbling, and spinning, wondering how his hip was going to survive its collision with the tile floor. At the last second, he threw out an arm and managed to get a death grip on the handlebar of the adjacent machine, spinning himself over and around it to break his fall.

Heads in the gym all turned to watch. They seemed to derive some sadistic satisfaction from his difficulties.

Jack came rushing over, his patron's smile didn't hide the mirth in his eyes. "Perhaps you need a little instruction, Judge," he volunteered.

"Huh," was all the Judge could manage, leaning over now, hands on his knees, trying to quell his suddenly panicked heart and stop hyperventilating. He made his way with as much dignity as he could muster over to one of the cushy lounge chairs in the massage waiting area and settled into its plush cushions, operating its controls to tip himself back into a semi-recline. A glass of iced tea was thrust into his hand, unasked, by the pretty young thing manning the desk. Maybe this wasn't so bad here after all. The Judge had his drink and then drifted off into what he considered was a well-earned nap given the gut-wrenching exercise he'd been through.

He was startled awake by a loud scream which erupted from the entrance door to the gym. A young woman stood there, screaming and screaming, and screaming, almost with rhythm. It was a testimony to her lung power and stamina that she was able to project over the blasting music.

CHAPTER 32
DAY 3
4:30 PM

.

"Get him out…" the girl finally choked out. "He's baking alive. Oh, my God… get him out…"

"Who?" asked Jack, rushing over, the Judge on his heels. "Where?"

"George… Mr. Walker, in the private room," she sobbed between hyper ventilations. She pointed down the hall behind her.

Jack and the Judge dashed down the hall, stopping midway at the brass door set in the middle of the long corridor, marked, *Private Spa Room.* The door stood ajar and Jack pushed it open to reveal the room with the two small pools the Judge had seen earlier. Everything looked in order, no one was in the room. The tray was still on the small table, the bottle of Ketel One half gone. Then the Judge noticed the door to the sauna. The inside layer of glass window set in the door was cracked, badly cracked.

"The sauna!" barked the Judge.

They dashed between the pools. The Judge saw the control on the wall next to the sauna door had been turned to max. The temperature gauge beside the control read *220 F.*

Jack got to the sauna door first. There was no doorknob, just a hole. On the floor sat the door handle and its shaft.

"I'll get the fire ax from the corridor," he screeched, turning and running back between the pools toward the door.

The Judge picked up the knob and shaft and carefully fit it back into the door. Even more carefully he eased the knob clockwise and nursed the latch out of the door frame and then carefully eased the door open.

Hot steam mixed with the scent of cooking meat assailed the Judge's nose and stung his eyes as he threw the door wide. Just inside the door on the floor was the interior doorknob. It had apparently come off when the occupant had tried to open the sauna door. There was a man slumped on the floorboards in one corner. Walker! He wasn't moving.

Jack was back with his fire ax, which he dropped, and the two of them hauled Walker out of the steam room and over to the double chaise lounge. His body was limp, unresponsive. His eyes were swollen shut and he wasn't breathing. His skin was covered with blisters, and patches of black and white... third degree burns.

The Judge put his hand to Walker's neck looking for a pulse. There was none. George Walker, Charlie's Chief Executive Officer, had been cooked alive!

CHAPTER 33
DAY 3
4:35 PM

The Judge picked up the handle from the sauna floor, and the screws and washers, wrapped them in a towel, and tucked the towel under his arm Then he made his way back to the gym, tired now. He sank down into the plush sofa this time, next to what had been the screaming girl, now sullen and silent, her face in a pout.

A yellow full-length bathing suit showed here and there under the folds of the girl's white terrycloth robe. One alabaster leg was hanging down in front of her, and one was tucked under her bottom, perhaps for security. She had a small face, a small flaming red mouth that matched her fingernails and toenails, short blond hair, and a slender build. She looked early twenties. Streaks in her pancake makeup were a silent reminder of earlier tears. She was chewing one side of her lower lip.

"Hi. They call me just Judge. What's your name?"

"Glenda."

"Glenda, were you supposed to meet Walker in the private spa room?"

"Yeah."

"Did you know George Walker well?"

"No. Not well. This was our third date."

"Where'd you meet?

"Here. On the ship. In the Sky Bar."

"Was it an intimate relationship?

"I don't know what that means."

"Did you have sex?"

"Yes."

"Did he pay you?"

"Of course. Why else would I go out with an old geezer like that?"

"What time were you to meet?"

"We made an understanding when we first met. Same time each day we're aboard together. George reserved twenty minutes for himself; hen I come later. But I was maybe twenty minutes late. I overslept."

"So, Walker may have been toasting for forty minutes in there at full heat."

"How the hell do I know? It was supposed to be just like before. I just show up, we spend some time together, he gives me a generous expense allowance, PPM, and I leave."

"PPM?"

"Pay per meeting. Are you going to pay me?"

"Me? Why would I pay you, Glenda?"

"You seem to be the one in charge. George booked me. Look, it's almost five o'clock. I've lost my time; someone should pay."

"Yes, I understand. Life can be cruel."

"That's not fair." A tear made its way out of one eye and ran down Glenda's cheek.

"Can you tell me what you saw when you walked into the room?"

"I came in through the corridor door just like before. George left it open, locked it after me. But when I came in today no one was there. The room was empty. But I smelled something funny, I don't know, just funny. I looked around again, saw the cracks in the sauna door's glass. Went over and peeked in."

She began to sniffle again.

"You saw Walker on the floor?"

"Yes. Like a hunk of burnt meat."

"Did you try to open the sauna door?'

"Yeah. The handle came right off in my hand."

"Then what?"

"What the fuck… What'ya think? I panicked. Started to scream. I ran from the room. All the way down the hall, to here."

"Did you see anyone outside in the corridor when you arrived?"

"No."

"When you left?"

"Fuck no."

"This is the third time you were to meet George Walker?"

"Yes. He reserves the private spa room daily, like clockwork. He is… was… kind of meticulous that way."

"So, his use of the private spa room is on the schedule."

"Yes. For today. For every day of the cruise."

"Did you tell anyone about your PPM, your date with George?"

"Just my roommate."

"Did she tell anyone?"

"I don't know."

"Where'd you tell her?"

"In the cafeteria, over breakfast."

"So, someone could have overheard you?"

"I guess so. I don't know. What the fuck. Who's going to pay me now?"

Glenda's small face puckered up into a pout again and she looked at her nails. Then she suddenly looked up at the Judge.

"You attached, Judge? Up for a little recreation?"

"Happily married."

"Damn. Yeah. Most of the more prosperous men on this cruise are. Makes it tough. I'm real tired of my windowless little box room up by the bow. And my roommate's endless jabbering. There's no one to have fun with here. Should have flown to Hawaii and just settled in an off-the-beach motel in Waikiki."

"Did Walker order food or drinks when you visited him the last two times in the private spa?"

"Of course. Munchies and a lot of booze. He drinks Ketel One and Ginger."

"It was all set up there when you arrived?"

"Yes."

"Did you see anybody in the corridor before you went into the private spa room?"

"No. Well, a mom and her daughter. Coming from the gym."

"Was the mom skinny, short, red hair, pale blue eyes?"

"Yeah."

"Daughter taller, a blonde, late twenties, wide of beam?"

"Yeah."

"Did Walker ever say he was concerned or worried about someone? Or maybe had been threatened?"

Glenda sat back in her seat, thinking. "He showed me a letter from his office last time. A kind of threat letter, he said. I didn't understand it."

"What did it look like?"

"Brown paper, like torn from a shopping bag. Cut out letters from a magazine or something pasted on it. Like in the movies. Didn't make much sense."

"What did it say?"

"I just got a glimpse. About his company or something. George said it was a stupid prank. Gets threatening letters all the time. Said he collects them. Seemed quite proud of it."

"Was there a threat in the letter, Glenda? Of bodily harm, or adverse consequences, or something.?"

"Shit I don't know. I only caught a peek."

"Thanks, Glenda. You've been a big help. Hope you find what you're looking for in Hawaii."

The Judge walked down the corridor to the elevator, and took it down to his deck, the towel with the door parts tucked under his arm, lost in thought. When he got to his room, he put his wrapped bundle into the drawer beside the bed and poured himself a stiff drink, a Redbreast Cask 12 that he'd purchased from the ship's duty-free shop. He wasn't a big fan of Irish whiskeys, but with Cask 12 one could make do. He hoped it would help displace the image of the over-done lump that used to be George Walker lying on the sauna floor.

CHAPTER 34
DAY 3
5:00 PM

The Judge left his cabin and made for the promenade deck where he could walk and think, mostly without interruption. He wondered where his bride had gotten off to; probably shopping. It was a blood sport with Katy, as with most woman, something in-bred that most males couldn't understand. Built into their genes for thousands of years as the gatherers had gradually taken over the earth and control of the nest from their swashbuckling males. What you could find worth buying on a cruise ship was beyond the Judge's ken, but he was sure Katy would find something.

He stepped out onto the promenade deck expecting sunlight but was disappointed. The sun was gone and everything skyward was dark grey and angry. He noticed the ship was beginning to buck a little and, walking toward the bow, he saw larger swells churning up ahead of the ship. The bow suddenly came up higher in the air as it crested the first mighty wave, then crashed down into the following trough with a vengeance, as though diving for the bottom. The second wave was similar to the first. When the ship recovered and began the climb up another, steeper wave, there was a kind of corkscrew motion that toyed with the stomach. There wasn't a soul on the promenade deck, and looking below at the pool deck, it was empty too, its pools beginning to slosh water out over the deck.

A howling wind had come up, sweeping along the decks, carrying salty spray into the Judge's face as he stared forward. Salt began to etch the lines of his forehead and his cheeks were pinkening from the slap of the wind.

The Captain had lied. It was getting really rough. This was far more enjoyable than the flat seas of the past two days. The Judge went back to his cabin to retrieve the ski jacket he'd insisted on packing over Katy's objections, and then took an hour to walk the deck, his storm sea legs coming back, his knees bent and flexible, his legs bowed. The Judge enjoyed the slippery deck, the wind whipping around him, striving to breach his jacket, and the blasts of salty spray. The sea was magnificent, all green and foam and churning, like an angry animal determined to do its worst to the floating tub caught in its midst.

The Judge finally returned to his stateroom to find Katy there, sick as a dog and vowing between trips to the toilet that she'd never go to sea again. The Judge tried to be sympathetic but admitted during one of the periods when Katy was coherent that he'd never been seasick in his life. Well, maybe once when he was twelve, but that was because it was a windless and flat day, hot and sticky, and his uncle with the sailing schooner had insisted on bringing out sardines and mayonnaise for his nephew and other guests.

This light anecdote didn't seem to brighten Katy's mood, who at the mention of sardines and mayonnaise threw her hand over her mouth and dived again for the bathroom.

The Judge decided he was doing no good staying with Katy as she didn't seem to appreciate his light banter. So, he left the cabin to make one more turn of the promenade deck before dinner, enjoying the angry sea boiling along the waterline as the light faded to dark black.

Shit, maybe this cruising wasn't so bad after all. The Judge felt more alive than he had in days.

CHAPTER 35
DAY 3
7:00 PM

The Judge entered the dining room and took his assigned seat, noting there were almost no guests there. His table was empty. As his soup course arrived Charlie stumbled in, displaying his utter lack of sea legs, bumping against chairs and tables as he lurched his way across the dining room to join the Judge like a drunken sailor. He eyed the Judge with subtle distain but seemed resigned to share the table with the only company available, waving Sean over to the table to order a Jack and Coke. The Judge ordered a Scotch on the rocks.

"How goes our investigation, Judge?" asked Charlie, immediately to business. Apparently, the only way he knew how to relate to people.

"I've talked to several people, but I don't have any concrete answers, Charlie."

"Well, why not. It's been forty-eight hours since you started nosing around. You must have turned up something."

"I have some suspicions; we'll see how they pan out. You didn't tell me about the threatening notes your executive officers received."

"Because they're not relevant, Judge. A bunch of malcontent noise makers. Been around me for years. That's what you get when you succeed, a bunch of assholes who try to pull you down out of jealousy. Impotent scumbags angling to be taken seriously when they're in fact no threat at all. Just big talk. Obnoxious bastards."

"How are things between you and your wife, Charlie?"

"That's not relevant to any of this."

"It could be. You gave me carte blanche to explore all aspects that might shed light on what has happened."

"How long you been married, Judge?"

"Eight years."

"Wait until you hit thirty years. These women never forget anything. They store it all up, then bleat it back at you, trying to make you pay over and over for each imaginary slight. Yes, things are a little rocky with Alice right now."

"I have to say, you're an interesting character, Charlie. How is it that you have yourself surrounded with pissed off people?"

Charlie took another large slug of his rum and Coke, relaxing back in his chair. "I'm one of the most straight-arrow guys you'll ever meet, Judge. I'm just misunderstood."

"Is that what Alice would say? What about your executive assistant? And I've heard is a long string of flings before Maddy."

"That's an interest questioning, Judge. It's perhaps easy for other people to judge me, not walking in my shoes. The fact is that Alice decided she didn't want to have sex any more with me about twenty years ago. I'm a man. I have needs just like other men. What was I supposed to do? I've stayed in the relationship, I've taken care of her and the kids financially, and in many ways emotionally. I could have dumped her back then, but I didn't. So, I play around a little… or maybe a lot. You can't call it cheating, or being unfaithful to your spouse, if your spouse denies you bedroom privileges, now can you.?"

"But why did she stop privileges in the first place?"

"I don't know. You'd have to ask her, Judge. But I wasn't mean to her. I didn't beat her or anything. She's always been secure financially, protected. She's always gotten plenty of money from me to run the household, with total discretion over how to spend it. I've given her the kids she wanted. You know, there's a lot more to a marriage than just sex. We were getting along back then, and we are getting along now… good companions, or were until Jay died."

"Tell me about Jay, Charlie."

Charlie's eyes blinked like he been hit. His eyes refocused over the Judge's shoulder, off to some distance space only he could see. Finally, he said, "That's certainly not relevant, Judge. Nothing to do with the accidents on this boat."

"Tell me anyway, Charlie. I want to understand."

"Not much to tell, Judge. Jay was Alice's favorite. He was twenty. About six months ago he woke me up in the middle of the night, like two a.m. Got me out of bed, dragged me downstairs, out to the driveway, threw gas over himself in front of me, set himself afire."

Charlie unbuttoned his cuffs, rolled up each sleeve, and put his arms out, pointing to the outside of each arm. Angry red flesh welted up in scar tissue there. "Second degree burns, trying to bat down the flames with my robe." Charlie sighed.
"Jay lingered in the burn center at UCLA for a week, Judge. Then he died. Alice blames me. She can't ever forget or forgive."

"Jay's suicide sounds like it was a very special message directed at you."

"Yes. It was awful. Jay was very sensitive, feelings easily hurt, very little self-esteem. I was supposed to be his role model, and God I tried. I tried to teach the ways of the real world, my love for business, how to assemble a business and make deals. I tried to show by example. Then, I'd take him into my confidence and explain my thought process. What I was trying to accomplish in a deal, and why.

But Jay wasn't interested. He just shined me on. Jay was… well, just Jay. He was never going to be me and we both knew it. I think the suicide was the only thing he ever carried through to the end… accomplished.

And that's very sad, I know. But was it my fault? Perhaps in part, and part Alice's, and part other people, and just life. But I believe some people are more prone to suicide than others. Jay was one of those. For him it was a viable solution to the internal pain he was experiencing. I could never get through to that pain, understand it, feel it, appreciate it. I just couldn't. We sent him off to therapy over various periods, but it didn't seem to help. Jay did what he had to do, but I didn't drive him there, didn't push him over that edge. I think we all have the inalienable right to just check out if we want. But it can be tough on the people we leave behind. It was particularly tough on Alice.

And me? I don't cry about it. But there's a gnawing hole in my life, in my spirit, with the loss of Jay. I celebrate what he was and try to forget what he wasn't. I'll always miss him. But it's something I keep private. I don't share my grief with anyone, except just now you, Judge."

"And what about Danny, Charlie? I understand he's been stealing from your company."

Charlie smiled. "Yes. Caught red-handed I understand. And tried to bull-shit his way out of it. It was stupid on his part. All I can say is, Danny's very young. He has some more growing to do to reach maturity. He'll get there. He's kind of a combination of me and Alice. I see that. Smart and tricky like me, but impulsive to jump into things without careful thought on the consequences, like his mom.

I've been hammering on Danny. Telling him, planning, planning, planning. Set your goal, chart the course, plan each of the steps very carefully, recheck your planning, and execute carefully. One step at a time. He's learning."

"But does he like you Charlie?... love you?"

"Love?... He respects me, he fears me, he perhaps underestimates me. And deep down, yes, I think he likes me. But he's very into striving for independence from me right now. That usually happens in your teens, breaking away from your dad, becoming you own person. He's a little late to be struggling with those issues, but that's where he is. Issues we all have to resolve about our dads as we grow into men.

What's the old saw attributed to Mark Twain? *'When I was fourteen my father was so ignorant, I could hardly stand to have the old man around. But when I got to be twenty-one, I was astonished at how much he had learned in seven years.'*

Danny's still somewhere along that continuum."

"And Laura?"

"Laura thinks I'm pretty cool, Judge. She's the one that's most like me. A little stunted on the sexual side, but she'll grow out of that. A world traveler. Has set her goal to have her own restaurant someday. She's very diligent in following her plan to accomplish just that. My teaching by example hasn't been lost on her. I'm very proud of her."

"And what about your executive officers who are now gone, Charlie? Were they your friends, or what?"

"Well Larry Cain was a friend. I loved that old man. He might not have been the best numbers guy. But he gave sage advice, always. I could always count on him for a fresh perspective. And a no bull-shit guy.

Always told it exactly the way it was. I'm going to miss him a lot."

"And George Walker?"

"George was a mixed bag. The investment bankers made me bring him on board as CEO. Wanted someone who would show better than me with my poor roots. He was fourth generation aristocrat, or something. And he served his purpose. He could schmooze and charm our investment bankers, and the lending banks and the press. Even the SEC at times.

But every time he opened his mouth, he expected people to drop everything and listen, just because of who he was, his background and breeding. And he opened his mouth a lot. Most of the time without thought. I never knew what he was going to say next, and unfortunately, neither did he."

"Did you two get along?"

"Oh yes. He was very loyal. He understood intuitively that he wasn't particularly good at business, but he was smart enough to take directions, so we got along fine."

"What about Kennedy?"

"Oh my god. What a disaster. A real spender. Trying to keep him on a budget was like trying to herd cats. I was continually yanking his chain, pulling him back from expensive plans he was eager to implement. He had no conception of profit and loss, gross margins, earnings per share, or anything like that. The world was his oyster, and unfortunately my company was a part of that oyster, available to pillage and burn to the ground if necessary to support the next new fad or idea he decided to pursue."

"Why'd you hire him? Why'd you keep him?"

"The answer to that is one word: Alice. She begged me re-hire him when he was down on his luck, begged me to keep him on many a time when I was ready to fire his ass."

"And you bowed to her wishes?"

"Sure. I knew she was sleeping some with Kennedy. Her toy-boy. As long as the two were discreet I didn't give a damn. It allowed me to have my pleasures too. Like Maddy." Charlie's eyes changed, sparking now with lust and pride.

"So, the affair wasn't a reason you might have wanted Kennedy gone… like dead?"

"Oh, no. He allowed me to feel guilt-free. I was happy to have him around, even though he wasn't much of an operating officer."

"Otherwise, you would have felt guilty, Charlie? Really?"

Charlie's eyes met the Judge's, dark pools now, impossible to read, but Charlie remained silent.

"And what about the last of your entourage, Ross Hamilton?" the Judge asked.

"Hah. There's an interesting character. When I was first starting out to take over the company I was a little short of capital and I talked Ross into joining me. He put up capital and acquired five percent of the company, which he still owns. Since then he's referred to himself as my business partner and wrapped himself in my accomplishments and success. The last few years he's become something of a pain in the ass. Pontificating on what the company should do next and trying to give me advice on this and that."

"Is he a friend?"

"Is a shark a friend, Judge? Perhaps occasionally when he's not hungry. Trouble with Ross is he's always hungry. He'll try to cross me one of these days I suppose. When he does, I'll squash him like the bug he is."

Charlie's eyes met the Judge's again, black and burning now, hooded. They sent a chill down the Judge's spine.

CHAPTER 36
DAY 3
9:00 PM

As the Judge pushed his stateroom door open and pocketed his boat security card, something slid with the door across the carpet. Entering the room, the Judge turned and stooped to pick up a plain white envelope that had been slid under the door. He tore the envelope open, expecting a bill, but it was a single piece of brown paper, much like grocers bag. The note had been carefully constructed using cut out letters from magazines which were pasted on the paper. Somebody must have a lot of free time, mused the Judge.

The Judge brought it over to the light from the balcony and read it twice.

"You've aligned yourself with the dark side. Now you must suffer the consequences."

He looked over to his bride, heavily asleep now. Oblivious to the continuing rocking of the ship. And just as well. Slight purring was emanating from under the sheet she had pull up mostly over her head, leaving only a small mop of taffy brown hair exposed out on the pillow. She seemed to be getting enough air under there to survive.

Had he inadvertently put Katy in danger again by poking into these so-called accidents? He wondered. Perhaps he should stick to law and let other people handle mysterious deaths. But Hell, this was so much fun.

The Judge folded the note and put it into the drawer beside his bed, gave a big yawn, and climbed in beside Katy, suddenly weary.

CHAPTER 37
DAY 4
8:00 AM

Charlie rolled over in bed and sat himself up on its edge. They said you might avoid a stroke if you didn't stand up right away. You weren't supposed to bound out of bed into a standing position immediately, as he used to do. Let your body adjust halfway first, sitting on the bed edge. He didn't know whether that was right, but his head hurt so much from all the Jack and Coke the night before that he wasn't able to stand up immediately anyway.

He looked across at the Prune. Alice was rolled up in her blankets for warmth. And maybe protection. From him…?

He wondered why they still slept together after all these years. There was no sex of course. Often animosity at various intersections of their relationship, particularly after the loss of Jay. But it still felt secure. A known quantity: one warm female body lingering there at the edge of his bed, at the edge of his consciousness as he slept. Softly breathing, still worrying about him here and there, still mothering him a little, angry as hell about Jay, even bitter, but committed to him just the same. Some basic instinct born when the race was young, attaching yourself to a mate and holding steady, holding on. Was he a prisoner of the same instincts?

He staggered up from the bed and carried his bulk into the bathroom, totally too small for him even in the luxury suite. 'Not enough room to swing a cat', his mother would have said. He fumbled through his shave kit for the aspirin and gulped three. Then dived for the antacid tablet bottle before his stomach cramped with the acid. Damn. Why was everything so hard in his world?

Despite its luxurious trappings, the suite smelled a tad moldy. What could you expect in the middle of the ocean? At least the ship had stopped rocking around. They were steaming forward through calm seas.

He went into the room and threw the drapes open wide to the morning sun, scorching every corner of the room in bright yellow, hearing with satisfaction the small squeak from the Prune as she lunged away from the windows and buried her head under the covers. The sky was all bright blue except for the sun and a soft mist radiated up from the distant robin's blue horizon. Beautiful.

He stepped out on to the veranda and looked over the rail at the sea immediately below, then running his eyes out to the horizon.

"*Oh, no… Oh Shit…!*"

CHAPTER 38
DAY 4
8:10 AM

When Katy woke the Judge was still sleeping. She untangled herself from his arm and rolled on to her back, reaching up to do a cat stretch with her arms and shoulders. Then she lifted her pelvis, making an arch. Her stomach felt empty, the sour taste of her troubles the day before lingering in her mouth.

She'd have to do double duty at the gym today to get the kinks out. She loved exercise. She got the endorphin high the Judge said he's never experienced. The Judge's idea of exercise was rocking in a rocking chair, or perhaps on the bridge of a rolling vessel at sea. She shuddered at that thought. He had no conception of how wonderful exercise could be. She felt sorry for him. He was missing something truly magical.

Thinking of rocking boats, she listened to the ship for a moment, felt it sway ever so slightly as it made its way through the sea like the precision machine it was. The giant village that was the ship, cast atop a wobbly hull, hung together, and controlled by giant stabilizers deep in its hull, was humming along perfectly, slicing through the water. They must have finally outrun the effects of the storm late the night before. Thank God for that.

She thought about coffee, could smell it in her mind, and perhaps an English muffin with a bit of that Knox raspberry jam. She'd order room service for them both: eggs, pancakes, waffles (the Judge loved his waffles), fruit, bacon, some yogurt for her (the Judge wouldn't get near that stuff), tea and coffee. Oh, and sticky buns. The Judge wasn't supposed to have sticky buns, or waffles for that matter, at least not the way he liked to load them up with butter and syrup. She kept a close eye on her Judge or tried to. But hell, they were on vacation. Let's cheat a little. The Judge would be happy.

When it arrived she would spread it all on the little table out on their balcony and they would watch the morning sun slowly distancing itself above the horizon, feel the breeze wafting along the side of the ship. The blue of the sea would reflect in the Judge's eyes and he would be calm, relaxed. He loved the sea. It would be like the impromptu picnics she used to enjoy as a child. What fun!

She threw open the curtains and stepped out on to their balcony, leaning over the rail to take a great breath of the sea air.... And then she started to screech... a high keening cry really, torn from her gut, expressing lasting sadness and calamity as only as a female can.

The Judge was awake and at her side in a heartbeat, adrenalin racing, ready to fend off whatever the threat. She turned and buried her face into his hairy chest, tears cascading in drops, speckling the veranda floor, her narrow shoulders shaking in grief. The keening rose higher in pitch, an outpouring of sorrow, and frustration, and anger at the stupidity of men.

CHAPTER 39
DAY 4
8:12 AM

The Judge gazed out over Katy's shoulder at the blue Pacific. Except, the sea wasn't an unbroken blue. It was crisscrossed and cut up by wide swaths of multi-colored surfaces, gleaming dully in the sun.... Plastic debris!

An ugly skin of floating plastic, snaking off in several directions into the distance, like some giant spider's web of death laid atop the water's surface in undulating strips. Lots of whites and clears, but also reds, greens, browns, and blues.

It looked like a solid path across the water you could walk on. But of course, it wasn't. As the ship cut through the mess here and there, objects were recognizable: disposable soda bottles, bottle caps, fishing line, plastic rope, pieces of floatation foam, and bits of color from all manner of wrappers and meal containers. There was the sad body of a seagull, belly up, its matted feathers plastered against its small frame.

There was a smell too. The pungent smell of the algae coating most of the material, reminding the Judge of the rotting smell of the red tide along the California coast. No wonder the sea creatures thought it was food.

It was the ugly, permanent legacy of seven billion stupid people, so stupid they could foul their own nest without a thought to their future. Or that of subsequent generations and other lifeforms.

The Judge sighed in disgust and held his bride tighter, biting his lip, wondering if this was man's destiny in the end. Like lice, over-populating, crowding, taking the good and trashing the unwanted without a thought, destroying species after species along the way. Infecting the earth to the point where the planet could no longer recover, no longer support its human infection.

CHAPTER 40
DAY 4
8:15 AM

The Judge and Katy pulled their little table inside their room (it barely fit) and awaited their room-service breakfast there, away from the smell and the view. Katy insisted on closing the drapes. But neither of them had much appetite.

Katy had stopped crying, but she hadn't regained her composure. She was frothing with anger now, directed at plastic manufacturers in general, and one Charles Westerman in particular.

"Look here, Judge," Katy said, gesturing at her smartphone. "One point six million square kilometers, or about twice the size of Texas. Gyres grinding plastic into smaller and smaller pellets, fish-food-sized, coating the plastic with algae. Of course the fish are going to eat it.

"It's elsewhere too, isn't it, Katy?"

"Yes. There are five major gyres: The North Pacific, South Pacific, North Atlantic, South Atlantic, and Indian Ocean. Due to currents, plastics from Asia make their way to this North Pacific gyre, creating the largest of the world's garbage patches. Our North Pacific Ocean is the most polluted of all the oceans of the world.

Sitting out there is an estimated two trillion pieces of plastic, representing a third of the total plastic found in the earth's oceans."

"Can't we just scoop it up? Send out cleaning crews?"

"No, Judge. Over time much of the plastic is broken down into tiny pieces, microplastics, by the wind, the waves, and the sun. These pieces can be anywhere from the size of a fingernail to the size of a grain of rice, or even smaller. Because they are made of plastic they will never decompose. Never, Judge.... Just never. They just go on becoming smaller and smaller, and more and more deadly.

Eventually much of the plastic is covered in marine biofilm, bacteria, and other microorganisms, and it sinks to the ocean floor as a sort of 'marine snow', tiny bits of plastic material carpeting the bottom. Once there, the bits get eaten by deep-sea life."

"What happens when the fish eat it, Katy?"

"The plastic will chemically contaminate the fish, or block its organs, or even just leave it feeling satisfied and full, so it stops eating and starves.

A first fish eats the plastic, then a larger fish eats the first fish, then a bird or a seal eats the second fish. The plastic poison moves down the ecological food chain like Drano. Poisoning everything. And we're digesting it too Judge, you and I. We risk it every time we eat the fish."

"Jesus. Where's all this plastic come from?"

"The top five polluters are China, Indonesia, the Philippines, Vietnam and Thailand. They dump more plastic into oceans than the rest of the world combined.

And the world's most powerful soda brand is also the biggest source of plastic pollution. The giant sugary drink company, valued at more the fifty billion dollars, emerges as by far the most common brand in audits of plastic debris found on beaches and in waterways, parks, and streets around the world. The other soda companies are equally at fault, like your friend Charlie's company. Pure greed that costs everyone, including future generations."

CHAPTER 41
DAY 4
9:30 AM

The Judge eased himself into the tight shower stall in the tight bathroom in the little stateroom they were cooped in. Katy had stormed out for a walk about, looking for a way to defuse some of her anger.

He was still sore from jumping off the gym's running machine. The water was hot in the tiny shower and unlimited in use. It felt good thrashing against his skin in the confined space and seemed to help the soreness. He heard the corridor door open into the stateroom and concluded that Katy was back from her walk. It had been a short one.

The bathroom door opened briefly and then closed, the Judge shouting over his shoulder from the stall, "Don't let my steam out, honey!"

He was halfway soaped up when he felt a buzzing in his ears. His eyes began to weep, his stomach felt rocky, and he was suddenly dizzy. He couldn't breathe. It felt like someone was sitting on his chest. Was he having a heart attack?

His stomach started to turn over and his breakfast was coming up fast. *Shit!* The tiny enclosure was starting to spin. He dropped the soap and threw the shower door open, plunging out into the steam filled mini bathroom. He stubbed his toe and tripped over something in the middle of the floor where there should have been nothing, barely regaining his balance.

Wiping tears from his eyes, he peered down at the floor through the misty steam in disbelief. There were six aerosol cans of insect fogger on their sides in the middle of the tiny space, each spraying out the dregs of its gas.

He charged to the bathroom door and tried to pull it open. It wouldn't budge. He fiddled desperately with the handle and the catch, but it was a no go. The lock seemed jammed in place from the other side.

He grabbed two towels, wrapped them around his shoulder, and threw his entire 220 pounds against the door. It bent but didn't give. He hit it again, and again. On the fourth desparate try there was a splintering sound, and on the fifth try the frame of the door gave way, the hinges coming out of the frame as the door bent the wrong way, out into the stateroom. He burst out into clean air.

He stumbled to the sliding doors and threw them open, collapsing into the small chair on the balcony outside, gasping for air. His lungs were burning from the toxic fumes, his eyes still streaming, and he leaned over to lose the bacon and eggs he'd stuffed into his stomach over his breakfast with Katy.

He closed his eyes and held his pounding head for a while, his breath gradually stabilizing, his pulse slowing. That was how Katy found him, wet, nude, collapsed into the balcony chair, trying to breathe.

CHAPTER 42
DAY 4
9:45 AM

The Judge reclined on the balcony chaise as Katy buzzed around him like an angry bee, pressing his eyes with a wet washcloth wrapped around ice, and forcing fluids. Water, not the single malt the Judge requested.

Their neighbor to their right, the old gal with the saggy tits, stuck her head around the privacy panel on the balcony to see what was going on.

"Shouldn't be sunbathing in the nude, young man. You'll get your balls burned," she cooed.

Katy turned beet red, made a dash inside for a ship's robe from the closet, and hurried back to ease the Judge into it.

Sophia, their floor maid showed up, peering with big eyes at the damaged state room door which had been jimmied to get in, the bathroom door and its shattered frame, and the twisted hinge hardware. She wrapped a handkerchief over her nose and mouth as she entered the bathroom, turned the poop fan on, scooped up the fogger cans, and fled for the corridor.

Finally, there was a buzz at their door and Katy let in a carpenter carrying a canvas toolbox and two pieces of trim swung over his back. After a bit of fiddling, hammering, and some muttering, the bathroom door and hardware were removed, new hinges mounted, new bare trim fitted around the frame, and the door re-hung. He then replaced the lock and latch on the stateroom door. "Can't stain the trim till we're in port and the guests have left, but that should serve," he the said as he left.

The Judge, feeling considerably better, got dressed in his never-wet trunks and t-shirt. He entered the repaired bathroom and turned on the shower full. Then he came out, closed the bathroom door tightly behind him, opened the suit's door and walked out into the hall. He closed the stateroom door and put his ear to its hallway side. He could faintly hear his shower spray drumming against the fiberglass floor. Anyone coming along the corridor could have stopped to listen and would have heard him in the shower.

He walked down the hall, looking for a cleaning supplies closet he assumed must be somewhere on+ the floor. Just after the hallway to the elevators and stairs amidships, he found it, curved into the interior wall, unlocked, its door standing open. At its back on the floor shelf he saw four cans of the same insect fogger that'd been used on him. Anyone could have come by and lifted the foggers out of the closet. This was clearly no accident. Not like the more ambiguous deaths of the three company executives. Someone had just tried to kill him.

CHAPTER 43
DAY 4
11:45 AM

After his discovery of the supply closet, the Judge stretched out on the bed for a nap, still trying to clear his head. He awoke with a start, leaving a nightmare of being trapped in a tiny cabinet with a drove of angry bees buzzing around him, intent on revenge for disturbing their hive.

He sat up, looking for his bride. A note on his nightstand read, *off to the pool to work on my tan.* The Judge found himself missing her now, after his close call and his bad dream. Drawing pants over his swimsuit and a plaid shirt over his t-shirt, he set off to find her. He circled the main pool, now crowded again with the return of smooth sailing. There were lots of pretty girls there, some giving him a glance now he was in his slacks and a sport shirt. But as for Katy, no cigar. He found himself fleeing rapidly back to the interior of the ship, away from the raucous music.

He buzzed around the buffet on the pool deck next, thinking perhaps Katy'd stopped for a snack, but no luck. Only the usual conga line of guests jostling with each other for position at the lunch buffet, vying to see who could load the most on their plates.

Back inside he glanced over the rail in the interior, into the big hole in the middle, gaping like the hole in a donut, and spotted what looked like it might be a familiar head eight floors down on the Plaza deck, camped on a barstool. That floor had reception and a small bar at the bottom of the hole. A young woman with light brown hair seemed to be leaning into an earnest conversation with a man at the bar there. She was wearing a frothy see-through turquoise cover-up over a skimpy bikini, barely meeting the dress code. A cover-up like Katy had brought.

He took the elevator down and walked out into the middle of the hole. Yep, it was Katy. She was flirting with a younger man, their bar stools slid together, leaning into each other in an intense conversation, drinking a Bloody Mary.

She turned, sensing the Judge's approach, blushing slightly, and fumbled through an introduction to Jerry, her new friend, then took a gulp of her drink, gasping a little from its heat and the pepper.

"Hi, Jerry," said the Judge, shoving out his paw and resisting the urge to pulverize the younger man's hand in the handshake.

"Jerry Barringer," the man said.

Jerry looked perhaps three years younger than Katy. He had a rounded face which matched the hint of chubby around his tucked in Hawaiian shirt and the thick furry legs below khaki shorts. His bright white teeth encased a contagious smile as he eyed the Judge with large innocent blue eyes. The Judge had met him or seen him before, he just couldn't quite place where.

Jerry was nursing his own Bloody Mary and couldn't keep his eyes off Katy, turning them back to her between sentences offered to the Judge.

"Where you from, Jerry?"

"San Diego. This is actually my first cruise. I just met Katy. Isn't she wonderful? I've been buying her drinks."

"I see that," said the Judge, looking over at Katy, who suddenly found something interesting to focus on across the lobby.

"Are you her uncle or something?" asked Jerry.

"No Jerry. I'm her husband."

Jerry's head snapped up, looking more closely at the Judge now. Then he blurted, "But you're so old."

The Judge smiled, keeping his anger under control, barely.

"She likes older men, Jerry, preferable a lot older, with oodles of money and no sex drive left," said the Judge. "I'm actually eight-five, well preserved for my age, and Katy… Katy…. Well, Katy is just slightly north of fourteen. We'd get in trouble with the law if we weren't married."

Jerry's jaw dropped open wide enough to drive in a truck.

"Now don't pick on my new friend, Judge. He's very nice," said Katy. "He's been filling me in on the Great Pacific Plastic Dump."

"Really?"

"Oh yes," said Jerry. "I'm a marine biologist. Been studying the Great Pacific Dump for some time. I'm just so excited now I've had a chance to actually see it. It's an absolute disaster, Judge. Don't you agree?"

"I don't know much about it, Jerry. Only what Katy's been telling me."

"Consider this, Judge. Think about next time you order that wonderful salmon steak on a rosewood plank from some fish house, fresh frozen and flown in, and you dig into that first bite. You may be ingesting a measurable amount of plastic beads into your stomach. It might make you feel unwell; you might even get sick. The plastic we saw today is entering our food chain at an alarming rate, polluting our fisheries across the world. Approximately three billion people rely on wild-caught and farmed seafood as a primary source of their protein."

Katy was nodding her head sagely, enthralled by Jerry's discourse. The Judge found himself a tad jealous of the attention Jerry was getting.

"But there are no concrete studies validating harm to humans from ingesting or inhaling a little plastic, are there?" asked the Judge.

"No, but tiny pieces of degraded plastic, synthetic fibers and plastic beads have turned up in every corner of the planet's seas, from Florida beach sands to Arctic sea ice. Their size—from about five millimeters, or the size of a grain of rice, down to microscopic—means they can be ingested by a wide range of creatures, from the plankton that form the basis of the marine food chain to humans. One study has estimated that a top

European shellfish consumer eats approximately eleven-thousand plastic particles annually."

"But that doesn't mean they're dangerous for humans, Jerry."

"Well, we suspect ingested microplastic particles may physically damage organs and leak hazardous chemicals, like hormone-disrupting bisphenol A, and phthalates, into our bodies. These substances may be compromising our immune functions, disrupting human growth and reproductive systems, and damaging our livers," sputtered Jerry.

"But there's been no proof of these suspicions."

"No. Research is only just beginning. But we'll get there."

"Where's all this plastic coming from?"

"Since the 1960s, plastic production has increased by approximately 8.7 percent a year, evolving into a 600-billion-dollar global industry. Approximately eight million metric tons of plastics enter the oceans annually, and conservative estimates suggest 5.25 trillion plastic particles currently circulate in ocean surface waters. While some plastics enter oceans from maritime operations, 80 percent is suspected to originate from land-based sources. Discarded plastic materials enter the marine environment as trash, industrial discharge, or litter through inland waterways, wastewater outflows, and by transport on the wind."

"Like single use soda bottles."

"Yes, exactly. Katy was telling me about your dinner companion, the Single Use Bottle King."

"So that's a big problem."

"It is. And not just in the Great Pacific Garbage Patch. Researchers have discovered explosive increases in levels of plastic in the seabed right off the coast of Santa Barbara. Scripps examined specific layers of sediment on the bottom from 1834 to 2010, and found that microplastics the size of lint began showing up in the fifties. And the concentration in the layers just keeps increasing year by year. Explorer Victor Vescovo found microplastics in the Mariana Trench, the deepest spot on earth."

"So, it's all over our oceans?"

"It gets worse… aaah… Judge," said Jerry. "You see, plastic doesn't biodegrade like other materials. Most of the 8.3 billion tons of plastic that has been produced by humanity since we discovered how to make it, is still here, somewhere, in our environment.

Researchers recently collected dust from supposedly pristine U.S. National Parks and wilderness areas and found microscopic plastic particles everywhere there. They measured more than 1,000 tons of tiny fragments raining down each year just on these areas alone. That's equivalent to between 123 million and 300 million plastic bottles' worth.

Plastic particle pollution is traveling on the wind and drifting down from the skies. Researchers believe particles deposited in wet weather originates from nearby. The plactic gets swept into the air by storms in urban centers and then falls again with the rain and snow.

But 75 percent of this plastic, the smaller, lighter particles, appear to be carried extremely long distances on currents high in the atmosphere. This plastic pollution has become a part of the cycle of global dust transport."

The Judge was listening now. This was not sounding good. "So, you're saying it's all over the world, Jerry."

"Yes. Italian researchers bought apples, lettuce, carrots and other fruits and vegetables in local markets around Italy and found traces of these microscopic plastic particles, likely drawn up by the plants from the ground water into their roots. Plastic particles have been documented in the water we drink, the beer we consume, and the salt we use, just to name a few of the many other contaminated food products, in addition to seafood.

Every nook and cranny on the surface of our earth now has microplastics. There minuscule plastic particles are in the air we breathe, in the water we drink, in the vegetables we eat, and in the protein we consume."

"So, it's already in our bodies, Jerry?"

"Oh, yes. We're eating and we're breathing in these microscopic plastic particles all the time."

"But are we as humans at risk from this, Jerry? You, me, Katy, my seven-year-old son?"

"The presence of so many fine particles in the air means we're all breathing it for sure. The health effects of taking in plastic particles into the lungs is not well known, Judge. But studies confirm the size of the particles detected in the air are consistent with the size of plastic particles that accumulate in our lungs.

Aggregate particulate pollution, which includes dust, soot, and other airborne threats, has been linked to heart attacks, strokes and respiratory disease. The World Health Organization estimates that small particulate pollution causes more than 4.2 million premature deaths annually. And studies of workplace exposure to higher levels of inhaled plastic particles has linked them to lung disease and tissue damage."

"What can be done?"

"It's an international problem, Judge. We need international cooperation to eliminate plastics from our goods and services wherever possible, and to develop a strict discipline for the disposal of the plastic where they can't be replaced with bio-degradable goods."

"How do we get there?" asked Katy.

"Organize a world-wide effort to clean up the plastic laying around our environment. Isolate and seal it so it can't escape.

Give up further manufacture of plastic, except where there is no alternative, and the part or product is critical to us. One place to start is to eliminate the sale of all single use plastic soda bottles. Someone like your Single Use Bottle King should be lynched. Him, and his entire executive staff. Or better yet, gassed. He's a pig. He and his ilk are destroying the oceans and the atmosphere and jeopardizing all of us only to feed their own greed."

"Wow, you really feel strongly," said the Judge.

"I do, Judge. Make no mistake, people like this Westerman and his management team are dinosaurs and need to be quickly wiped from the face of the earth."

"Someone seems to be trying, Jerry. Three of the company's key executives are dead. Died on this boat."

"Good. Glad to hear it, Judge. Glad to learn someone is doing something."

"I didn't say they were murdered, Jerry. It may be just a coincidence of accidents. In any case, I think it's time for me to take Katy off your hands. The old guy here needs some private attention over lunch."

With that the Judge slid Katy's arm around his waist, hauled her off her stool, and guided her toward the elevator, deliberately leaving Jerry to produce some sort of tip for the bar. Katy came willingly, giggling a little now, all the vodka hitting her. She turned her head back to Jerry and did a silly little wave with her free hand.

"That was fun, Judge. He was actually flirting with me."

"*Harrumph.*"

"Oh, come on Judge. You never flirt with me like that anymore. It was good for my self-esteem. You should try to flirt some, like when we first met."

"I follow the advice my father passed down from his dad, Katy."

"Which is…?"

"You don't chase the trolley after you're aboard."

"Ouch!" yelped the Judge. Jesus, Katy's elbow was vicious.

CHAPTER 44
DAY 4
12:10 PM

The Judge guided Katy to the dining room and they settled into their table for lunch. Everyone was there: Charlie, Alice, Danny, Laura, Maddy, and of course Ross Hamilton, eyeing the Judge with obvious distaste as they sat down. It was a profoundly uncomfortable grouping, perhaps because of the three empty chairs where Kennedy, Cain and Walker had sat. The Judge supposed it was the dining equivalent of the Missing Man Formation. Charlie, though, was his usual robust self, loud and boisterous as ever, with the appetite of a horse.

Ross, in his power trip seat at the opposite end of the table from Charlie, periodically glared with ill will at the Judge from under his bushy eyebrows but refused to talk to the Judge or to Katy. Katy glared back.

Alice didn't say much and didn't eat much. Heavy makeup was layered across her face covering what must have been a tearful night, highlighting her red rimmed eyes. Danny seemed to relax a bit after the soup course, which they all initially sampled with suspicion before digging in. He chattered a mile a minute about trivial stuff the Judge tuned out. Laura listened to Danny's ramblings with good natured attention. Maddy listened to Charlie, to every word, resting her chin on her hands, a tableau of the student learning from the great master.

Katy was in a combative mood. The Judge could tell by the way she kept her chin lifted. She waited for the salad to arrive, then lobbed a broadside across the table at Charlie. "We've just met a fascinating marine biologist this morning, Charlie, who explained how your single use soda bottles are destroying the planet and infecting us all."

"You've got it all wrong, little lady."

Katy's eyebrows reached for the ceiling.

Oh boy, thought the Judge. *This is going to be good.*

"The liberal press asserts with no proof at all, Katy, yet with unshakable faith in their ability to divine truth out of thin air, that most of this plastic debris floating at sea comes from land-based sources."

"As it does."

"No, Katy. You don't know that. There's no direct evidence to support such an assumption. Consider this. Since 1984, stranded debris has been recorded along the west coast of Inaccessible Island, a remote, uninhabited island in the central South Atlantic Ocean that has a very high macro-debris load.

Plastic drink bottles show the fastest growth rate, granted, increasing at 15 percent per year compared with 7 percent per year for other debris types. In 2018, they examined 2,580 plastic bottles and other containers, one-third of all debris items, that had accumulated on the coast, and a further 174 bottles that washed ashore during regular monitoring over the course of 72 days."

"So, so…."

"So, let me tell you. The oldest container was a high-density polyethylene canister made in 1971, but most were polyethylene terephthalate drink bottles of recent manufacture. Of the bottles that washed up during their survey, 90 percent were date-stamped within 2 years of stranding.

In the 1980s, two-thirds of bottles were derived from South America and carried 3,000 kilometers by the West Wind Drift. By 2009, Asia had surpassed South America as the major source of bottles, and by 2018, Asian bottles comprised 73 percent of accumulated bottles, and 83 percent of newly arrived bottles, with most made in China."

"Well, there you go."

"Yes, but Katy, the rapid growth in Asian debris, mainly from China, coupled with the recent manufacture of the items, strongly suggests they couldn't have come from Asian land-based sources. They just arrived too soon at Inaccessible Island to come from China."

"That doesn't make sense."

"It does if it was the ships, Katy. It had to be the ships. Maybe cruise ships like this one, maybe container ships, probably both. It's the ships that are responsible for most of the bottles floating in the central South Atlantic Ocean. The result of intentional or unintentional violation of the International Convention for the Prevention of Pollution from Ships." Charlie relaxed back in his chair; certain he'd set the little lady straight.

"That doesn't mean the North Pacific Gyre was created by ship pollution," snapped Katy, "But it's irrelevant, anyway, Charlie."

"It's irrelevant that it's the rule-breakers rather than the plastic manufacturers who are responsible for the mess?"

"You just admitted it's the single use plastic bottles that account for the largest part the problem. I don't care whether its land-based or ship-based, it's got to stop. And it's your bottles. Even if you're not legally responsible, you can't just throw up your hands and say, 'not my problem.' You've got to start giving back a deposit, say a dollar a bottle, two dollars a bottle, whatever, for the return of each of your plastic bottles. Build it into your cost structure. Make it a big enough a reward so that people will return the bottles for the cash, whether it's the initial drinker, or a dumpster diver. You've got to stop people throwing away the bottles. You have to make it stop."

Charlie was agitated now, leaning forward in his seat, practically sputtering, his voice rising in falsetto. "We can't do that. We'd be out of business. No one would pay an extra buck for our soda just so they might collect a buck someday, somewhere, somehow, for a return. That's nuts. That's not what our customer wants. He wants a cheap drink in an easy throwaway container."

"You'll poison the whole food chain, Charlie; there won't have any customers left to sell to. It's going to happen." Katy pointed her finger at Charlie as though it were a weapon. "Either voluntarily or by international fiat. With or without your consent, Charlie. If you stand in the way, you'll simply be replaced. You and your greedy company."

"*Harrumph!*" was all that Charlie could manage in response.

CHAPTER 45
DAY 4
2:00 PM

Charlie sat back in his bar chair, resting his back against its high back, in the Dragon-Fly bar on top deck. The bar perched over the back half of the ship with the pool, jacuzzi tub and four terraced decks stretched out below. Soft mood music was playing in the background, so soft he could barely hear it. *Beyond the Sea*, or something. The pretty bartender was wafting a coconut perfume, its scent drafting out to enshroud the bar stools, empty except for Charlie. Her girlish figure was wrapped in a jade sarong with embroidered golden dragons strung over it. The sarong made a stark contrast to her thick black hair, braided, and strung down her back. Her round Malaysian face, dark sparkling eyes, and flashing white teeth reminded Charlie of other times, other places, and other women who'd excited his nights and driven him wild. *God, the scent of a new woman was so intoxicating.*

He smiled at the thought, took a big breath, and let it out slowly, finally relaxing for a bit on this crazy ship. He pushed his bucket glass over for another Jack and Coke. He was expecting his long-time business partner to join him for an unhappy pow-wow, or maybe a happy pow-wow, depending on your perspective. He sensed the change in the ether well before Ross strolled up with exuberance and deposited himself on the bar chair next to him.

"A drink, Ross? They're on me since they're free."

"No, Charlie, I think not. Perhaps we best keep this meeting short and sweet." There was a touch of gloating in Ross's voice that couldn't be missed. The lion was going to pounce and then he would boast of his victory. And of course, that's exactly what was going to happened, thought Charlie. The only question was, 'Which one is the lion?'

"It's been a long and sometimes bitter bunch of years I've lingered in the shadows as your minority partner, Charlie. Never able to take control. Never able to right the company ship and put it on a proper course. Never able to counter-mand your childish mistakes and stamp out your petty quarrels that have cost us time and money, over and over. And the capricious and arbitrary manner in which you manage has left you with lots of enemies. You are aware, I think, that our employees all hate you. What's left of our management hate you. Our bankers hate you. Our distributors hate you. And I hate you."

Charlie smiled. "Nobody ever made money by being a boy scout, Ross."

Ross smiled too, but there was no humor in his eyes, only malice. "I'm throwing you out Charlie. Out on the street. I've acquired another five percent of our stock on top of the five percent I've held. I hold ten percent of our stock now."

"That and three dollars will get you a Starbucks, Ross."

Ross's face turned red in reaction to Charlie's taunt, and he clenched his hands into fists on the bar, barely controlling his anger.

"I've enlisted Anderson & Sparks, Charlie. They've set aside a large war chest to make a tender offer for another twenty-five percent of our stock in the market. That will give me thirty-five percent to your thirty and working control. And they have agreed to fund a proxy fight to solicit proxies from the rest of the shareholders so we can vote in a new board, my board. I'm going to clean house, Charlie. We're going to dump your remaining cardboard executives and directors and put real people in under *my* direction. You're done. The only way you'll get close to *my* company again is by buying one of our sodas."

Ross sat back in his stool, arms folded across his chest, the glow of victory coloring his cheeks.

"The announcement will hit the press tomorrow. But I thought I'd give the news to you the personally, Charlie."

Ross leaned forward against the bar now with his mean smile, savoring his moment, waiting with anticipation for the explosive response from Charlie that would make it all the sweeter.

Ross waited… and waited… and waited. But Charlie didn't even look at him. Charlie took a last sip of this Jack and Coke and casually slid the bucket glass over to the coconut scented bartender for a second refill.

"Well?" said Ross.

"I'm not surprised, Ross. I've already heard about your little effort at a coup."

"Kennedy told you, didn't he, Charlie? I knew the bastard would run to tell you. I knew the moment I tried to recruit him and he waffled. Knew unless Kennedy was stopped somehow, he'd go to you and give you a warning. But I figured old Kennedy'd want to wheedle some concessions out of you in trade for his information. He wouldn't come out and just tell you. There'd have to be a negotiation about what he'd get. I'd hoped when Kennedy died in his soup that he'd not had the chance to spill his guts."

"You're right. Kennedy didn't tell me. I heard from other sources."

"The asshole lawyer, of course. The pontificating piece of shit that goes around referring to himself as the 'Judge' and thinks he's Don Juan. And I know just who gave him the information too.

But it doesn't matter, Charlie. There's nothing you can do. I have the commitments in hand; the capital is set aside in their trust account. It's like an automated train moving down the tracks. And it's going to flatten you. The tender offer's going forward, the press campaign will start tomorrow, the phones and internet will be flooded with my vote solicitors, stacking proxies to throw you out, Charlie. And buying up the public market for the company. Not your company. Not anymore. It's about to be my company. You're going to be out on the street, looking in."

Ross rubbed his hands together, his eyes bright, leaning further forward to leer at Charlie.

"Did you kill Kennedy, Ross? Charlie fired back. Were you the one that dumped peanut oil into his soup?"

Ross just smiled. It was a non-committal smile Charlie couldn't read.

"Does it matter, Charlie? Kennedy is gone. As are Cain and Walker. You will be gone shortly too. It's the grand game we're playing and I'm about to sweep the board."

"Just like that?"

"Just like that. And once I've control, I'm going to initiate a public investigation that ferrets out every dime you've taken from company coffers, every dime you've stolen to spend on yourself and your stupid family. I'm going to get charges filed, I'm going to go on talk shows and blast your incompetency and your looting. I'm going to spread the word about your thievery at business conferences and to the financial community. When I'm done, you won't be able to find a job as a janitor in any company."

Ross's face was livid with rage now. Charlie suspected he might froth at the mouth.

"Why, Ross? Why? After all these years?"

"Why…"

"Yes. Why, Ross? Why all the hate? Look at you, Ross. You're enraged. Why? What have I ever done to you? We've been partners holding stock in this company for thirty years, building it together. I thought you were my friend, my compadre, my partner."

"You still don't get it, Charlie? You still don't see?" Ross's face opened in amazement. "We started out as equal partners. But you immediately set on a strategy to minimize me and take control, Charlie. Oh, you were subtle in the early years. You pretended to be my friend. But all the while you were buying up shares, manipulating stock bonus programs, setting up secret stock buying pools offshore, chipping away at diluting my share ownership until my percentage in the company was whittled down to nothing, minimized. Till you had control."

"But you could have bought shares along with me, Ross."

"Bullshit. No one knew. You didn't tell anyone. Until one day I suddenly was no longer an equal partner, and you had control. Then you stepped in and rearranged everything. I was off the Executive Committee, no longer an officer, no longer a director, demoted to a half-assed consultant."

"We both went off after that SEC investigation, Ross. It was for our own protection."

"No, Charlie. I understand now. The SEC was just a smoke screen. You brought in your stooges, Walker, Cain, and later Kennedy. Your people, not mine. Put them on the board. Manipulated them like the puppets they are.

Gradually my consulting fees were cut, then eliminated. My position was demoted. My stock bonus program was terminated. Next, I lost my retirement program, then my key man insurance, and finally even my medical. All I have left is my shitty little office in the back that's the size of a shoebox."

"We were cutting costs back then, Ross. We had to or the company wouldn't have survived."

"That's fuck-all crap, Charlie, and you know it. No one cut your salary, your benefits. You stayed the most expensive outside consultant any company has ever had."

"I was doing the deals, Ross. I acquired eight companies for us in the space of eighteen months. It was those eight acquisitions, the terms I negotiated, my force of will to make them happen, to close them, that made all the difference. Overnight I turned our company into a major international player in the soda business. Without me there'd be no company today.

Of course I got well compensated. I saved the day, I righted the ship. All you did was sit on your hands and whine, back then, and every day since. What did you expect?"

"You didn't treat me fairly then, partner, and you don't treat me fairly now."

"You have no clue what I do now, Ross. Or how the company would still be a nothing company if I hadn't taken control. I'm the fixer. I've got relationships everywhere. With senators and congressmen, with the President's Chief of Staff, with the head of the FDA, with the president of our primary bank, with the heads of the firms that serve as our market makers for our stock. I'm cozy with our suppliers and their parents, with our distributors, and with the heads of the countries in which we operate. Everywhere.

Who do you think got approval for the single use plastic bottle? Who got us out of the infernal business of dealing with deposits and return of bottles? Who shut down our major competitor when they tried to bring out a look-alike product that tasted like our primary brand? Who monopolized the best ad agencies so our competitors couldn't use them? Who discouraged our competitors from mounting a self-defeating price war over the cost of soda? This company can't survive without me."

"Well it's going to have to Charlie, because shortly you're going to be long gone."

"No."

"What?"

"No."

"What do you mean, 'No'?"

"I'm not going anywhere, Ross. You're the one leaving. You've been around a long time, Ross. And you've mostly felt comfortable, like an old slipper. I'm going to miss you. But you shouldn't have stepped out of your sandbox to play with the big kids."

"What do you mean?" There was a savageness in Ross's voice.

"I mean I heard about your planned coup d'état and have taken steps to defuse it. I think if you call Anderson & Sparks… in the morning I guess, it's after hours there now… you'll find they no longer have any interest in funding your play. And their account guy who's been working with you has been let go."

"No. You're lying. It's not possible."

"I never lie about money matters, Ross. You should know that after all these years. And, oh yes… I'm afraid the broker who extended you the margin so you could buy the additional five percent of our stock is going to want payment in the morning, or he's going to sell you out. You no longer have margin credit at that brokerage."

Ross's face went beet red, his breathing ragged, his hands opening and closing in tight fists.

"You bastard…. They wouldn't do that. Anderson & Sparks wouldn't back out. I have written agreements. And my broker's been my broker for thirty years. You're lying."

"Fraid not, Ross. Look, here's a message from my attorney in New York, sent just before they closed down."

Charlie produced his Note cell phone from his inside pocket and leaned over to share a text message with his former partner.

'Confirmed Anderson Sparks shut down Campaign, fired account manager. Brokerage has called Hamilton's Margin… Chuck.'

"You mother fucking bastard, Charlie. I don't believe you. I don't believe any of it. They wouldn't all turn on me like that."

"Believe what you like, Ross. I could care less. But on our return, you'll need to remove your personal things from your office. My company needs the office space and we're eliminating your office and your presence at *my* company."

Ross clenched and unclenched his teeth several times, his hands shaking.

"If this is true, Charlie…. If this is true…. You're a dead man. A dead man walking, Charlie. A dead man."

Ross got shakily off his bar seat and marched off, stiff legged.

Charlie didn't bother to watch him go. But he did savor the warm glow in his belly, always there after he'd turned the tables. It was a blood sport he relished.

CHAPTER 46
DAY 4
3:00 PM

As the Judge strolled along the promenade deck, trying to substitute walking for the gym workout Katy was lobbying him on again, he found himself walking fifteen feet behind Charlie and his wife, Alice. They were walking into the wind and their raised voices carried back to the Judge, voices engaged in bitter verbal combat. Too focused to notice the Judge behind.

Alice turned to Charlie and snarled. "You just take it all, Charlie, don't you? You just take it all. You can't leave me anything. Nothing to be joyful about. Being with you is like being smothered under a black felt blanket!"

"What do you mean?"

"You killed Jay, and now you've killed Kennedy."

"I didn't kill your lover, Alice. He was your lover, wasn't he?"

"Yes. I knew you knew."

"How could I not? You flaunted him in front of me before, and now again."

"Kennedy was a wonderful lover, Charlie. He had a big dick, not like your little pencil. He touched places in me you couldn't even dream to reach. He was a sweet and romantic lover, taking sex to an art form you'd never understand. Your idea of sex is a series of grunts over thirty seconds and then you roll over and go to sleep. You're such a pig, Charlie."

Charlie bit his lip, his face turning pink. "I'm surprised you'd remember, Alice. It's been years since you last allowed sexual contact."

"You smell, Charlie. And you sweat. Your hands are like ice. And you used to slobber all over me. And on those rare occasions when you got it up for more than a minute and a half, well you were quickly all done. And your sperm smelt like the sewer. I'd have to scrub myself, over and over, inside and out, just to get away from the scent afterward. You're a rotten lover, Charlie. Anyone that sleeps with you does it only for the money. You're a big zero as a man."

"How would you know, Alice? All you were able to attract was that burned-out hulk Kennedy."

"Fuck you, Charlie. I know you were livid about Kennedy. Before and now. So, you got even, didn't you? You got rid of Kennedy forever."

"I didn't kill Kennedy, Alice. He died of a peanut allergy for Christ sakes."

"Don't give me that, Charlie. We saw him repeatedly jabbing that EpiPen into his thigh. The panic on his face. Somebody rigged it so the pen wouldn't work. Someone killed him, Charlie. It was you. You tampered with Kennedy's pen and set him up to die."

"I did no such thing, Alice. I didn't kill Jay either."

"You did, Charlie, as sure as you poured the gas on my baby yourself. You badgered him, bullied him, made him feel small and worthless. Always the criticism. Always the taunts. Always the disgust with whatever he tried to accomplish. You had no love for him in your heart, Charlie. No affection. Not even empathy for another human being. He was just a useless appendage to your family you'd sooner do without."

"That's not true, Alice. That's all fantasy. It's true Jay was weak, lazy, unimaginative, a hanger-on. He'd never have accomplished much. But I tried to set a good example for him. I encouraged him to make something of his life. I was saying all the time to Jay, '*Look at me. Look at how I do it. Follow my thinking. My lead. Let me show you.*'

Sometimes I wish there was a shot of wisdom we could just jab into the arm of kids so they instantly had our experience, see the issues that lie ahead, and the path around. But you can't, Alice. They mostly have to make the same mistakes we made as young people, experience the world and their own failures, try again, work it out for themselves. But Jay never seemed to get past his failures, was never able to work anything out."

"You gave him no chance, Charlie.... Nothing! You just crushed him every time." Alice was almost hissing now. "Jay had my softness, my sweetness. My great heart, my empathy for people. He was a rich human being. Not a money-grabbing goon like you, Charlie. You disgust me."

"You're not soft nor sweet anymore, Alice."

"No. you've worn through my softness. All I have left is contempt... for you... for your company... for your money."

"Jay was soft, lazy, disoriented. In the end he couldn't take it so he chickened out. And Kennedy was a worthless piece of shit I spent money on, took back into the company just for you, Alice. So you could carry on your illicit affair with your toy-boy."

Alice stopped abruptly, turning to Charlie.

"Oh my God. I just realized... I get it now. You knew, Charlie, didn't you? You *knew*."

"About what, Alice?"

"About Jay."

"Of course, I knew. I always knew. You think I'm stupid, Alice?"

"You're ridiculous, Charlie, a joke. A caricature of a real person, devoid of any human emotion or understanding. I hate you."

Alice increased her walking pace dramatically, pulling ahead of Charlie, not looking back, her head high, her arms swinging with vicious energy. Their skirmish was over for the moment.

As Charlie's shoulders sagged in Alice's wake and his gait slowed, the Judge slowed too so as not to catch up.

And the Judge thought about how nature had created females as the weaker sex, but only physically. Nature had evened it out. Giving females the ability to cut a man to ribbons with their words. They were verbal creatures, adept at tearing a male down, destroying his self-esteem, his self-confidence, flattening his ego, inflicting emotional damage with verbal cut after cut. They were able to string sentences together to flay a man's hide and gut him like a fish.

CHAPTER 47
DAY 4
5:30 PM

The Judge settled into a window table in the Buffet Room after fighting his way through the food line, buffeted by heavyset guests scrambling to fill their plates and waddling to tables to chow down early. An early dinner? Or perhaps a first dinner. It was unclear. After all it was free food, wasn't it?... sort of.

He sipped at his watery coffee and crunched on his sticky bun, savoring the sugary treat Katy wouldn't have allowed if she'd been around. She wasn't.

Suddenly the late afternoon sun coming through the window and over his shoulder was blocked by a curving shape which stormed around the table to the other side and settled into the chair there, materializing into the form of Barbara, his long ago ex. She didn't look happy. She glared at him from beneath plucked eyebrows pulled down into a slouch, her mouth set in a mean line slashing across her face.

"You bastard, Judge. You miserable fucking asshole bastard."

The Judge put his coffee down, wondering if he needed to physically defend himself. Barbara had bright red splotches on both cheeks and her hands were shaking she was so angry.

"What's the matter, Barbs?" He tried to put some light and merriment into his tone. But it only seemed to inflame her more.

"You know what the fuck's the matter. You told him, Judge. You told Charlie about Ross's plan to take control. You sold me out, gave away my secret, the whole plan, to Charlie. A secret that wasn't even mine. It belonged to Ross. A secret I shared with you in confidence as a friend, as a lover, as an attorney. What the fuck happened to attorney-client privilege? You're a real bastard."

"What are you talking about, Barbara? What's happened?"

"Charlie has put the kibosh on Ross's whole deal with the underwriting firm; got the brokerage firm to call in Ross's margin loans, has put Ross into financial ruin."

"Why am I not surprised, Barbara? Charlie is a tough customer. But I didn't say anything to him."

"The Hell you didn't. It had to be you, Judge. You're the only one who knew. Now Ross blames me for the leak, as he should. Never wants to see me again. And fuck. I couldn't be with him now anyway. He's flat broke. He's got no money to take care of me. Five months of my loving time and attention wasted, down the drain."

"It wasn't me, Barbara. I didn't tell anyone about Ross's plan. It would have been hard to keep it secret in any event, but it wasn't me."

"Sure, Judge. Sure. It wasn't you." Barbara's voice was rising now, turning heads in the crowded restaurant.

"It was a troll under our table, right, Judge? Listening in when I asked for advice. You're such a lying jerk. This is twice you've ruined my life. Twice! Before, when you wouldn't wait to marry me. You just abandoned me, remember? And now, destroying my happiness and my financial future once again, out of pure malice. I never want to see your ugly face again."

With that, Barbara rose, reached across the table, and shoved his almost full cup of coffee off onto the Judge's lap with a splash.

CHAPTER 48
DAY 4
6:45 PM

After a shower and fresh pants, the Judge leaned against the rail on the pool deck and watched the descending sun, enjoying his solitude now that the pool music had ceased for the day. Katy was napping, having worn herself out on the treadmill.

"Hi, Mr. Judge."

The Judge swung around to see Jerry Barrington, Katy's new friend, leering at him with an ear-to-ear smile. The drink in his left hand was cola-colored, but his breath as he leaned forward, extending his right to shake, told of rum. He was heavy into his rum and Coke.

Jerry looked chubby in his boxer trunks, bright panels of satin red in front and back, matching panels of white on either side, supporting a tubby waist and white chest, devoid of fur. Like a beached animal that could only tolerate the water or the shade.

Jerry's trunks brought back memories of four nights before, in the jacuzzi. Shit, that's where he'd seen Jerry before. This asshole was the phantom groper in the jacuzzi.

"I thought we could chat for a minute, Judge. I've often wondered what it would like to be a lawyer."

"It's great fun, Jerry. And they pay you well to have fun. Nothing better than that. But sometimes you have to sue people who try to smear your reputation, make false representations, claim you're a co-conspirator in a grope party or something. You get a judgment and then you lien their house.

"Oh, cool." Jerry seemed oblivious to the Judge's subtle threat.

"What did you really want to talk about, Jerry?"

"Oh, I don't know. I was just wondering about all these deaths aboard. Rumors are flying the ship is jinxed. I heard you were investigating them. Were they all accidents, Judge?"

"I really can't comment on that, Jerry. The police will have to decide. I'm just gathering the facts, trying to determining what really happened."

"All are officers of this ugly soda company, I heard. Serves them right if you ask me. They're societal criminals. Ought to be tried by a world court, convicted, and put away, or hung. Like Nuremberg!"

"That's crazy, Jerry. You don't really mean that."

"I do. What they've done impacts us all. But I heard the real culprit, the one who controls the company and its polluting policies, might be this shareholder guy, this Charlie Westerman?"

"I can't comment on that."

"Guy like that ought to be stopped, Judge. Locked up. Or maybe just thrown overboard. He's a social menace. Maybe he's killed his own officers. Maybe we can get him on that and put him away. Stop the plastic rain."

"What makes you think he'd kill his own officers, Jerry?"

"Oh, I don't know. A guy that like that who pollutes the oceans, he's got to be lower than whale shit. I heard he's quite a lech, too."

"Why do you say Westerman's a lech?"

"Oh, well, I just heard… you know, heard he was running around with a girl half his age. Guy like that. That old. Ought to have learned by now how to keep it in his pants."

"Is that any of your business, Jerry?"

"Well… no… of course not. I was just wondering. Rumors are flying."

"What about a guy who would crawl into a crowded jacuzzi and start groping young women under the water? What should be done with someone like that, Jerry?"

"Oh. That. It was so crowded in that pool, Judge, it was impossible not to have contact with the person sitting next to you. Perfectly innocent. But, well, I've got to be going now. Nice talking to you. See you around."

Jerry backed away from the Judge, then darted around the corner, rabbit like. The Judge gazed at the corner where he'd been. Wondering. How much violence was the guy capable of? Could Jerry Barringer be the missing piece in the puzzle?

As the Judge stood there, he felt a tug at his arm. He turned to find Maddy Stevens at his side, watching him with wide eyes. She'd changed into something elegant, a canary yellow halter dress, full length. She looked delicious, a vast panel of pelt exposed down her chest to her waist, her breasts slightly undulating under yellow material that didn't quit cover around the edges. The Judge was impressed.

"Watch out for that guy, Judge," Maddy whispered.

"Jerry Barringer?"

"Yeah. He's an asshole and a stalker. He's been following me around forever."

"You know him?"

"Unfortunately, I do. I joined one of these online dating services about five months ago. Just before I met Charlie. Wasn't on it long. But I had a date with Jerry."

"And?"

"He got me into his condo and tried to make a move on me. I had to slug him in the nuts to get out of there. He yelled after me that I was a tart for being on the site.

But after that, wherever I'd go, whomever I'd date, Jerry would just happen to be there. The same club, the same restaurant, the same movie, the same show, even the God damn same beach. It got to be really creepy."

"So, what'd you do?"

"I called the police. They said as long as he wasn't talking to me or harassing me or anything, there was nothing they could do."

"That must have been scary."

"It was. When I started seeing Charlie, I told him about it. That very evening we went out to Nobu on La Cienega, and Jerry showed up fifteen minutes after we sat down and maneuvered himself into a table nearby. I got really upset."

"What happened?"

"Charlie went over to Jerry's table and introduced himself. Then he leaned over and whispered something in Jerry's ear. Jerry's face got real red, I could tell he was barely holding in his temper. He looked like he was going to explode. Anyway, Jerry quickly settled his bill and left."

"Did you ask what Charlie told him?

"Yes. Charlie said he explained to Jerry in a nice way that if he saw Jerry anywhere near me again, he'd have someone cut off Jerry's balls."

"Wow. And did that work?"

"It seemed to, until this cruise."

"Jerry's been following you around on the boat?"

"More or less, yes."

"Did you tell Charlie?"

"No. I didn't want to ruin the cruise for everyone… well, for Charlie, by causing a lot of trouble."

"So. Charlie doesn't know Jerry's on the boat?"

"Well, he didn't at first. But then Charlie saw Jerry yesterday. Jerry was just sitting across the pool, staring at me. Charlie, went over and talked to Jerry some more."

"Do you know what Charlie said?"

"No. But Jerry left in a hurry. Anyway, watch out for the guy. He's a creep."

"How are you and Charlie doing??

"Great. Charlie left Alice this morning and has moved in with me in Kennedy's room. I think I've got him now." Maddy gave the Judge a bright smile that was all dimples and joy.

CHAPTER 49
DAY 5
11:30 AM

The Judge caught up to Charlie at the pool bar. There'd been a message Charlie wanted to talk. Charlie was in a celebrating mood, down at least two Jack and Cokes already and reaching for his third. He was as relaxed as the Judge had seen him. The Judge slid on to the stool next to him and ordered a Scotch.

"Just wanted to hear you can vouch these were unfortunate accidents, Judge. Kennedy, Cain, Walker."

"I can't do that, Charlie. I'm still investigating but it's looking more and more suspicious."

"Oh, come on, Judge. There's no indication of foul play anywhere."

"What about the notes, Charlie?"

"Notes? What notes?"

"The ones your officers received. Ones threatening dire consequences if your company didn't get out of single use plastic bottling."

"You mean the mash notes? Like this one?" Charlie reached into his back pocket and pulled out a crumpled brown piece of paper, apparently torn from a brown paper shopping bag. It had *Von's* stamped on one side. Charlie shoved it across the table to the Judge, a look of disdain on his face.

The Judge uncrumpled the paper and spread it out on the bar so he could read it. Letters had been cut out of a magazine and pasted on the paper with what looked to be Elmer's white glue to form a short message.

"No more warnings. You and your managers are the worst of the worst and will be removed from this planet you've chosen to pollute."

The Judge looked up at Charlie, who had a sneer on his face as he set his third Jack and Coke down and crossed his arms in a protective manner.

"Where'd you get this, Charlie?"

"Piece of crap, isn't it Judge? These pseudo-terrorists think they can scare big corporations with their rants, spelled out on brown paper bags. What a joke. We get this crap all the time. Liberal tree-huggers who don't have a clue about the real world. How competitive it is. How we're just giving the consumer what he wants."

"This is like the other notes your officers have been getting back in LA?"

"Yes. Our executive officers get them all the time."

"I mean just like this, spelled out in pasted letters on paper from a brown paper bag."

"I don't know. They don't come to me. This one Kennedy gave me the day we came aboard."

"So, it was Kennedy who got this note?"

"Yes. I think he brought it along to show me because he was proud. Added a little flair to his dull life. I don't give any credence to such crap."

"Is that how Kennedy felt?"

"Kennedy said he got two other notes over the last ninety days like this. All demanding we either cease putting our soda in single-serve plastic bottles, cold turkey, or provide a one hundred percent redemption policy with a hefty deposit return fee. He didn't give it any credence to them either."

"And now Kennedy's dead."

"Yeah, but unless you can prove it was something different, I believe it was a mistake in the ship's kitchen. Incompetence and negligence. We're going to sue."

"And what about your other two executive officers."

"Bad timing, an unfortunate coincidence, Judge. Shit like that happens to me sometimes."

"It didn't happen to you, Charlie. It happened to them. They're the ones dead."

"People behind notes like this are all talk, Judge. They can talk the talk just fine, but they don't have the guts to walk the walk."

"I don't know, Charlie. Someone sent me a threatening note as well. It was a note tucked under my stateroom door, using pasted letters on white butcher's paper. And the next thing I knew, someone was trying to gas me in my own shower with bug bombs."

Charlie's head swung to look the Judge in the eye, much like a disturbed shark. "You mean you got attacked here, Judge, on this boat?"

"Yes."

Charlie sat back in his chair, his eyes narrowing, suddenly scanning the frolicking people behind him cavorting about the pool, drinks in hand, clustered in small knots of noisy animals, determined to have a good time now the ship was on even keel again and their sea sickness long forgotten.

"Is it possible someone on this boat is sending these note to my Company?" whispered Charlie

The Judge nodded. "It's possible, Charlie. Or it could be a red herring. An effort by an insider in your group with a grudge against one or more of your officers. A person who engineered these… 'accidents'. Now seeking to cover his tracks ahead of my investigation, with the blame to fall on an anonymous malcontent sending angry notes"

"Like Ross Hamilton?"

"Perhaps, or maybe someone even closer to home."

"Speaking of home, Judge, I'm in Suite 632 now, two doors over from my larger suite."

"You moved?"

"Yes. I took Kennedy's old suite. I'm shacked up with Maddy for the moment." Charlie's dark eyes sparked for a second. "I've moved out on Alice, perhaps for good. She's gone too far with her vitriolic diatribes.

Anyway, if you need me, I'll be there. I'm going to take a nap."

Charlie eased himself off the bar stool and slowly toddled off around the pool, walking stiff and erect as he headed for the interior and the elevators, barely avoiding bathing suits of one stripe or another. Charlie was loaded to the gills.

CHAPTER 50
DAY 5
1:45 PM

The Judge watched thoughtfully as Charlie walked away. The man was hard to figure. Charlie seemed to callously shake off the death of his three officers, just, the Judge supposed, as he had shaken off the death of his son, Jay, six months earlier. He'd only shown concern for an instant at the prospect that a murderer might be aboard. Then again, no one had sent Charlie a Black Spot note. And why would they? Charlie was neither an officer nor a director, merely an unconcerned shareholder….

And Charlie had seemed cowed by his wife on the promenade deck. Yet now he'd moved out on Alice to shack up with his administrative assistant. That must be a little uncomfortable for Alice, what with Charlie and Maddy so close, just a stateroom between.

Charlie seemed oblivious to the environmental damage he was doing with his single use plastic bottle. And he would not accept criticism of his company's plastic production policies, disputing every allegation.

Yet, he inspired what sounded like a fierce loyalty from Maddy Stevens, and apparently from his employees. Even Cain and Walker, now deceased, had expressed a fondness and a respect for Charlie. That had surprised the Judge.

Charlie was loved by his daughter, Laura. But he was disliked by his son Danny, who seemed to be running a con game with the company's cash as much to spite his dad as to secure wealth for himself.

What drove a man to be so many different people all at once?

The Judge watched the pool crowd for perhaps a half hour, nursing his drink. He particularly enjoyed the young pretty girls with the skimpy suits, never meant to get wet. After all, he was a male and it was okay to look, right? Okay as long as Katy wasn't near anyway. He supposed he was turning into a dirty old man. He smiled at the thought. He wasn't turning into anything new, the only thing that had changed was his age. He'd always enjoyed watching beautiful semi-clad women. It was how guys were built; natural hard wiring that kept the human race going.

As the Judge watched the unfolding scene around the pool, he sensed the stool next to him being filled by a warm body. A body scented by coconut sunscreen applied liberally smelt familiar.

He turned to meet the brown eyes of Maddy Stevens again. But this was a very different Maddy from a half hour before. Her eyes no longer soft and smiley, but now puffy, red. And perhaps a bit panicky. Mascara was running around the edges and her lipstick was lightly smudged around a bitter smile as she glared at the Judge.

Her blond hair was pulled back so tight in a ponytail it looked like it might come out at the roots, and there was a brittleness to her body that suggested she barely had herself under control.

"You were right, Judge. Charlie Westerman's a pig. He's just thrown me out. Back to my windowless cubby in the bow. Says he might go back to Alice. The waffling bastard."

Turning to the barmaid she snapped, "Give me a double Scotch, and quick."

"What happened, Maddy?

"That's the thing. Nothing happened. I went back to the room from the after we spoke and he just turned on me, told be to get out. Said we were over. I was fired. Just like that. No reason. No argument. No discussion. Just get out. I'm in shock. I still can't believe it.

I thought I had him this morning when he changed rooms. Left Alice. But when I went back to the room, he just threw me out. The man's a psychopath. Thing is, I would have been good for Charlie. Would have slowed him down a little. See he had some fun and not all business, business, business. I was going to make a difference for him."

A small tear appeared in one brown eye, which she blinked back. The Judge was unsure if it was a tear of anger or a tear of sorrow. Perhaps both.

"I might have said some awkward things the other night when we were in that bar together and I was loaded, Judge. About me, about Charlie. You didn't say anything to Charlie about that, did you?"

"Of course not, Maddy."

"I don't know what happened then. He just turned cold and cruel for no reason." She gulped the last two fingers of Scotch out of her glass. She scribbled the number for her old room and a large black X on the tab the barmaid had set down with the drink and slid unsteadily off the stool.

"By the way, Judge, did he show you the note he got?"

"He showed me the note, the threatening note. He said it was sent to Kennedy before you folks started this cruise."

"That's it. He's so stubborn, doesn't want to admit the note was sent to him. I found it in an envelope shoved under the door."

"At the office, Maddy? In L.A.?"

"No, Judge… No. Here…. This morning. Under the door to Kennedy's stateroom after Charlie moved in."

"Jesus. Do you think it was directed at Charlie, Maddy?"

"The envelope was addressed to Charlie, Judge."

"The writer of these notes to the officers must be aboard this ship, Maddy. He even sent a threatening note to me. If Charlie is the last person to get a note, it may mean Charlie is the next target for a fatal accident."

Maddy's chin came up now, her eyes blazing.

"And I hope they get him, Judge. He is so cavalier with people's lives and emotions; he really deserves to die. I might just push him off this God damn tub myself."

"Look, Maddy, this changes a lot. I've got to talk to Charlie. Where is he?"

"Probably still in Kennedy's room. I don't know, and I don't care."

Maddy started to tear up again, turned, and, holding her hand over her mouth, slowly walked away toward the elevators, bent over in distress.

The Judge asked for his bill, which seemed to take an inordinate time to come. The barmaid was busy flirting with the skinny steward, Ajay, at the other end of the bar. He finally got something to sign, jumped off his stool, and headed for the elevators, pushing the down button for Kennedy's floor.

CHAPTER 51
DAY 5
2:20 PM

Charlie stepped out on to the balcony of Kennedy's room with a fresh Jack and Coke.

He'd just thrown Maddy out, and good riddance. God damn conniving females. He'd found the pregnancy testing kit by accident in her luggage, at the bottom, while searching for aspirin. He knew immediately what it meant; her scheme was crystal clear. He wasn't going to sire any more children. And he wasn't going to be with anyone intent on trapping him into parenthood.

Besides, he'd met someone else who'd caught his eye. Barbara… Barbara something. Ahh, the scent of a new woman…!

He leaned way out over the rail on his toes now, gazing down the length of the ship, trying for a moment to recall how many Jack and Cokes he'd had.

Charlie felt a presence behind him; Was Maddy back again, like a bad penny? He started to come off his toes and lean back in. But it was too late. The full weight of someone struck him from behind, low, just below the knees, grabbing his legs and thrusting them up and outward, away from the rail. Shifting his center of gravity, pivoting him on his belly over the rail headfirst, shoving his legs over the rail after him with venom.

The was no chance to grab the balcony rail. The force of the attack, coupled with his weight, took over, pivoting him over the rail and sending him into a head-first dive, down… down.

He careened off the rail of the balcony below his, smashing his nose and forehead, flipping him over on to his back as he fell past the next floor. Falling toward the foaming grey green sea at the ship's side.

A blur of decks and sea and then sky as he tumbled, clawing uselessly at the passing rails of two decks below, unable to catch a hold. His long shrill scream was cut short as he slammed onto the deck rail three levels down, his spine absorbing the damage, his vertebrae collapsing in several places, taking his breath away.

He bounced off the rail inboard rather than overboard, landing with force on his face on the deck. Then blackness… nothing.

CHAPTER 52
DAY 5
2:21 PM

As the Judge got off the elevator on Charlie's floor, he heard a muffled scream. It was a short panicky scream. It didn't bode well, coming from around the corner where Kennedy's old suite was. The Judge dashed around the corner, hearing a door close somewhere along the corridor ahead, spotting the open door to suite 632, now Charlie's suite.

The Judge dashed into the room. It was empty. He moved out the sliding glass window to the veranda and looked over the rail and three decks down. On the promenade deck below he saw a figure sprawled on its stomach, head turned to the side. A big man, crumpled, one arm underneath him, his face just a blur of blood. Liquid was puddling on the deck under and around him. Unconscious or dead? The Judge couldn't tell.

As he stood there panting from his dash, stunned by the tableau below, something caught his attention. A smell. A scent, really. Something he'd smelled before. What was it? A scent of musk, citrus and the woods.

By the time the Judge got down to the promenade deck a small crowd had formed around Charlie. He was still breathing, his nose smashed and to the side of his face, his breath coming in heaving gasps. And he was unconscious. People around him were afraid to move him for fear of doing further damage. But someone had taken a wet handkerchief and wiped the blood from his eyes and from around his nose and mouth. The flow of his blood seemed to have slowed to a trickle.

Paramedics arrived with a stretcher. They started to carefully move Charlie over and on to the stretcher. As they lifted him, Charlie regained consciousness and gave a blood curdling scream. Whatever his injuries, they were clearly excruciating.

After the ship's doctor arrived, a procession with the stretcher in the lead headed for the elevators, the Judge bringing up the rear. Maddy joined the procession at the elevators, her face a blur of tears and more running mascara as she squeezed her way over next to the stretcher. The doctor had given Charlie a shot of morphine and when Charlie recognized Maddy, he smiled, and took her proffered hand to hold. The procession re-formed outside the elevator and moved past the Morgue on Deck four and on to the Sickbay.

The Judge and Maddy settled into deep leather chairs in the waiting room. Alice and Laura and Danny showed up five minutes later and they all huddled together in the confined space, awaiting word. Alice leaned against the wall on the other side of the room from Maddy, as far away as she could get, and occasionally threw hateful looks Maddy's direction.

Maddy ignored Alice, locking her arms around her torso, and gently rocking in her chair in absolute distress.

After forty minutes of mostly silence, the doctor came into the little room to talk to them, officially directing his comments to Alice, as Charlie's wife.

"Three crushed vertebrae I'm afraid. His motor mechanisms are shut down below the waist. A broken nose, broken arm, and a nasty concussion. The other injuries will heal, but… I expect he'll never walk again. I'm sorry."

Alice bit her lip and turned away, while Maddy started to sob. Laura and Danny looked at each other in shock.

The Judge got up, extended his condolences to everyone, and shuffled out, his mind operating at warp speed, trying to assess what had happened.

CHAPTER 53
DAY 5
3:30 PM

The Judge returned to his stateroom to find Katy waiting for him. Word had spread through the passengers and crew about Charlie's fall, and Katy was concerned to make sure the Judge was okay.

They settled into the tiny veranda table for an afternoon drink and to watch the view. The plastic sea had disappeared. The ocean was again its traditional blue, tinted by the sky with its colors. It was their last afternoon on the cruise. In the morning they would dock at Hilo, and the Judge and Katy would get off what the Judge had come to think of as the 'cursed boat' and continue independent travel through the islands.

Katy raised her margarita to toast, clinking glasses with the Judge, a rueful smile on her face. "Here's to tomorrow's end to this interesting cruise, dear. Not the relaxed and soothing voyage I'd anticipated for you. You seem to invariably find yourself in a pile of bodies wherever you go. But at least you had something to occupy your time. In fact, I think you've actually been having fun since death started stalking the guests."

The Judge smiled too, staring into Katy's beautiful aqua eyes, backgrounded by the deep blue Pacific. "You make me sound like a ghoul, Katy. But okay, I admit it. It's been a lot more interesting than I anticipated, but only after we moved our dining table and met Charlie and his posse."

"So, Judge. Do you have a theory about what has happened?"

"I was going to ask you, Katy. You're usually the power behind my image who susses out what really happened and who the culprits are."

"So, who do we have as suspects, Judge?"

"With Charlie and his group, the suspects are everybody."

"Do you think one of the deceased killed Kennedy, and then there was a daisy chain of killings?"

"I don't, Katy. The method of each death was designed to look like an accident. That's a signature of a single killer."

"Okay, Judge, who is it? Do you know?"

"No. And we seem to have lots of suspects."

"Who do we suspect, Judge?"

"Well, there's Ross Hamilton, Charlie's now ex-business partner. He hates Charlie and he hated the officers Charlie had wheeled into the front to officially run the company. He was in the gym area before George Walker died and buzzing around the area where Larry Cain took his deadly fall."

"But he was at our table talking to me when Kennedy died. How could he have gotten peanut oil into Kennedy's soup?"

"I don't know. Maybe he leaned over Kennedys soup and covered his movement somehow. Ross was sitting at the end of the table, perpendicular to Kennedy."

"It's possible. In fact, he did lean out and stretch briefly after Kennedy left to take a whiz. And it was just after the soup arrived."

"What about the bottle of peanut oil I found in the kitchen?"

"Maybe that had nothing to do with the peanut oil in Kennedy's soup."

"Then why was the empty bottle stolen from our quarters?"

"Oh."

"Then there's Danny Westerman, Katy. He's been stealing from his dad's company. Kennedy knew it, Cain knew it, and Walker knew something of it. Now they're all dead."

"How would he have gotten the peanut oil in Kennedy's soup?"

"He and Laura went to inspect the kitchen while the soup was being portioned out. That gives either or both the opportunity to lace the soup. And it puts them in the same location as the discarded peanut oil bottle."

"What about Cain?"

"Danny may have been on the floor Cain started down before his death fall. When I went up there,

Danny was coming out of the elevator, looking a little fishy. But he might have already been on the floor; pretending to come out of the elevator as a cover."

"And in the Gym?"

"Yes, I saw him in the corridor on the way to the gym."

"So, he's a live suspect too."

"Yes, and so is his sister, Laura. She hated Kennedy from what I can tell. She was in the kitchen with Danny before Kennedy keeled over. And she was in the corridor leading to the gym with Danny."

"Maybe they did it together."

"Maybe, but I'm not convinced."

"That leaves the executive assistant, and Charlie's wife, Alice. Everybody else who was at our table is dead."

"Maddy was livid when Charlie broke up with her, threw her out of his cabin. But I haven't found any motive for Maddy to want to kill the officers."

"Maybe you were looking in the wrong direction. Too much concentration on her boobs and ass; too little on her motivations."

"Katy…"

"You know it's true. You men are all alike. You can't see the forest for the nipples."

"What about Alice, Katy?"

"How do you get her into a position to poison Kennedy's soup? Besides, she loved Kennedy. Did you see her face when he died? She didn't kill Kennedy."

"Well, maybe you were right before; maybe the murders were committed by different people, in sequence. Maybe Alice offed Larry Cain, or George Walker, and someone else killed Kennedy."

"Or perhaps Charlie killed all three and has been using you has his goat, Judge."

"I'd make a good goat, Katy. The old goats are the best."

"You're my Old Goat, Judge, just remember that. What about Charlie's fall? Was that an accident?... or attempted murder?"

"I don't know, Katy. I spoke briefly to Charlie down in sick bay. He's paralyzed, you know. Several broken vertebrae. The doctor said he doesn't think Charlie will ever walk. Charlie was very evasive about what happened."

"Protecting someone?"

"Perhaps. Maybe a son or a daughter, Katy."

"Or a wife or girlfriend?"

"Who knows. From what I overheard on the promenade deck; Alice was really angry at Charlie. It wasn't only the affair with Maddy. Alice blamed Charlie for the suicide of their son, Jay, last year. And there was something else, something about Jay. I couldn't tell what it was, but Alice suddenly flew into a rage. It was pretty ugly."

"So maybe Alice killed Cain and Walker, Judge, and pushed Charlie overboard, but someone else killed Kennedy. Maybe Ross."

"Perhaps."

"Or maybe, Judge, when Maddy got told she wasn't going to ever be the Mrs. Westerman she'd planned to be, she exploded like the ticking time bomb she is."

"You think Maddy's a ticking time bomb?"

"She looks to be really tightly wound. I think there's a lot there boiling under the surface. But I don't know, Judge. It's a puzzle."

"It is Katy. And then there's a whole other aspect I've been thinking about."

"Tell me, Judge."

"Not yet, Katy. I need to work it through a bit more in my head. But I think we need to organize a dinner, maybe a captain's dinner, and get everybody there who's touched the facts surrounding the three deaths and Charlie's fall."

"Just like Hercule Poirot, Judge."

The Judge just smiled.

"Of course, if it were Poirot, the gardener would have done it," said Katy.

"That reminds me, Katy, of someone else we've forgotten."

"Who?"

"Your toy-boy, Jerry something or other."

"He's not my boyfriend."

"Well, you were practically sitting in his lap when I showed up at the bar."

"I beg your pardon. I was doing no such thing. I was merely pumping Mr. Barrington for information."

"Is 'pumping' the word for what you had in

mind, Katy?"

Katy's elbow was quick and accurate. "Ouch…!"

"Jerry Barrington had nothing to do with this and you know it, Judge."

"I don't know it. The guy seemed pretty wacko to me. Talking about gassing Charlie and his officers. Maybe it was him."

"Jerry was just upset after stepping out on his veranda and finding himself in the middle of a plastic sea, as were we all."

"Perhaps, Katy. Or perhaps Jerry's been stalking Charlie and his officers all along, waiting for his chance to put them all away. He's young, and he's a liberal tree-hugging marine biologist. Just the sort who would follow through with something crazy."

"You're ridiculous, Judge. Besides, there's another person we've left out."

"Who, Katy?"

"Barbara, your ex-lover."

"Oh, well, now that is truly ridiculous."

"I don't know, Judge. Charlie has ruined Barbara's greedy plan. She was going to ride off into the sunset with Ross Hamilton. She could have been working with Ross the whole time to eliminate his competition. She was going to be rich. She was going to be married to the man who controlled a huge company. The hussy was so close to marriage and riches she was salivating. Charlie ruined all that, destroyed Hamilton, broke him. Now everything's off. And

Barbara's got quite a temper, particularly when she's been drinking, which is most of the time. Maybe she stopped by Charlie's suite and dumped him over the side to get even."

Katy sat back in her chair, proud of herself for marshalling the facts in such an attractive way.

The Judge just sighed. For Katy, Barbara would always be the villain.

CHAPTER 54
DAY 5
4:15

The Judge went down to Deck 7 where all the duty-free shops were, and into a shop selling expensive liquor and perfume. A pretty Croatian girl, perhaps thirty, long jet-black hair and sparkling black eyes under long eyelashes, immediately stopped taking inventory and came over to the Judge, sensing a significant sale.

"Perhaps you can help me," said the Judge. "I have a lady friend who likes a perfume called *Aoud Absolue Precieux*. Do you carry that?"

"Ooh la la, my friend, your girl has very expensive tastes. I know it. It's *Roja Musk Aoud Absolue Precieux*. I think we have one small bottle back in the locked part of our stock room. Let me check. We may not have it."

Four minutes later the girl was back with a tiny silver cannister about the size of a lip stick. "This is all we have. It's the spray. And it goes for five hundred dollars U.S."

"Five hundred for that tiny spray?"

"Yes, Monsieur. Can I show you something else?"

"Can I smell this *Roja Musk*, or whatever it's called?"

"But of course." The girl flipped off the top, sprayed just a touch on her wrist, rubbed her wrists together, and then offered one delicate hand for the Judge to sniff.

The Judge took one whiff, nodded his head, and said, "Okay, I'll take it."

"Oh, Monsieur, I think your woman is one lucky female."

"Actually, I think not, but then life isn't always fair, is it? Can you put it in a bag?"

The girl produced an expensive looking felt bag of silver-gray with pretend ruby draw strings, stuffed it with tissue and a card baring the shop's logo, and then deposited the canister inside.

The Judge left the shop and took the elevators up to the bridge deck, looking for the captain. The captain was in fact on the bridge but came out on to the walkway to talk.

"How goes the investigation, Judge? Do you have news for me?"

"I'm very close to answers, Captain."

"We're running out of time, Judge. You got an extra day at sea because of the storm, but we'll be in Hilo tomorrow morning."

"Yes. I understand. I thought perhaps you could throw a Captain's dinner party tonight. It's our last night aboard. You could host this dinner party in your private dining room, and we could use the opportunity to sort this whole thing out. Put it to rest."

"Tonight?"

"Yes."

"I can do that if it will help bring clarity to what has happened. Who would you want to invite?"

"I have a list, Captain." The Judge took it from his pocket.

"The Captain scanned the list, his eyes widening a little. "You didn't leave anybody out, did you, Judge? This is quite thorough. I'll get right on it and have invitations delivered personally."

"There may be some who will be reluctant to come. I think it's important we have everybody. Can you lean on everyone to show up?"

"It's my boat and I'm the Captain, Judge. Don't worry, they'll all show up."

"Thank you, Captain. I think we can put an end to this unfortunate business tonight."

CHAPTER 55
DAY 5
8:00 PM

The Judge and Katy arrived five minutes late to the assigned door on the 17th deck, marked with a small brass plaque as the *Captain's Dining Room.* Katy had delayed them with last-minute adjustments to her makeup, leaving the Judge to pace up and down their tiny suite until she was ready. He knew over some years of experience that come Hell or high water nothing would move Katy from her mirror in the bathroom until she was entirely done painting her face. It was a ridiculous quirk; he'd told her once she may as well be Korean. That hadn't sat well, and she'd not spoken to him for a day and a half. Now he kept his mouth shut, but it irritated him they were always a little late to everything.

Katy had her eye on the silver-grey felt bag the Judge carried at his side, dying to know what was in it and who it was for, but too proud to ask.

The Judge rang the doorbell and the heavily varnished door swung open, manned by a steward in whites, including gloves. It was Ajay, the pool MC turned Captain's steward again. His tan face broke into a brash smile that displayed matching ivory teeth as he recognized the Judge.

Inside, the dining room was paneled in soft mahogany and intricate moldings. Several seascapes hung on the walls, each with its own spotlight. The carpet underfoot was a plush green. The room was perhaps twenty feet long by fifteen feet wide, with large bouquets of flowers set in silver pots in its four corners. The long table stretching the length of the room was set with fresh linen, and two tall candelabras were spaced a third of the way down each side; their twinkling candle flames sparkled down onto the gold rims of the Vera Wang Wedgwood china and the Christofle silverware.

A second waiter in whites greeted them after they stepped in and offered them a glass of champagne from his silver tray. It was Sean Cross, their waiter from the dining room. Katy and the Judge selected glasses, toasted each other, and drifted down to the far end of the room where a small huddle of people were in conversation. The Judge saw Captain John Quincy Smith, in his blue uniform but no cap, and beside him his first officer, Rex Edwards. The Captain was talking animatedly with Danny Westerman and his sister Laura, holding forth with stories of working his way up in the great cruise line to Captain.

Behind them Ross Hamilton was engaged in some serious conversation with Alice Westerman. Leaning against the wall to the right in a corner was Maddy Stevens, looking faintly uncomfortable and out of place. She'd placed the knot of people between her and Jerry Barrington, who was on the other side of the room inspecting one of the oil paintings.

Charlie of course wasn't there; he was lodged in the ship's infirmary with his broken back and couldn't be moved. The Judge and Katy joined the Captain's small clutch of admirers as the doorway to the small galley kitchen opened. Sophia, their floor maid, dressed in a black uniform and white apron, offered the Judge hors d'oeuvres from the tray she carried. The Captain finished his story of near double tragedy when his ship had assisted a tanker taking on water. Turning to the Judge, Captain Smith said in a boisterous voice, "And how is your investigation coming, Judge? Have you a suspect?"

"Actually, I have, Captain."

"Oh." The Captain's head came up and the Judge found himself looking down the barrels of two steely blue eyes; Captain John Quincy Smith had iron under his jovial exterior.

"Have you ever heard of the Earth Liberation Front, or ELF, Captain?" asked the Judge.

"Uhh… no."

"The Earth Liberation Front has claimed responsibility for thousands of terrorist acts against property, including the 1998 arson of a ski resort at Vail where twelve buildings were simultaneously set alight to the tune of twelve million in damages. And the arson of a San Diego condo complex in the early 2000s that caused fifty million in damage. In March of 2008, ELF torched luxury homes in the swank Seattle suburb of Woodinville because it claimed the housing development was not green as advertised. In September of 2009, the Front claimed responsibility for the destruction of two radio towers in Seattle. The list goes on and on. In the five years ending in 2008, the FBI estimates eco-terrorists were responsible for over two hundred million dollars in property damages."

"What motivates people to commit such violence and arson Judge? I don't understand how they can justify such acts."

"Eco-terrorism is a form of radical environmentalism that arose out of the same school of thought that brought about deep ecology, ecofeminism, social ecology, and bioregionalism, Captain," piped up Jerry Barringer, as if rising to the surface for bait.

"Eco-terrorists believe in biocentrism, that the human species is just one more ordinary member of the extended biological community. They believe all living things should have rights and be protected under the law, including the creatures in the sea. Many members want to return the environment to its natural, or pre-industrial, state. They believe that human society is responsible for the depletion of the environment and, if current society is left unchecked, it will lead to the complete degradation of the planet. And given our Sea of Plastic, they have a point."

"Perhaps," said the Judge. "But more recently, they've started to go beyond property damage, beginning to inflict personal harm on those they perceive as polluting the planet."

"You think someone from this organization, this liberation movement group, has a hand in these accidents?" The Captain leaned forward toward the Judge, intense.

"It's not exactly a group, Captain. More like an idea. The Earth Liberation Front was founded in 1992 and calls itself an eco-terrorist organization. But the problem is, it's not really an organization at all. It's more like a loose collection of relatively autonomous 'cells' that act independent of central planning or control, but shelter under its name and claim credit for terrorist acts on its behalf. It's a clandestine movement that seeks to inspire self-starting individuals to confront environmentally harmful corporations and government actors through militant resistance and terrorist acts."

"And you suspect I have one of these people here, aboard my ship?"

"Yes."

The room went silent. Everybody had been listening or eavesdropping as the Judge spoke. And now there were staring at the Judge, uncertain what to say. Finally, the First Officer spoke, "I'm certain we don't have anyone like that aboard our ship, Judge. I can vouch for our crew. And our passengers are almost all well-heeled Americans. I don't think we can attribute these unfortunate accidents to a phantom group."

But the Captain held up his hand, shutting his executive officer off. "Let's hear what the Judge has to say, Rex."

Just then, Sophia rang a small gong on a side table, signifying it was time to sit for dinner.

"After dinner then, Judge," said the Captain. "Let's enjoy our scrumptious meal."

Name tags were arranged in front of each chair, and the Judge found himself at one end of the long table, with Captain Smith at the other end. Katy was to the Judge's right, and Danny was to the Judge's left.

Dinner was quite a lavish affair, if not particularly festive. The remaining family members were despondent over the three deaths and the tragedy that had befallen Charlie.

There was a shrimp cocktail made with giant shrimp, followed by a Caesar salad that lacked the garlic kick the Judge gave it when he made his. Then a white clam chowder that was a tad pedestrian, but filling. The main course was New York steaks, which the men dove into with relish; the women were more restrained, likely wishing there was a vegetarian alternative. But there was not.

By unspoken mutual agreement there was no talk of the plastic sea they'd now left in their wake, nor of the three mysterious deaths, nor Charlie's suspicious fall.

CHAPTER 56
DAY 5
9:00 PM

As dessert was passed around the table, individual plates double-loaded with a slice of Key lime pie and a slice of New York cheesecake, the Captain turned to the Judge and said in a voice that carried around the table, "Okay Judge, let's hear more from you on your investigation."

"Of course, Captain, I can relate what I know. But first I wanted to commend you on your magnificent dinner. It was thoroughly enjoyed by all here tonight."

"My pleasure, all." The Captain dipped his head in a seated mock bow.

"The only thing I missed was the Indian spiced carrot soup with ginger."

"Well, yes. I'm sorry about that Judge. And that reminds me. Let's have our serving staff come out for an acknowledgment."

There was movement behind the Captain where the three crew members had been lingering to eavesdrop. Then Sophia, Sean and Ajay stepped out and moved to lean against the dining room wall behind the Captain.

"Give them a hand for preparation of this scrupulous meal," said the Captain.

There was polite applause from the table.

"And at the Judge's request, we tried to get Ajay to make his famous Indian spiced carrot soup," continued the Captain. "But he ran out of one of his key ingredients and was unable to oblige. When a crew member has a special dish, like Ajay's soup, they carry their own home spices and things aboard to assure it's authentic."

"Ah, yes. And…" said the Judge, turning to face the dinner staff now. "Tell me Ajay, where is home.?"

The scrawny kid took a step forward, made a slight bow, grinning from ear to ear, and said, "Home for me is India."

"And exactly what town, Ajay? Where did you go to university?"

Ajay nodded his understanding, and said, "The Junagadh Agricultural University in Junagadh."

"And what was the missing ingredient that made it impossible for you to make your famous Indian spiced carrot soup?"

Ajay's smile faded a little. "Just some local spices."

"Oh, come now, Ajay, don't be coy. What didn't you have in your trove of local foods and flavors you brought aboard because you'd already used it up?"

"An… oil."

"What kind of oil? Olive oil?"

Ajay's smile was gone, replaced by a panicky look.

"Just an oil…"

"Kind?"

"It's not important."

"Is that because it was peanut oil?"

"What?"

"Peanut oil. Was it peanut oil you lacked?"

"The recipe doesn't call for…"

"Oh, but it does. I looked it up myself. No self-respecting guy from Junagadh would make the soup without using the local peanut oil. But you had no peanut oil left, did you Ajay?"

"Well…"

"You had no peanut oil left because you loaned the bottle to Sean, who finished the bottle off lacing Kennedy's soup."

Heads turned toward Sean, who suddenly found something to stare at on the back wall of the dining room, his face set in stone.

Ajay said, "No. No. I had nothing to do with Kennedy's soup."

"You know it was laced with peanut oil."

"I'd heard a rumor."

"And you knew Kennedy had a bad allergy to peanuts?"

"Another rumor, but…"

"There's no use lying about it, Ajay. I found the bottle of peanut oil in the trash in the dining room kitchen right after his death. It was labeled as produced by Rachana Seeds Industries Private Limited, of Dolatpara. Where is Dolatpara in relation to your University, Ajay?"

Ajay was stuttering now. "Well, I'm not sure exactly."

"Oh, come now, Ajay. We both know that Dolatpara is a suburb of Junagadh where you grew up and went to school."

"It's not my fault Kennedy's EpiPen wouldn't work. If it hadn't mal-functioned he'd be alive now."

"Oh, but it is. Because you had an accomplice who tampered with it."

Ajay flushed and shut his mouth tight.

"You see, when Larry Cain fell down the stairs, I caught the flash of a white deck shoe and an ankle on the landing above before the person departed the scene. A small foot. And the flash of an ankle bracelet with the initials, M.Y. on it. Do you know what M.Y. stands for?"

Ajay shook his head, his face changing now from red to white.

"It could stand for lots of things, I suppose, like for instance, Motor Yacht. But in this case, it's the international abbreviation for 'Malaysia'. That's because the tag I saw is the same tag that's currently on the ankle bracelet your co-conspirator, Sophia standing next to you, who is wearing. The ankle she is unsuccessfully trying to tuck behind her other foot.

"Aren't you from Malaysia, Sophia?"

It was Sophia's turn for her face to go white, panic in her eyes.

"Sophia is the floor maid for my section of staterooms. That includes both my room and Kennedy's suite. One of the three of you accessed the guest dining accommodations records and found out that one of your targets had a serious peanut allergy.? And, Sophia, you went rummaging through his things for his EpiPen, likely while he was at the pool. You emptied the EpiPen's contents and then returned it to his coat pocket, creating a trap waiting to be sprung. Did you not?"

Sophia was shaking her head no, her mouth open to speak, but no words came.

And while you were in my cabin cleaning that evening after dinner and the attack on Kennedy, you lifted the pieces of evidence I'd taken from the dining table: the sample of his soup, the empty bottle of peanut oil, and the doctored EpiPen, and threw them down the trash chute, didn't you?"

Sophia looked like she was going to be sick.

"And it was you, Sophia, on the upper deck landing before Cain had his fall. You who screwed a small hook into the wall, four inches above the second stair down from that floor. You who ran the invisible fish line across to wrap around the stair rail support.

You yanked the fishline tight as Cain started down the steps, tripping him into a headlong fall down the stairs, in which he broke his neck.

You had to get rid of the fish line and remove the hook as soon as Cain fell. That's why I saw your foot on the landing above as we examined Cain at the foot of the stairs.

All eyes were on Sophia's ankle bracelet; and the little tag that dangled there.

"And of course, we can't forget Sean, can we Sean? You had several parts to play. You spiced up Kennedy's soup with the entire bottle of Ajay's peanut oil concentrate. And you went into the private spa room after George Walker entered the sauna. You used a screwdriver to unscrew the outside sauna handle and jam the mechanism so the sauna door wouldn't open from the inside. Sealing George Walker in, trapping him. Then you set the sauna thermostat to max, condemning Walker to his own hellish oven and baking him alive."

Sean's face was filled with rage.

"Walker had it coming," Sean hissed. "They all had it coming. Destroying the oceans with their foul plastic."

"Yes, you thought so, didn't you, Sean. You and your little group. Your cell. Here is the napkin I pulled out of the trash after the three of you met in the crew's cafeteria. See the initials Sophia was doodling: ELF. That stands for the Earth Liberation Front, doesn't it?"

Suddenly the three of them dashed for the door, squeezing out and disappearing down the corridor before the First Officer could reach them.

As the First Officer thundered after them, the Captain wiped the shocked expression from his face and replaced it with a grim smile. There was fire now in his blue eyes.

"Don't worry, Judge. We'll get them. I don't know where they think they're going to go, on my ship, in the middle of my ocean. Let's enjoy our dessert."

CHAPTER 57
DAY 5
9:15 PM

"Unbelievable," said the Captain. "They committed three murders on my ship, and an attempted murder."

"Three murders, yes, Captain. Three meticulously planned out murders. Premeditated for sure, although they of course couldn't be sure Kennedy would die from the peanut oil, or that Larry Cain would break his neck in his fall down the stairs. And they risked someone finding George Walker before he cooked to death."

"Indeed."

"But the attack on Charlie wasn't planned like that. It was a crime of opportunity. Charlie told me he was leaning over the rail when the attack occurred, scanning the sea, more than a bit tipsy. The person couldn't know Charlie would be in that cabin, Kennedy's old cabin, at that time, or and leaning way out over the rail, or smashed."

"True."

"The attack on Charlie was carried out in an entirely different manner. I believe it was committed by someone else."

"Someone else?"

"Yes. Someone who saw the opportunity and, in that split second of assessment, went for it. Crouched low behind Charlie's legs and hoisted him up over the rail, using the rail as a fulcrum. Toppling Charlie over with hatred and passion in the spur of the moment."

"Could it have been Sophia, seeing an opportunity when she let herself in to clean the room?"

"I don't think so. I think it was someone Charlie knew well."

"Who, Judge?"

"Someone entered the room after Charlie wobbled in and the door swung closed, as it does."

"Was it Maddy then?" asked the Captain, swinging around to look at Maddy, who had her hand over her gasping mouth now.

"I thought about that. Maddy was one of the last people to see Charlie before his fall."

Maddy's head snapped up to look at the Judge.

"You don't seriously think I had anything to do with Charlie's fall?"

"You were incredibly angry," volunteered Ross Hamilton. "I could hear you screaming through the walls of my suite about something". I'm in the next suite over, 630. And the walls are thin."

"The son of a bitch said he was going to dump me."

"Charlie?"

"Yes. Dump me for some stupid blonde he met aboard. Barbara or something. You're God damn right

I was angry. That doesn't mean I pushed him over the rail."

"The yelling stopped," said Ross. "And then his door slammed next door as someone angrily left. It rattled the whole corridor. Whoever left was really angry. And then five minutes later I heard Charlie scream. It must have been as he plummeted down from his balcony."

"There you go, Judge. As you heard, I left," said Maddy.

"You could have come back, Maddy."

"But I didn't go back. I went to my tiny interior stateroom on Deck 5 in the bow. I was so angry I never wanted to see Charlie again."

"Do you still have the key card to the room?"

Maddy snatched up her purse from the floor beside her, rummaged through it, pulled a key card out, and flung it across the table at the Judge. Her face contorted in anger now.

"Calm down, Maddy. I checked with the floor maid on Deck 5. She confirms you went into your interior room and didn't come out until there was a commotion over Charlie's fall."

Maddie slouched back in her chair.

"The desk says they gave Charlie one key card when he took over the room," said the Judge.

"Yes," said Maddy. "That's right."

"Did you get that card?"

"No. They didn't change the code on the lock. Charlie gave me Kennedy's card to open the door and move my stuff in when he moved me over. That was before he got his key card at the desk. That key card that was in my purse, on the table now, is Kennedy's old card."

"According to the desk, when Kennedy checked in he was given two key cards. Those two plus Charlie's card make three," said the Judge. "One key card was in Charlie's pocket when they found him on the deck. One is right here, from your purse. Where is the third key card?"

"I don't know. I never saw it. I suppose it's still in the room."

"I searched the room myself," said the Judge. "There was no keycard in the room."

"Well that maid, Sophia, had a master key card anyway. Maybe she used it to get in and get at Charlie," said Katy.

"Even if that's true, it still leaves the third keycard outstanding," said the Judge.

The table got silent, people turning to look at each other, questions in their eyes.

"But when you think about it," continued the Judge, "isn't the answer obvious?"

More silence.

"Who would Kennedy have given the second key card to?"

"Mom," Laura blurted out, then slapped a hand over her mouth.

"Exactly. Kennedy's lover, Alice."

All eyes turned toward Alice, who shifted uncomfortably in her seat.

"Do you still have the keycard, Alice?"

"No. I turned it in when Kennedy died."

"There's no record of your turning it in."

Alice's eyes blazed. "Well I did."

The Judge walked over behind Alice's chair and swung her purse off the back of the chair where it hung.

"Do you mind if we look?"

"You've got no right. Give me my purse."

"The Captain has the right. It's his boat."

The Captain reached over and grabbed the strap of the purse, hauling it away across the table, barely avoiding a last-ditch effort on Alice's part to snatch it back.

He reached in, poked around, and came out with two key cards. Alice had taken a sharpie and marked a large 'K' on one of them.

Heads turned again toward Alice, whose face had gone white.

"There's something else," said the Judge, turning to reach behind his chair for the silver-grey felt bag he'd brought along. He opened the bag and produced the small silver canister. The gold engraved letters on its side declared, *Aoud Absolue Precieux*.

"Is this your perfume, Alice?"

"What if it is?" Alice's hands were shaking now. She darted them under the table onto her lap.

"I was the first one in Charlie's room, perhaps a minute after his fall at most. Whoever was there before me had left the door wide open as they fled. I went to the balcony. There was a vivid scent there. A musky scent of citrus and woods, quite distinctive. The scent of *Aoud Absolue Precieux*." The Judge held up the bottle for all to see.

"Whoever had just been there with Charlie at the rail of his balcony was wearing this perfume. It's a distinctive scent. Your perfume, Alice. I remember it from when we shook hands five nights ago at our first dinner."

"Why would I try to kill Charlie?" Her voice went up an octave. "We've been together for thirty-two years. We had three children together. Charlie had just made it clear to the little bitch," Alice nodded at Maddy, who scowled in return, "that he was not leaving me. Why on earth after all these years would I try to push him into the sea?"

"I wondered about that too, Alice. Until I thought about the snippets of conversation I overheard walking behind you and Charlie as you had your big blowout out on the promenade deck."

"So what? We often fought. It doesn't make me the one who pushed Charlie over his rail."

"But this fight was different, wasn't it, Alice? You have each been living a lie for over twenty years."

"What are you talking about?"

"Your lie, Alice, was that Jay was Charlie's son."

Alice gasped.

"And Charlie's lie was that he pretended to believed Jay was his son when he knew full well Jay wasn't his son."

Alice's mouth dropped open, but no words came. It was almost as though she were making a silent shriek

"Jay was Kennedy's son, wasn't he, Alice? The product of a liaison between you and Kennedy over twenty years back when Kennedy was working for the soda company the first time. A time when Charlie was traveling a lot for the business.

But you didn't know that Charlie knew about it, knew about it from the beginning. You figured it out yesterday, on the promenade deck."

Alice looked at the assembled dinner guests with the eyes of a cornered animal, starting to rise from her seat, in flight or fight mode. Then she collapsed back into her seat, her body going slack like a punctured balloon, her eyes focused on the table knife in front of her. She sat there for perhaps thirty seconds, silent, then her head came up and she looked at the Judge.

"I… I… I… Aw shit. The bastard deserved it. I thought he'd just go overboard and disappear forever. Charlie has always abused me with his psychological games. Bullied and beat all of the softness and joy out of me, 'til there was nothing left. Nothing but bitterness and hate. I can't even breathe anymore when he enters the room. He just sucks all the life out of me. He deserved to die."

"But that's not why you did it, Alice. Is it?"

"No, Judge. I did it for Jay.

All these years, I thought my secret was safe. Kennedy left the company shortly after I got pregnant and never knew. Charlie never gave any indication he thought Jay was not his own. Then last night, when I realized Charlie knew, had always known, I saw that Charlie had deliberately set out to crush Jay.

And he did. Charlie killed Jay. Charlie hated Jay, belittled him, destroyed the least little suggestion of independence or self-assuredness in Jay. Made Jay feel small, defective, useless. Abused him physically when he was small, abused him emotionally his entire life. From the day Jay was old enough to understand, he was belittled, criticized, told he was stupid, worthless, graceless, a dead weight, a miserable child that no one loved or wanted.

Charlie told Jay every day how everybody laughed at him, how everybody knew he was ugly, stupid, selfish, and a worthless piece of shit. Can you imagine what it does to a child when he is told that over and over, from his earliest moment, every day for twenty years? How he is unloved, unwanted? How he is stupid and useless?

Charlie often would say to Jay's face that Jay should just go check out, jump off a bridge or something, put himself out of his misery. Is it any surprise Jay committed suicide?

Charlie wasn't very nice ever to any of us. But only yesterday I understood how especially cruel he'd been to Jay. And why. Charlie hated Jay because Jay wasn't his. And even worse, Jay was walking, breathing proof that 'his' wife had slept with another man. He set out to destroy Jay, and he did. What was left committed suicide six months ago in front of Charlie. But that wasn't Jay. That was a husk of a young man hollowed out by the hate and destruction rained down on him from someone he thought was his father.

Charlie deserved to die… and so, I tried to kill him."

"It wasn't planned out, was it Alice? Not premeditated?"

"No. I'd come to the cabin to confront Charlie. Him and his tarty little executive assistant. Tell him I wanted a divorce. I didn't knock, just used Kennedy's card key. The slut wasn't around."

Alice shot another mean look across the table at Maddy, who sat straighter in her chair, chin up, angry.

"I saw Charlie out on the balcony, leaning way out.

I charged in hard and low, lifted his legs up as high as I could, and shoved with all my anger and hate. He pivoted right over the rail. It was a wonderful feeling. Like freedom. My only disappointment was he didn't scream much. Just one long squeal on the way down.

Anyway, you are right, Judge. I did it. And I'd do it again if I had the chance. If I were a man, I'd have cut him up into small pieces and fed him to pigs. But I'm not a man. I saw an opportunity and I took it. And I am glad I did. I hope he never walks again. I hope his new life in a wheelchair turns into a rolling hell for him from which he never escapes."

She looked up then and around at them, bitterness in her eyes. "My only regret is that I didn't do it sooner. And I didn't see what was happening to Jay and protect him."

Then she slumped down further in her chair and closed her eyes, her face going relaxed, almost serene.

CHAPTER 58
DAY 6
9:20 AM

The ship pulled into Hilo and it was finally time to get off the damn boat. The crew in their wisdom required everyone out of their cabins at 9 a.m. and then insisted everyone sit around in the dining room, or on the stairs, or wherever they could find a seat, until their color coded number was called for their group to disembark. Apparently the ship company considered this an orderly process, with little concern for the passengers who got high numbers, like Katy and the Judge, and who would be sitting on their duffs for some hours before their turn came to get off.

The Judge lasted almost twenty minutes. He spent the time fantasizing how nice the master suite at the Four Seasons Resort Hualalai was going to be, with a bed long enough so he could stretch out his legs and stretch his hands behind his head and still not touch the walls. And the fine restaurants, real restaurants run by individual master chiefs with discriminating palates; goodbye to five days of homogenized food that tasted like cardboard.

It was just too much. He stood up, declaring to Katy he was leaving the boat now. The crew had no legal right to restrict his ability to leave. Any attempt to restrain him would be akin to false imprisonment he muttered.

Dragging Katy and their luggage, discarding the brown tags around their necks in a trash container, he elbowed his way into the line of first departing passengers making their way to the gangplank who wore yellow tags. They breezed through without objection from the crew, giving up their ship's identity cards at the hatch. They marched across the bridge and then crisscrossed down the ramps and into the big grey entry hall. They across its checkered floor and fell in line toward the turnstile that led to the parking and the taxi line.

Five minutes later a large man and his small wife ahead of them proceeded through the turnstile and out into the sunlight. As the Judge pushed forward with Katy to be the next passengers through the turnstile, the ship's officer at the gate suddenly put his hand up to press his earpiece further into his ear. Then he moved deliberately in front of the gate, blocking their exit.

"Oh, for Christ sake" muttered the Judge. "I'm not going to remain a prisoner here just because I lost my colored placard."

Other men in ships uniforms were moving in from either side to stand outside of the gate, adding to the blockade of the Judge's exit. The Judge could feel his blood pressure rising; he so very much wanted off this tub.

The ship's officer turned to look at the Judge, his eyes wide.

"I'm sorry sir."

"What?"

"I'm truly sorry, Sir." the ship's officer said again. "We've just discovered Norovirus in several of our passengers, a particularly unpleasant stomach bug. The entire ship, crew and passengers, cannot disembark. We're all now under quarantine for four days."

The Judge looked over the officer's head at the sparkling sunshine beckoning just beyond, dreams of master suites and fine dining shattering in his mind. So close, and yet so God damn far.

Damn,... Damn... and... Double Damn...!

CHAPTER 59
DAY 6
EPILOG

Charlie awoke with a start, memories of his situation slowly flooding into his consciousness. The hospital bed, the sprints and swaddling of bandages, the lack of feeling in his legs. His inability to move his lower torso.

There were new noises now, and the subtle rock of the ship had stopped. The ship must be in port. He could faintly hear the bustling of the crew, at a rush, double duty, to clean the ship, get the passengers off, and reset the common area and the staterooms for the next flood of passengers. The ship-board cycle of life for a ship's crew.

He remembered what had happened to him now, and why. He was in the ship's infirmary. They'd told him Alice was a few chambers away, locked in the ship's brig. He felt sorry for her in many ways. He'd ruined her life.... Of course, now, she'd ruined his as well, sort of a cosmic justice he supposed.

He heard a disturbance at his door, a fumbling or something, a squawk of the latch. Perhaps the big-boned nurse with the large tits was back. He waited expectantly, hungry for lunch now as he thought about it. The door opened a crack, and a hand came through to quietly swing the door inward. It was a large hairy hand, certainly not the big-boned nurse.

Then a face appeared. A faced containing a grimace for a smile and squinted piercing eyes filled with hate and loathing. It was his old partner, Ross Hamilton.

He wondered if Ross had come merely to gloat, or for something worse.

He hoped for the latter….

The End

xxxx

SOME ADDITIONAL NOTES

For those who want to read more about the Great Pacific Garbage Patch:

Curious what the Great Pacific Garbage Patch looks like on the surface? Here is a link to a video which show what the ocean's surface looks like.
https://www.youtube.com/watch?v=QHK2Zg5OibI

And what makes up the Great Pacific Garbage Patch? A link to another video showing some of its content.
https://www.youtube.com/watch?v=nU6xmmII0sk

If you want to learn more about the microscopic plastic particles in the air, start with Editorial Column in the Los Angeles Times, page A-11, July 6, 2020, "**The Plastics You Don't See Might Kill You**."

And this link to the New York Times article of June 11, 2020: **Where's Airborne Plastic? Everywhere, Scientists Find.**
Link:
https://www.nytimes.com/2020/06/11/climate/airborne-plastic-pollution.html?campaign_id=57&emc=edit_ne_20200611&instance_id=19319&nl=eveningbriefing&regi_id=81663552&segment_id=30707&te=1&user_id=e4cfb82cf1bade7b829e50d1efcbf9f7

Also: The United States contribution to coastal plastic pollution worldwide is significantly larger than previously thought, possibly by as much as five times, according to a New York Times article on Oct 30, 2020.

See Link: **https://www.nytimes.com/2020/10/30/climate/plastic-pollution-oceans.html?campaign_id=57&emc=edit_ne_20201030&instance_id=23675&nl=evening-briefing&regi_id=81663552&segment_id=42957&te=1&user_id=e4cfb82cf1bade7b829e50d1efcbf9f7.**

If you think death in a sauna is a little far-fetched, see this article from the Daily Mail: It tells of the killer sauna where a mother and daughter died after being trapped inside for 90 minutes when the door handle came off. Link: https://www.dailymail.co.uk/news/article-4417924/Pictured-Sauna-two-died-door-handle-came-off.html.

ACKNOWLEDGEMENTS

Thanks to those good friends who helped me to write and edit this book. Dr. Alexandra Davis, who was the first to see every word; my amazing editor, Jason Myers, who did yeoman work on the edits and kept me on the straight and narrow; the multiple good friends who agreed to read and comment on the early draft, and Dane Low, (www.ebooklaunch.com), who helped me design the distinctive cover.

Thank You All.

Davis MacDonald

This is a Work of Fiction

The Cruise is a work of fiction. Names, characters, businesses, organizations, clubs, places, events, and incidents depicted in this book are either products of the Author's imagination or are used fictitiously. Any resemblance or similarity to actual persons, living or dead, or events, locales, business organizations, clubs, or incidents, is unintended and entirely incidental. Names have been chosen at random and are not intended to suggest any person. The facts, plot, circumstances and characters in this book were created for dramatic effect, and bear no relationship to actual businesses, organizations, communities or their denizens.

About Davis MacDonald

Davis MacDonald grew up in Southern California and writes of places about which he has intimate knowledge. Davis uses the mystery novel genre to write stories of mystery, suspense, love, and commitment, entwined with relevant social issues and moral dilemmas facing 21st Century America. A member of the National Association of Independent Writers and Editors (NATWE), his career has spanned Law Professor, Bar Association Chair, Investment Banker, and Lawyer. Many of the colorful characters in his novels are drawn in part from his personal experiences and relationships (although they are all entirely fictional characters).

Davis began this series in 2013, with the publishing of THE HILL, in which he introduces his new character, the Judge. Here is a bit about each book in the Series, in the order they were written:

THE HILL. The Hill is a murder mystery and a love story which also explores the sexual awakening of a young girl, how sexual manipulation can change lives forever, and the moral dilemmas love sometimes creates.

THE ISLAND, set in Avalon, Catalina, continues the saga of the Judge and his love Katy, as the Judge finds himself in another murder mystery, and forced to make some key decisions about his relationship with Katy. The story explores the dysfunctional attitudes of a small town forced to drop old ways of thinking or face extinction.

SILICON BEACH, set in Venice, Santa Monica, Playa Vista and Marina del Rey, opens with a sundown attack on the Judge on the Santa Monica Beach, and carries the reader through the swank and not so swank joints on the Los Angeles West Side, as the Judge tries to bring down killers before they bring him down. The book takes a close look at the homeless, who they are, where they came from, what their lives are like, and offers a novel political solution.

THE BAY, set in Newport Beach, Balboa, and the Orange County Coastal communities, finds the Judge pressed into service by the FBI to solve a murder of one of their own, stumbling into a terrorist plot that could devastate Orange County. The story takes a close look at Islam in its many strains, as it exists in the United States.

CABO, set in Mexico, finds the Judge and Katy on a holiday in Cabo San Lucas which turns deadly as they unravel a stealthy double murder, and go head to head with human traffickers in Baha California.

THE STRAND, set in Manhattan Beach, Hermosa Beach, and Redondo Beach, tracks a murder. And also a controversial case centered on a pre-school and alleged child-abuse. A case that triggers prosecutorial misconduct and a rush to judgment by the D.A.'s Office and the Press, ruining reputations and destroying the lives and asset of the accused in reliance on 'creditable' sources that are not creditable, long before the defendants are ever brought to trial.

THE LAKE. A best friend dying in your arms. His last desperate words a cryptic message of death to thousands. What would you do? The Judge sleuths out the facts, exposing the shocking private lives of people he thought he knew. Uncovering the greedy that would risk the world for financial gain. Blind-sided along the way by Katy's sudden unhappiness, the love he expected to last forever seemingly unraveling, the relationship wobbling. What are the right words, the right steps, to touch her heart again? To put something fragile back together and fuse it so strong it lasts a lifetime ? Can the

Judge hold off the dark in his personal life, while exposing killers so cold, so calculating, they give the word Evil a new meaning?

THE CRUISE. The Judge and Katy are on a relaxing cruise to Hawaii when one of their fellow passengers has a deadly accident. And then a second deadly accident,… and a third. As the number of 'accidents' becomes statistically improbable, the Judge weaves his way through the conflicts, animosities and rivalries of a fractured business family and the Ship's guests and crew, seeking the truth. But the more the Judge learns, the more he puts himself in harm's way. When the ship is blown off course into the Great Pacific Garbage Patch, business partners become adversaries, family becomes the enemy, old lovers become bitter, and polite facades are dropped to reveal ugly motives, jealousy and hate.

Theft, embezzlement, avarice, greed, infidelity, sex, and of course… 'accidents'. Lots and lots of suspicious accidents. The primal violence seething underneath humanity's surface comes to a boil in the pressure cooker of a six-day cruise across the Blue Pacific. Follow the Judge as he risks all to ferret out the truth, on… THE CRUISE!

VEGAS, a murder mystery set in Sin-City Las Vegas, will be published in the Fall of 2021. The first Chapters of Vegas are included at the end of this book

All books are available on Amazon on Kindle and in paperback, and other fine bookstores, and available at online shopping platforms. Audio books are available for the first four books in the series. Watch for Audio Books to come out regularly on the remaining books in the series.

HOW TO CONNECT WITH

Davis MacDonald

Email: Don@securities-attys.com

Website: http://davismacdonald-author.com/

Twitter: https://twitter.com/Davis_MacDonald

Facebook: Davis MacDonald, Author

Blog: http://davis-macdonald.tumblr.com/

LinkedIn: Davis MacDonald

Amazon Author's Page: Davis MacDonald-Author

New in 2021: VEGAS

Look for **VEGAS** from Davis MacDonald, Book Nine in the Judge Series, to be published in the Fall of 2021.

What follows are the Prologue and the first two Chapters of **VEGAS**:

VEGAS
A Mystery Novel

by

DAVIS MacDONALD

Prologue

The sun was drying him out like an old piece of leather. The sun, the sand, the reflective heat, and the temperature, 110 degrees. No liquid for hours now. How many hours? He'd lost count.

He'd like to see his grandchildren again. Just once more. The hope for the future. But it wouldn't be. A picture of the four, three little girls and a boy, flashed in his mind; blurred, he couldn't seem to hold the image.

He'd been afraid. Thought he'd be shot in the head as he sat blind-folded and someone pushed him out of the Jeep and into the sand. But he hadn't. Hadn't touched him. Just dumped him. Out here in the middle of the Nevada desert. In the middle of nowhere.

He tried to laugh through his cracked lips, but it was more of a croak. As he'd thought about it he'd realized they'd been cruel. Why couldn't they have just used a bullet? This was far worse. Slow, agonizing, awful.

He stumbled and fell. Couldn't get his burned hands up in time, his face buried in hot stinging sand. He tried to spit the sand out of his mouth but there was no saliva.

His vision was going now, turning the desert dark around him in the middle of the day, almost hiding the shadow of the predator birds overhead. Circling, waiting, patient.

He got onto his knees, but there was no strength to stand. He lingered there a bit, on his knees, then crashed headfirst back into the sand....

Letting go.

CHAPTER 1

The Judge picked up his cell on the second ring. 11:30 on a Saturday morning, September in Palos Verdes. It was a soft day, cooler, with the broad expanse of the Santa Monica Bay outside his window glittering a bright blue. He'd been in the middle of doing his taxes; receipts and documents for which were spread all over his dining room table.

"This is the Judge."

"Detective Marsh, Judge, Vegas. You asked me to keep an eye out for your buddy who'd gone missing…a Robert Hanson."

"Yes. Have you found him?"

"We have, but the news isn't good."

"Tell me."

"Deceased. We found him in the middle of the desert, thirty miles from any road."

"What?"

"Yeah. No obvious marks on him. No bullet holes. No clear signs of trauma from an assailant. The coroner will have to decide, but we think he died of terminal dehydration and heat exposure. I figure someone took him for a joy ride out into the desert north of Vegas and just dropped him off. No water, no food, no shelter, no nothing."

"Shit!"

"Yeah. A miserable way to go."

"Who found him?"

"A couple of young guys in dune buggies. Decided to extend their range beyond the twenty-mile network of trails. Came across what was left of Mr. Hanson. He had his wallet with his driver's license, credit cards, and several hundred dollars in large bills in it. Dental records confirm it's him. I'm sorry."

The Judge set the cell down and stared at the litter of receipts, bank statements and canceled checks carpeting the top of the table, and the half-full file box sitting on the chair next to him. He took his arm and ran it flat across the tabletop, sweeping the papers into the box. It took him three sweeps and two heavy press-downs on the box's contents before he got everything in. But it was a satisfying. He slammed the lid down on the overloaded box with a vengeance and set it over by the door. Then he picked up his cell and did what he should have done at the outset. He called his accountant.

Ninety minutes later he was in his car nosing his way up the beginning of the Cajon Pass, the jagged and lofty trail that cut through San Berdo Mountains like a marauding snake and now was Interstate Highway 15 to Las Vegas. Katy, his bride, had been unhappy of course. Even wanted to get a nanny for their son and come along. But his instinct told him it wouldn't be wise for her to accompany him on this trip. What he had to do, he had to do mostly alone. It wasn't going to be fun, or for that matter, safe. He'd have enough trouble taking care of himself this time; he didn't want to risk Katy too.

Robert Hanson, or just Bob, had been a long-time friend, and more recently a client. They'd gone to USC together, fraternity brothers, and then on to the USC Gould School of Law. They'd been study-group pals, initiated in the Hell that was first year Law. Held up to the scalding intellect and scathing public interrogation of their overbearing professors. Publicly humiliated each time they were called upon to speak. Found wanting again and again and again… Until suddenly they weren't. Suddenly, they were thinking like lawyers.

Bob had been in the Judge's first wedding to the wife before Katy, and the Judge had stood beside Bob at his wedding, and at a christening of Bob's first child, a son, three years later. In the end neither marriage had worked out; many didn't in 21st Century America. Perhaps because the females had a lot more options now; and if they chose a career, a lot more stress.

Ten years ago, Bob had left the practice of law and begun doing real estate deals, riding the upswing in property values and doing well for himself. You had to be a bit of a gambler to succeed… Bob was.

The Judge stopped in Barstow and stretched his legs, grabbed some coffee, and wished he'd taken the plane. He was stiff as a board, and another two and a half hours to go. He thought back to the last time he'd seen Bob, three weeks before at the project. Bob was a large man, all big chest, gut and hind quarters set upon short spindly legs that left him a bit breathless at the top of stairs, and on long marches around the perimeter of his project. An unruly shock of hair, prematurely gone white, tapering down the side of his face in carefully manicured sideburns, framing his ruddy complexion. Large blue eyes under white winged eyebrows, always friendly and filled with good cheer for everyone. A tad too trusting in the Judge's opinion. An aw-shucks grin that slightly showed teeth white and perfect like polished ivory.

But behind Bob's smile there'd been a sense of desperation. His fortunes as a real estate developer had been a lot of ups and downs, the nature of the business. But too many downs on his last projects. As though he saw his latest project, the Spire, as his last chance to crawl out of the hole and score big on the brink of settling into his senior years. One last grab at the brass ring that would assure security, an expansive lifestyle into the future, and proof of ultimate self-worth and success in what had been a checkered career.

After stopping at the Mad Greek for a strawberry shake, sixty miles out, the Judge brought out his cell phone and dialed a Las Vegas number. Cindy Hanson, Bob's ex-wife who had kept her married name, answered immediately. The soft quiver in her voice as she said tentatively, "Hello", told the Judge she knew.

"Hello, Cindy. I'm so sorry."

"Oh, Judge." She let all her air out in a huge sigh.

"If there is anything I can do, Cindy…"

"No… No. The kids are on the way over. I can't believe it. I just can't believe Bob's gone". Then her voice changed, rising in anger now.

"Did you hear how he died, Judge? What they did to him? God, it was so cruel. He was eaten. Eaten alive by God damn turkey vultures." Cindy's voice changed, racked by a sob.

"Yes."

"Find them Judge." Cindy screeched into the phone. "Find the bastards that did this to Bob. See that they fry."

CHAPTER 2
The Peak

As the Judge traversed the last of the great Mojave Desert, up, over and down hills of dry, hot sand and scrub, maneuvering the Mercedes along the grey asphalt ribbon that jagged its way through the desolate space like an errant zipper, he thought back to eighteen months before, when Bob had sought his help.

Bob Hanson had come to the Judge seeking legal advice for a new project. A typical Hanson project, a real estate play he'd bet his entire net worth on.

His project was to build a time-share hotel in Vegas, just off the Strip. And of course, the Judge had said yes. It was always fun to work with Bob. The guy was always up, always smiling, always seeing the best in every turn of event and every person he met. He could charm anybody with his dancing blue eyes, broad smile, warm handshake, and the embrace he instinctively gave even to casual acquaintances. The Judge was going to miss his friend. It shouldn't have happened. Not to Bob. Not this way. Not any way.

They'd spent a lot of time together from that beginning, sorting out the legal and financial aspects of Bob's project, 'The Peak'. The Judge had enjoyed that time. And they'd watched the project grow out of the ground into a beautiful twenty-story boutique condo-hotel.

But the hotel had gone over budget, surprise, surprise. And had taken longer to construct, surprise, surprise. Bob had run through his own capital, the capital of the syndication he'd put together, and his construction financing. He'd pounded the pavement for additional money to complete the project, talking to sources he'd avoided disclosing to the Judge. But the real estate market had tanked.

Two weeks ago Bob had disappeared. And now he was dead… Shit!

Later the Judge pulled off the freeway, crossed the Vegas Strip on Flamingo Road, turned right on Koval Lane, and pulled into the sweeping driveway of the residential tower pyramid called The Peak.

Driving past the glistening silver structure on Koval, just behind Bally's, people instinctively slowed their cars, just to have a close look. It was an awe-inspiring structure clad in a reflective silver skin. Reminiscent of a church with its sweeping single-sided spire pointed to the heavens.

The footprint of the building was set by its first floor, a rectangle structure, its length along Flamingo and its short end on Koval Lane. Above the first floor, the structure soared ten stories on one side, part of a giant triangle, its tall side on Koval and its angular plane running from its peak down to the top of the first floor facing the strip. In the center of its angular plane was a rectangular hole cut down to the ground floor, creating an open-air rectangle plaza in its middle. The shared green space inside the cutout was an 'urban oasis' with its two pools and verdant green-scape entwined with patios and a walking path.

The Peak's shape changed, depending on the viewer's vantage point. From the west, it was a hyperbolic paraboloid or a warped pyramid. From the east, The Peak appeared to be a slender spire.

By keeping three corners of the block low and lifting the east portion of the building, the courtyard opened with views towards the Strip and its massive light show at night and caught the low western sun deep into the block in the late afternoons. While the courtyard was a private space and a sanctuary for residents, it could still be seen from the outside, creating a visual connection to the Strip and its intense activity. At the upper levels, the condominium units were organized on a fishbone layout, orienting the units towards the view of the Strip. Large terraces carved into the warped façade maximized the views and light into the units.

The building was… well… magnificent. And it was all built, its interior complete… except. Why was there always an 'except'?

Except that half the bathrooms were not installed. The City Building Department refused to issue an occupancy permit until all interiors were complete. But Bob had run out of money. All financing had dried up with the economic downturn; and after payments weren't made, the construction lender initiated a foreclosure on the construction loan to take the property over.

Bob had taken the only course open. He'd put the project into a bankruptcy forty-five days ago. Was there a connection? Between bankruptcy for the Peak and Bob's one-way ride into Hell?

The Judge wondered…

XXX

Look for the Mystery Novel, **"VEGAS"** to be available on Amazon and in bookstores in the Fall of 2021.

A Personal Note from the Author

I hope you enjoyed your read. Here are the other books in the Judge Series, (in order). If you've enjoyed one or more of these Mystery Novels, please leave a Review on Amazon and help us spread the word.

Davis MacDonald

THE JUDGE SERIES

Book 1: THE HILL

Book 2: THE ISLAND

Book 3: SILICON BEACH

Book 4: THE BAY

Book 5: CABO

Book 6: THE STRAND

Book 7: THE LAKE

Book 8: THE CRUISE

Book 9: VEGAS (out in late 2021)

(On Amazon search under 'books' for Davis Macdonald to find a complete list of the books. All are available in paperback and on Kindle. Books 1 through 4 are also available on audiobook, and book 5, Cabo, will be out on audiobook shortly.)